Up for Heir

Up for Heir

RUTH CARDELLO

Montlake
Romance

Published by Montlake Romance, Seattle

www.apub.com

Amazon, the Amazon logo, and Montlake Romance are trademarks of Amazon.com, Inc., or its affiliates.

ISBN-13: 9781542045919

ISBN-10: 1542045916

Cover design by Eileen Carey

Printed in the United States of America

*To my husband for being the kind
of dad who wouldn't hesitate to get
into a bounce house with our kids.*

Westerly

Family Tree

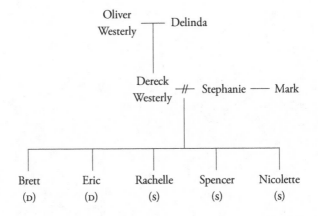

Prologue

Desperate times call for desperate measures, but surely I can do better than this.

Seated at her Queen Anne writing desk, Delinda Westerly tapped her perfectly manicured nails absentmindedly and studied the bold redhead across from her. "You don't look like a detective."

The woman pursed her wine-colored lips in a childlike pout that didn't diminish the intensity of her gaze. Her tan pantsuit was understated but tailored to fit. Expensive camouflage. She reminded Delinda of a Siamese cat she'd once had who purred and preened but pounced mercilessly and without warning. "That's the goal, wouldn't you say?"

"Victor Andrade said you're the best."

"I am."

"He said you work with Dominic Corisi. Considering his reputation, that's hardly reassuring."

The detective maintained unblinking eye contact. "And yet, here I am."

Delinda sighed. "Yes." She picked up a black card that had only the woman's phone number written in white. "It's a delicate situation. No one can ever know I was involved in this part."

"A secret assignment. My favorite kind," the woman said with a smile.

"Cockiness leads to sloppy mistakes, and I have no tolerance for either, Alethea Narcharios." The redhead arched an eyebrow. "Did you think I didn't know your real name?" Delinda tapped her nails again. "Rule number one in any engagement: never underestimate a person's connections. The Andrades are close friends of mine, and they consider Corisi one of their own. I know all about you. The background report your friend Jeremy gave you about me? I helped him write it."

Alethea's eyes widened, then she threw back her head and laughed. "It felt too perfect. Well played, Delinda. Not many people surprise me."

"I really don't see what you find amusing." Delinda narrowed her eyes. "According to Victor, you are dangerously curious, often manipulative, and consider yourself above the law."

Looking more intrigued than insulted, Alethea leaned forward. "Something tells me those are traits we share."

After pressing her lips together briefly, Delinda circled back to her concern. "I can't afford another mistake. I need to know I can rely on your discretion. Money is no object if this is done well."

"You've been misled if you think I care about the money."

Delinda wanted nothing more than to dismiss the brash redhead. *Unfortunately, I need her.* "It's about my grandson, Spencer. I thoughtlessly said something last year that hurt him deeply. I hoped that reconciling with his mother, Stephanie, would be the bridge back to him, but as personally cathartic as that reunion has been, it hasn't helped with Spencer. He is distancing himself from the whole family, determined to prove he doesn't need anyone. His older brother, Brett, is getting married soon, and Spencer has announced he won't be attending. I want him at that wedding."

With a look of amusement, Alethea said, "How exactly would you like me to change his mind?"

Delinda took a photo out of her desk drawer and laid it down, facing Alethea. "Hailey Tiverton. She and Spencer dated in college.

Stephanie said it ended abruptly, and Spencer pined for her for a long time. She's the only woman his mother thinks he's ever really cared about. I want you to find out why they broke up and bring me a full report on her. If I approve of her, you'll arrange for her to come work for me."

Alethea smiled slowly. "Delinda Westerly, you're a romantic at heart."

In response, Delinda touched the tablet on her desk to wake it and then turned it to face Alethea. She gave the woman a moment to absorb the headline of the online article, as well as the photo of Spencer leaving a club, looking as disheveled as the scantily clad woman on his arm. "I want my grandson back—he's a good boy. Not this. He's miserable."

"He doesn't look miserable."

Delinda spun the tablet back. "Are you interested in helping me, or not?"

The PI took a moment, as if she were debating the same question. "I am." She paused, then asked, "When you said I'll 'arrange for her to come work' for you, what did you mean?"

"This is where your skills come into play. You'll close every door around her until I'm the only choice she has."

"That's a dangerous game."

Delinda stood. "And here I thought dangerous was your forte."

"It is." Alethea rose to her feet. "I'd just hate to see you hurt by this."

Raising her chin, Delinda answered, "My dear, at my age, pain is a friend of mine. Time is the enemy. It has been a year. My grandson needs a shake-up, and if he felt half as much for this woman as his mother thinks he did, I'll have him married and in my life again by the holidays. First, though, we need to get him to attend Brett's wedding. It'll break Brett's heart if he's not there."

Alethea whistled. "I have to admit, I admire your confidence."

Confidence or desperation? It didn't matter. "Michael," Delinda called out to her butler, "please show Ms. Narcharios out." Before the detective left the room, Delinda added, "I'll expect that report by the weekend."

Alethea nodded before turning to leave.

Alone, Delinda sank back onto her chair and picked up the photo of the woman she'd sent Alethea to investigate. *Bring Spencer back into my life and you'll have everything you've ever wanted—in abundance.*

Hurt him again and you'll discover exactly how much fight is left in this old broad.

Chapter One

Hailey Tiverton reached across the taxi seat and took the hand of her seven-year-old niece. "It's going to be okay, Skye. You'll see. I hear there is a private beach, and you love the ocean. The guesthouse is twice the size of my apartment in Mendon. We'll be happy here. You'll see."

Her niece didn't say anything, but she'd hardly said a word in the year since her parents died in a car accident. Just thinking about it had Hailey clinging tighter to the child that her brother, Ryan, had entrusted her to raise, a little girl she was still desperately trying to reach. "I know you didn't want to move, baby, but we're not that far from our old place, and we didn't have a choice. I couldn't afford the rent hike and . . ." *I lost my job because I've used every last one of my sick and vacation days to be with you.* Hailey let out a shaky sigh. Skye didn't need to know how frustrating the months of unsuccessful job hunting had been or why they'd taken a taxi instead of the car Hailey couldn't yet afford to fix. Things were just about to turn around for them. Working as a personal assistant for an elderly woman after being a purchaser in retail was hardly a dream come true, but it promised good pay and stability.

Life had an odd way of circling back to what a person preferred to forget. It figured that the woman who was stepping in with a job offer when Hailey most needed one shared the same last name as the man who had done nothing for her when she'd needed him the most.

Spencer Westerly.

No. I refuse to do this to myself. I haven't thought about him in years and I won't start thinking about him now.

Yes, he had the same last name as the woman who'd hired Hailey, but Spencer needed odd jobs to scrape together enough money to buy used equipment for his garage computer lab. His mother was a nurse. His father had been a physical therapist. Delinda Westerly, on the other hand, was an heiress with a mansion by the ocean. *Doesn't mean anything. All it does is remind me of another time in my life when I felt this lost.*

But losing Spencer taught me that I didn't need him to survive. It made me stronger.

"This will be good for us," Hailey said, as much for herself as for Skye. Beyond the modest pay, the job included housing along with, most importantly, health insurance.

Parenthood had come suddenly and without instructions. After the funeral and a rough week of realizing how little her brother had planned for such an event, Hailey had tried to get things back to normal for Skye.

As if that were possible after such a devastating loss. Hailey had sought the advice of friends and counselors at Skye's school. So many conflicting opinions. In the end, Hailey had found an apartment in Skye's school district so her niece could have consistency with friends and her teacher.

A good plan, until Skye had refused to go to school and when forced, had reacted with such despair that more experts were brought in. Skye completely shut down then—refusing to speak a single word. No one expected it to last, but it had.

In the end, on the recommendation of the school and her therapist, Skye began homeschooling with a certified teacher. Months later,

Skye was still withdrawn. She refused to see any of her old friends or speak. Hailey was beginning to panic. The therapist Skye saw once a week was expensive, even with insurance. Financially, they'd been sinking even before she lost her job.

This is a fresh start for us. The therapist said Skye was over the worst of it and that the rest would simply take time. Skye's teacher, Mrs. Tillsbury, said she was working above grade level as long as all assessments were done in writing. All Skye seemed to enjoy was reading—and only the books Hailey had taken from Skye's old home. Hailey had tried to speak to Skye about Ryan and Erin. Skye withdrew from any mention of them, but she would sit and listen to Hailey read the stories they had read to her. Hailey didn't know if those stories made it easier or harder for Skye to heal, but she felt Ryan would want her to keep his memory alive.

Hailey hadn't expected that the hardest part of raising a child would be the uncertainty of doing any of it right. The therapist accepted Skye's silence and her quiet nature, as her teacher did, because they hadn't known the free-spirited, boisterous child she'd once been.

But I did. Hailey blinked back the tears she refused to give in to. *Don't give up on me, baby. I may not have known what to do at first, but I'm learning as fast as I can. We'll figure this out together.* She looked out the window briefly to regain her composure. The taxi pulled off the street and turned onto a massive driveway that led to a stone-fronted mansion. *One paycheck and I'll have my car repairs done. Every step forward is one where we don't fall back.*

Even though it felt intimidating to just pick up and move into the guesthouse of a woman she'd spoken to only briefly on the phone, Hailey forced herself to be optimistic. The job had come like an answer to a prayer. Two weeks earlier, on the way back from a disappointing interview, Hailey had found a newspaper on the bus seat beside her. It had been folded open to the employment section, and this job had been circled. The description had fit exactly what she needed. Fate? A message from Ryan? She wanted . . . no, needed to believe so.

When the taxi stopped in front of the house, a stately-looking older man in a gray suit approached the vehicle and opened the door. Skye's hand tightened on Hailey's.

"Welcome, Ms. Tiverton. My name is Michael." He offered his hand to help Hailey out.

Before taking it, Hailey looked back at Skye. Their eyes met and held. "We need this, Skye. Trust me. Please, honey. I know it's hard, but I love you. Home is wherever *we both are*." Skye nodded solemnly and scooted out of the taxi as Hailey did. Skye seemed afraid, but she was putting on a brave face. Hailey wanted to hug her, but she was afraid it would reduce them both to tears.

"You must be Miss Skye. We're happy to have you." He leaned down in a confidential manner. "Even Mrs. Westerly. She loves children."

"She does?" Hailey asked, a sense of relief washing over her. Her only impression of her employer had been from their brief phone interview, during which the older woman had sounded stern.

Michael straightened and smiled. "Just don't tell her I said so." He paid the driver before Hailey had a chance, then collected the luggage from him. "The boxes you sent are in the guesthouse. I'll walk you over. Take time to settle in. Mrs. Westerly is expecting to meet with you before dinner, which will be at six. She'd like to speak with you first, though."

"Today?" Hailey had hoped she'd have a day to adjust. She could hardly say no to meeting with her employer, but she hadn't lined up anyone to stay with Skye. Mrs. Tillsbury had always been okay with staying extra hours if Hailey made arrangements and paid her for her time. She closed her eyes briefly. *This is not how I was hoping day one would go.*

Skye stepped closer to Hailey. Separation in the new place would not be easy. It broke Hailey's heart not to be able to give her more time, but they both needed this job to work out.

Hailey turned and bent until she was eye to eye with her niece. "We *can* do this."

Skye nodded but held her silence.

Panic nipped at Hailey, but she pushed it back. *Our lives were getting smaller and smaller where we were. We didn't have a choice.*

Michael cleared his throat and started walking. "Miss Jeanie is our cook, and she makes chocolate chip cookies from scratch. I'll tell her I'm craving some, and if I see Miss Skye in the house later, perhaps she could join us for some. You have to eat them fast or Miss Jeanie will scarf them up herself." He turned and winked. "We should keep that last part between us, also."

Hailey smiled and nodded toward Michael. "Homemade cookies? What's better than that? I say yes, but on one condition."

Skye frowned in question.

Hailey caressed her niece's cheek. "You have to promise to save me one."

Skye nodded and some of the tension seemed to leave her.

Hailey straightened and started to walk forward, relieved when Skye fell into step beside her. Under any other circumstances, Hailey would have taken time to appreciate the elegance of the guesthouse and the impressive view of the ocean behind it. All of her attention, though, was on the little girl beside her.

They stepped beyond an ornate wooden door and into a beautifully decorated hallway that was flanked on one side by two sitting areas. One had a fireplace and bookshelves. The other was more open with large windows that brought the outside in. They followed Michael farther inside to the first bedroom, where he deposited Hailey's luggage. It was a feminine master suite with long drapes and thick carpeting. Michael gave them a brief tour of the adjoining bath area, then led them to a room across the hall.

"We didn't know what you would like, but we did our best to prepare the room for you," Michael said.

The room was decorated in purple and light green, Skye's two favorite colors. If someone had sat with Hailey and given her a limitless budget to design the perfect room, this would have been it. It was youthful but with just enough sophistication. A castle bed dominated half the room. In general, Skye had outgrown her fascination with princesses, but this bed was delicately crafted. A staircase led to a bed above. The section beneath had a built-in desk along with several bookshelves and a tuffet reading chair. Skye let go of Hailey's hand and walked toward the bed. She ran her hands over the books, her books, that filled the shelves. Her attention turned to a package on the desk. She touched it, then looked to Hailey.

Michael said, "I believe it has your name on it."

"Open it," Hailey urged.

Skye slowly, carefully unwrapped it and held up a chapter book, *Billy and the Lion.*

Michael said, "Mrs. Westerly said her grandchildren used to love that book, and she hopes you will as well."

There was a time when Hailey would have asked Skye to thank Michael, but she held back the words. Skye was looking like she might be able to accept this move and that was enough for now. Hailey asked, "Do you like it, Skye?"

Skye held the book up, then tucked it against herself and nodded.

Michael smiled in a way that warmed the room. "Well then, I'll tell Mrs. Westerly you said so and she'll be pleased." After a pause, he said, "If there's nothing else you require, I'll return to the main house."

Hailey walked with him to the front door, encouraged by the fact that Skye stayed behind to explore her new room. She held out a hand toward Michael. "Thank you. For everything." Part of her wanted to explain Skye's silence to him, but it was neither the time nor the place to do so, and he didn't seem to need it.

He nodded politely, stepped outside, and reminded her that she was expected at the main house before dinner. Hailey said she would be there and closed the door. She almost allowed herself to slump against it in relief but then caught Skye watching her, so she squared her shoulders and forced a smile to her lips.

It had been a year filled with loss, but the worst of it was over. As she walked toward Skye, she reminded herself she was a survivor. *Skye is, too.*

I know all about loss, honey, but I also know you can't let it beat you. Although Hailey had been older, she knew how devastating the death of a parent was. Her mother had walked out on her family when she and Ryan were very young, leaving her father to raise his children alone. She'd survived that loss because her father and brother told her she would. They'd watched over her, and she remembered her childhood as a happy one.

Her father had worked long hours to make sure she and Ryan could go to college. Worked too much. He had put off seeing a doctor about chest pains because he hadn't wanted to take a day off.

One day, Hailey was looking forward to her sophomore year in college, with a perfect boyfriend and amazing friends; the next, she was a shell of herself who returned to school and simply went through the motions.

Oh yes, Hailey understood how one needed to withdraw from everyone they knew. It wasn't that people hadn't cared. Her friends relentlessly tried to drag her out, but drinking, even a little, brought too many emotions to the surface, and Hailey ended up crying and embarrassing herself rather than having a good time.

And Spencer? The very side of him that she'd loved in the beginning, his obsession with his garage lab, had been more important to him than her. His all-consuming drive to start his own tech company took priority over anything she felt. He'd said he was determined to be somebody important.

He didn't understand he already was.

To me.

I didn't care if he ever made it big. I loved the way he looked at me, how we laughed together, the way his touch lit a fire in me. After Dad died, though, I needed him to notice that I was falling apart. Hold me. Tell me everything would be okay.

She'd tried to explain it to him once, using an analogy of pie and cake. A person could have pie every week and never tire of it. It was always good. Always reliable. She'd desperately needed Spencer to acknowledge that the under-celebrated comfort pastry was more important than a flashy, ten-tiered cake. He had defended his love of cake with the stubbornness of a man with no clue that such an argument could end a relationship.

Just as it had.

After that fight and weighed down with grief, she'd called her brother and said she wanted to go home—home being with the last of her family. She'd retreated from her schooling, her friends, and Spencer . . . needing more than anything the feeling of safety from having family in the next room. She'd expected Spencer to see how he'd hurt her and come for her. Not for a moment had she thought it would really be over.

He did call. He'd even said he loved her, had been going out of his mind without her. They'd made plans to get together, but he didn't show. She'd waited for him for hours in a coffee place near her brother's apartment. Called. Texted. No answer. Eventually, sad and confused, she'd gone home and gotten drunk for the first time in her life.

When she'd woken the next day to a killer hangover and still no word from Spencer, she let herself cry. It wasn't a time in her life that she was proud of. Life had knocked her off her feet, and instead of standing, she'd curled up on her brother's couch and cried until she felt numb and empty.

Her brother had come to her, trying to console her, and said, "Life sucks sometimes, Hailey. I don't know why. It's not fair. It's not pretty, but you don't ever let it beat you. Do you hear me? Dad raised us stronger than this. One foot in front of the other. Your life won't get better if you don't get off your ass and make it happen."

"You just want me to start paying rent," Hailey had joked.

"That, too," Ryan had said before mussing her hair and telling her to go take a much-needed shower. Funny how some moments stayed vivid in a person's memory. She credited every success she'd had, from finishing college to getting a job for a large retail chain, to that pep talk from Ryan.

When she'd needed someone, the most support came from family, not her other relationships. Family carried a person through and even gave a person a kick in the ass when needed. They were what mattered. *I learned that I am stronger than anything life can throw at me and, God willing, I'll show Skye that she is, too.* Hailey looked into the sweet, sad eyes of Ryan's daughter and said, "We're going to be okay."

Seated on the very top step of the Kukulcán pyramid at Chichén Itzá in Mexico, Spencer Westerly took a moment to appreciate the early-morning calmness of the ancient Mayan site. The view of the Temple of the Warriors against a backdrop of jungle never became less awe-inspiring. There were tweaks still left to be made, but the stone beneath him was warm to the touch and the breeze increased in force the higher one climbed while containing precisely enough humidity to allow for comfort as well as authenticity.

Spencer stood on the plateau of the pyramid. "Run conference type E. Connect Cohen." Slots on the wall opened and a table and chair were realistically represented via the combination of hologram and physical planks. A business partner, Jordan Cohen, appeared beside him. The two had been friends since high school, and their shared obsession with coding had blossomed into WorkChat, their virtual reality software design company.

Over the past year, their goal of getting contracts in New York, California, and London had been realized. Beijing and Australia were next. Already expectations were rising as clients began to integrate the simulators into their daily routines. What was considered a breakthrough one day could be considered mediocre and subpar a month later. In the world of big investors, perfection was not only expected but vital for a tech company's survival. Others were attempting what WorkChat was already bringing to the market. It was only a matter of time before the playing field would be crowded with competition. Building a reputation for excellence as well as solid infrastructure was imperative. Spencer often reminded his lead team that almost anyone could make a computer, but most consumers purchased only a handful of brand names. Reputation and infrastructure. Companies bought technology that was reliable, connected, and cutting-edge. They invested in programs that increased productivity, especially in a global community where traveling was becoming an inefficient use of time and resources, increasingly dangerous, and costly.

With WorkChat, the physical location of employees didn't matter. As long as simulators were available at each site, teams from around the world could conduct conference meetings anywhere—even from the top of a Mayan pyramid. WorkChat, though, wasn't simply about making it appear as if people were in the same location; it was about fooling their senses into believing they actually were. Easier to achieve until one had to cycle back in the practical aspects of conducting business, but they were doing it. If he seemed hard on Jordan, it was only because everything they'd worked for was suddenly within reach. "It shouldn't be this windy in the conference area, and the temperature needs to lower gradually. No one should feel as though they stepped in front of an air conditioner. Make it seamless."

"I always do."

Spencer paced beside the conference table. "We do this one right, and Bylon in Australia is next to sign on."

Jordan leaned his chair back and stretched. "We're good. Relax."

Slapping his hand down on the table, Spencer said, "Good is not good enough. It never has been."

Rather than looking intimidated, Jordan propped his feet up on the edge of the conference table. "Here we go. What has you all wound up today?"

There were days Spencer regretted working with someone who had known him long enough to have no fear of him. He rubbed a hand over his throbbing forehead. Hangovers had become the norm, but they still sucked. "Nothing."

"You look like shit, so I'm guessing you went out again. I ran into Jade at the bistro. She was looking for you. I told you not to go out with her a second time. She thought you were dating."

"I told her I don't do relationships."

"How can you be such an ass to women and get laid as often as you do?"

"Can we talk about something that matters? Like our looming deadline? I need to know I can step away and not have this project go to shit. You have two weeks to polish Chichén Itzá if we plan to upgrade the systems this summer. It's time to get serious."

"Serious? I all but live here already." Jordan dropped his feet to the floor and leaned forward on the conference table. "So do you. Lighten up. You sound like your father." Jordan never missed a chance to call him on his shit, another *benefit* of knowing him for so long.

But on this one he was wrong.

Dereck Westerly is not my father. Spencer's hands fisted, but he kept his gut reaction to himself. Jordan didn't know the truth. No one outside of Spencer's immediate family did, and that was how Spencer wanted to keep it. Anger about unchangeable past events distracted him from the one thing that did matter—WorkChat. Logic couldn't be applied to the drama that lately came hand in hand with spending any amount of time with his family. Debugging, tuning, and designing required a clear head.

Avoiding his family didn't fix anything, but he was in survival mode. He couldn't handle hearing his mother apologize again for not telling him that his biological father had been her second husband, Mark, and not her first as she'd led everyone to believe. Affairs happen. People get lonely. Her justifications were limitless. What neither her apologies nor her explanations did, though, was give him a chance to have one final son-to-father conversation before his real father died.

He didn't have the stomach for another round with Rachelle, his older sister, as she explained again that good people could make horrible mistakes without it making them bad people.

The definition of a good person is someone who doesn't selfishly fuck up other people's lives; a good person doesn't confess to lies only when they're caught.

The one he felt sorry for was his younger sister, Nicolette, because she was still wrestling with uncertainty when it came to having her own paternity confirmed. Not knowing was torturing her, but she feared the truth would be something she wasn't ready for. Feeling sorry for her, though, didn't mean he knew what to say to her or that he wanted to talk about it again.

His brother Eric chose to hide in Europe rather than get involved. That much hadn't changed.

In stark contrast, Brett, his eldest brother, once distant and work absorbed, was as annoyingly persistent to have a relationship with him. *I don't have time to pander to his midlife crisis, either.*

That sounded colder than Spencer meant for it to, even in his thoughts. It wasn't Brett's fault that their mother had cheated on, then left Dereck Westerly. Nor was it his fault that Spencer had spent most of his life wondering why their father had kept two of his sons with him, raised them in a life of luxury, while essentially ignoring the three children who'd been left with their mother.

Being disowned by their father had been confusing. *Why didn't he fight to keep us? Why did we have to work to support ourselves and our dreams while Brett and Eric were handed everything on a platinum platter?*

At least I don't have to wonder anymore.

Too much drama. Only work made sense, and Spencer was determined to make that part of his life a success.

"You really *are* in a bad mood. Run beach with summer crowd C."

The table and chairs withdrew into the wall, and the two men were transported to a sandy beach where bikini-clad women were basking in the sun, wading in and out of the water, and playing volleyball. The simulation had started as a joke, but Jordan had obviously been working on it, as it was now impressively realistic. *No wonder he's falling behind.* "What the fuck is this?"

Jordan grinned boyishly. "Heaven. That's what I call it. Take a moment to soak it in."

Spencer didn't bother. "End program. Maintain connection." The beach faded away, and the two men were standing in a neutral screen room. "We are not courting the porn industry. Focus, Jordan."

Jordan shrugged. "What's wrong with having a little fun? There was a time when you would have laughed. Okay, okay. I know how to cheer you up. I've been working on something that will blow your mind." He waved a hand. "Run photo album two." The room transformed again, and they were transported into a virtual representation of their old college campus. "Your mother kindly sent me your old flash drives full of photos and copies of her pictures. I used our basic facial recognition feature, added a dash of artificial intelligence, and voilà—a person literally *can* go home. Tell the program who you want to see and the backdrop you want them to appear in. It requires clients to upload their own location videos and photos, but if we pair this with devices to make it simple, we'll dominate the entertainment industry as well as the business sector. The awesome part is you can opt to put yourself in or take yourself out. Numerous photos of the same person allow the computer to generate a 3-D representation. Movies allow them to move through the space. This is a game changer, Spence. What do you think?"

"End program. Maintain connection. No," Spencer said decisively. There was nothing in the past he wanted to see.

"That's it? No? I put months into this."

"Exactly. You wasted months, which is why you need to get your ass in gear now and finish up the Chichén Itzá simulation. We need it perfected and out to our customers, along with upgrades."

"I created the album simulation on my own time."

Spencer threw his hands up in the air. "Do you want us to fail? Is that why you're dicking around?"

"'Dicking around'?" Jordan let out an audible breath. "What's with you? Seriously."

Running his hand through his hair, Spencer asked, "Me? Who just put us behind schedule while he tweaked his *Girls Gone Wild* simulation? Fine, I'm an asshole because I want to meet deadline and not muddy my brand."

"*Our* brand. Don't talk to me like I work for you." With a sound of disgust, Jordan glared at Spencer. "I cut you slack because your brother is marrying your ex-fiancée and I know it's bugging you, but you weren't even into her. And honestly, she dodged a bullet because you're a real dickhead lately."

Spencer's head snapped back beneath the criticism from someone who had been like a brother to him for over a decade. A better brother than his biological ones had ever been. "This is business, Jordan. You can't do whatever you want."

Jordan raised his hand and pointed at him, moving fast enough that his hand temporarily blurred, a fact that made the perfectionist in Spencer wince. "That's what's wrong with you. You used to enjoy this. We both used to. Now it's all about the contracts and connections. I don't want to sit around kissing the asses of big business. I want to create things I'm excited about. I want to want to be here. I *need* to want to be here."

"You can *create* whatever you want after you finish this project."

"It's like talking to a wall. Whatever is fucking bothering you, it's changing you. You like to say you don't need anyone; well, you're about to find out if that's true. Finish Chichén Itzá on your own. I'm outta here. End connection."

Fuck.

Jordan and Spencer had always been different, but that had been their strength. In high school, Spencer had balanced his passion for programming with sports. He'd ruled on the football field while Jordan fully embraced the geek lifestyle. They'd each brought something different to the table.

Of course I've changed; it's called growing up. Spencer slammed his hand against the blank wall of the simulator, then threw open the door and strode out of it.

His secretary looked up with a smile that faded as she noticed his mood. "Your sister is on line one. I was just about to tell her you were busy. Would you like me to put her through to your office?"

"Do I look like I want to talk to anyone right now?" Spencer growled.

A red flush swept over his secretary's face, and she blinked several times before saying, "I'll tell her you're in a meeting . . . again."

Thank you. Do I have to think for everyone? "Lisa . . ."

"Yes, Mr. Westerly?"

"Go home early today." He was done with her as well.

Tears sprung to her eyes. "Please don't fire me. I just got a new apartment."

God, I really am a dick. "You're not fired. Just go."

"It's barely three o'clock."

He gave her a look that must have expressed how he was feeling because she quickly told his sister that he was in a meeting, turned off her computer, grabbed her purse, and bolted for the door. Alone at last, he went into his office, closed the door, and sat down on the leather couch, burying his face in his hands. This should be the best year of his life, but in stark contrast to how well WorkChat was doing, his personal life was spinning out of control.

He'd only felt like that once before, and Jordan's mention of college brought that back to him as if it was only last week. In college, he'd fallen in love with a woman who claimed to feel the same—until she didn't. Hailey Tiverton. She'd broken up with him because they favored different desserts. How fucked up was that?

For a moment, he was there again, sitting in his car with a bouquet of flowers in hand, an apology ready, having his heart torn out of his chest and thrown back in his face. Hailey had left school without explanation, but he hadn't needed one when he'd seen her in the arms of another man. He'd wanted to rush over and demand to know how long she'd been cheating on him, but he held back.

He hadn't wanted to know.

Some questions were better left unanswered.

He'd learned then, and was recently reminded of, one of life's simple truths: *people can only hurt you if you care, so it's better not to.*

I don't need Jordan to finish Chichén Itzá.

I don't need the shitfest of drama that is presently my family.

I'm better off on my own.

Chapter Two

A few hours later, Hailey and Skye walked to the main house to meet with Delinda Westerly. It was a warm evening, so Hailey had chosen cotton dresses for them both. Skye seemed to understand the importance of making a good impression. She'd brushed out her hair and had her new book tucked to her side.

"I'll keep the meeting as brief as I can," Hailey promised. "You have your book. We'll leave the door open. If you read you won't even miss me. She's expecting me to stay for dinner, but I'll tell her I can't."

Skye nodded without meeting her eyes. Hailey raised her hand to ring the doorbell, but the door opened suddenly.

"Come in," Michael said, holding the door open wide. "Mrs. Westerly is in the solarium waiting for you." They entered the house, and then he closed the door behind them. "She's looking forward to meeting you, Miss Skye. She asked me to send both of you in."

Skye's eyes widened.

"Oh, I thought—" Hailey stopped herself and looked down at her niece. "That's very nice of her, isn't it, Skye?"

As Hailey expected, Skye stepped closer to her and took hold of her arm. Six months ago, Hailey would have turned around and left with Skye, but she had to trust in the progress they'd made. Ryan would have said it was high time that both of them hid less. She laid her hand over Skye's and said, "I like her already."

Skye tipped her head in question.

"She made you a beautiful bedroom, gave you a thoughtful gift, and now has included you in our meeting." Hailey tapped her nose lightly. "There is no surer way into my heart than to be kind to you."

Skye's smile lit up her eyes.

In that moment, Hailey would have promised to work for Mrs. Westerly for free. She cleared her throat and said, "We shouldn't keep her waiting, should we?"

Still holding on to her arm, Skye walked with her into the solarium.

Although Hailey had nothing to base it on, she'd imagined Delinda Westerly as a tall woman, when in fact she was the opposite. She stood as they entered, and the top of her white curls came up to Hailey's shoulders. What she did have, though, was a strong presence. Hailey felt as if she were visiting the queen.

There was an uncomfortable moment as the older woman looked her two guests over. "So you're Hailey Tiverton."

It was an odd greeting from a woman who had yet to smile. "Yes." Hailey fought the urge to tuck Skye behind her. Instead, she said, "And this is my niece, Skye. Thank you so much for everything you've done to make us feel welcome. Her room is amazing. She absolutely loves the book."

Mrs. Westerly bent until she was eye to eye with Skye. "Do you really like it? You can tell me if you don't."

Skye tensed beside Hailey.

"She doesn't—" Hailey started to say "speak," then stopped when Mrs. Westerly straightened.

"Doesn't what? Doesn't like it?"

Dry-mouthed and fearing it had been a mistake to mention it at all, Hailey said, "She doesn't talk."

The older woman showed very little reaction to the announcement. She bent again and addressed Skye. "You look like an intelligent young woman. One day soon, tell your aunt she needs to stop speaking for you."

Hailey gasped audibly and was about to tell the older woman . . . well, she wasn't sure what she would have said because, before she chose her words, she noticed Skye was no longer clutching her arm. Her niece wasn't afraid of Mrs. Westerly. Her all-too-frequently hunched shoulders were squared and her chin was high.

Not sure what to think, Hailey watched the two of them size each other up.

Mrs. Westerly straightened. "You'll do. Both of you." She raised her voice ever so slightly. "Michael, bring in the tea, would you?" She returned to the chair she had been seated in when they'd arrived. "Come. Come. I sit more often than stand nowadays, and I prefer if those around me do the same."

Michael rolled in a tray of tea, finger sandwiches, and small pastries. He uncovered a small plate. "And for Miss Skye, cookies fresh from Miss Jeanie's oven. Where should I place them?"

Skye took the seat next to Mrs. Westerly and put the book beside her. She smoothed her dress and turned her hands upward to accept the plate.

Michael handed them to her, and Mrs. Westerly looked at Skye as if waiting for her to thank Michael, but Skye held her silence and looked away.

Michael poured tea for all of them, then faded out of the room. Hailey opened and closed her mouth a few times, rethinking what she was about to say before uttering a word. She cursed herself for not fully explaining Skye's situation before arriving. She'd hoped to get to know her employer before introducing the two. *I always think there will be more time. When will I learn? Life has its own schedule.* "You have a beautiful home."

"Thank you," Mrs. Westerly said between sips of tea. "It used to be one of my favorite places, but now all the empty rooms make me sad."

She put her cup aside. "The job description focused on potential duties I may require, but this is mostly a companion position."

The announcement took Hailey by surprise. "I see," she said, although she had no idea what that would entail.

"Where does Skye attend school?" Mrs. Westerly asked.

"She's homeschooled by a full-time teacher who thankfully has agreed to make the drive here."

"One?"

"Yes."

Mrs. Westerly's nose wrinkled. "I'll need to meet this teacher of hers. Is he or she multilingual? Where did they graduate from?"

What is she doing? Hailey's chest constricted. *This is what I get for accepting the job in a rush. I should have come out to meet her in person first. I should have had this conversation before we moved in. I never considered that Mrs. Westerly would want to know so much about Skye.*

When your back is to the wall and a solution presents itself, you don't ask too many questions. You close your eyes and leap. "Please don't worry yourself about things like that. Skye adores her teacher, and I'm pleased with how both of them are doing."

Mrs. Westerly's eyebrows rose. "Every child who has lived in this house has had only the finest educational opportunities. If you're worried about the cost, I'll assume it, of course. The foundation one lays down early determines the choices available later."

Hailey turned to Skye. "Honey, could you take your book and your cookies out to the chair we saw in the hallway?" Slowly, reluctantly, Skye rose and picked up her book before making her way out of the room in a painfully slow fashion. She didn't close the door, so Hailey lowered her voice and turned back toward her employer. "First, I am so grateful for the opportunity to work here."

Mrs. Westerly folded her hands on her lap, but the move was neither docile nor compliant. "Yes. Yes. I'm sure you are. What is it, though, that has you gasping like a fish out of water?"

Hailey took a calming breath. "Skye has had an extremely difficult year. She's okay, but it's a delicate situation."

"And you'd prefer I not involve myself in your family's business."

Shit, I'm going to get fired, but she needs boundaries. "Yes."

With a wave of her hand, Mrs. Westerly said, "I'll never understand people. All I want is the best for her. How could you not?"

The question cut through Hailey. Her face warmed as her temper rose. She stood, hands clenched at her sides. "With all due respect, you don't know her or me. Skye is my responsibility, and her welfare comes first . . . always. Even if that means not remaining here."

"Sit down," Mrs. Westerly said in a harsh tone.

Hailey remained standing. Part of her wanted to storm out of the house, but there was nowhere to storm to. *Shit.*

With a sigh, Mrs. Westerly said, "Please."

Hailey sat tentatively.

"I've offended you, haven't I?"

Seriously? If I answer honestly I can probably kiss this job goodbye. Which might be for the best. "I—you—"

"Are you afraid of me? What is robbing you of your ability to articulate what you think? I had higher hopes for you."

"As did I for you," Hailey said under her breath.

"What did you say, dear? Speak in a clear, crisp voice if you want to be taken seriously."

Sitting up straighter, Hailey said, "I had hoped you would be someone I could enjoy working for."

"And you've already decided that I can't be?"

"It's definitely harder to imagine."

After a short, dramatic pause, she added, "My eldest grandson said I need to soften my approach, or I'll die alone."

Hailey coughed nervously. "I'm sure he was joking."

"He was not."

They sat in tense silence for a few long moments.

Mrs. Westerly looked Hailey over from head to foot, then said, "I don't want you to resign any more than you want to look for a new job."

Breathe. This could work out. Crazier things have happened. "For me, it will all come down to if this is a healthy environment for Skye."

"Your dedication to your niece is admirable." Mrs. Westerly leaned forward. "Help me understand why you won't accept my assistance with Skye's education."

Feeling she had little left to lose, she decided to lay the truth on the table. "In the past year, Skye lost her parents, the home she grew up in, her friends, and now my apartment as well. I appreciate your offer, but I couldn't afford to continue with any option you'd choose if this job doesn't work out." Hailey looked down and then raised her eyes to Mrs. Westerly's. "Skye needs consistency, and I'm trying to give that to her. I won't be the reason she loses anything else."

Mrs. Westerly nodded. "I like you, and I don't like many people."

Do I still have the job? Oh my God, I think I do. "Thank you."

"I only have one more question."

I hope it's not about how fast I type. I may have exaggerated about that. "Yes?"

"What is your version of why you and my grandson Spencer broke up in college?"

Hailey's jaw went slack in shock. Mrs. Westerly was Spencer's grandmother? *No. No. No.*

Mrs. Westerly added, "And do enunciate, because my hearing isn't what it used to be."

Spencer dropped his computer bag on the counter as he entered his apartment. It was nearly two in the morning, and although he was exhausted, his mind was still racing. He grabbed a six-pack of beer from the fridge, placed it near the couch, then opened one as he stepped out of his shoes.

Long day, but that was nothing unusual.

He sat down and took a gulp as he went over the end of the night in his head. He'd finished the Chichén Itzá simulation and proved that the project didn't require two lead programmers. Without Jordan, both Spencer and WorkChat would survive. What Spencer hadn't expected was how little satisfaction that knowledge brought him.

He closed his eyes and remembered the call with Brett earlier that night. "What do you need, Brett?"

"Just checking in. I heard you were courting Incom. I've dealt with them in the past. If there is anything I can do—"

"I closed on the deal this morning."

"Under the terms you wanted?"

"I wouldn't have accepted anything less."

"Good. That's good. How is everything else?"

"The same." It was obvious that Brett had something he wanted to say, so Spencer prodded, "And you?"

"Great. Alisha and I were hoping we could lure you out to dinner with us this week."

That wasn't going to happen. "This week? I'm slammed."

"How about next week?"

"The new contract is going to keep me busy for a while."

"We'll drop by your office."

"Please don't. As I said, I'm slammed—"

"We have news we want to share. Something we'd rather say in person."

Fuck. "Alisha's pregnant."

Brett was quiet for a moment, then he said, "Yes. We didn't want you to hear it from anyone else."

Spencer had stood and paced his office. As messed up as the situation was, he knew how much family meant to both Brett and Alisha. "Mom must be over the moon."

"We haven't told her yet. We wanted to make sure you heard it from us first."

"Although I appreciate the gesture, it's unnecessary. We've been over this. I'm fine with you marrying Alisha. Our engagement wasn't real, and you two seem happy enough together. I don't know what else you want me to say."

"How about congratulations?"

"Congratulations," he said tiredly. He'd known Alisha for most of his life, and she'd always been a good friend. No one else would have gone along with the crazy idea of marrying him to help him get his inheritance early. She deserved this happiness.

"Have you talked to Mom lately?"

"No."

"She really wants to see you."

"We don't all get what we want, do we?" Spencer asked and punched the wall.

"Spencer, you need to let this anger—"

The last thing Spencer wanted was another lecture. He already felt like shit. "I'm not angry; I'm busy. If you haven't noticed, WorkChat is soaring. Sorry if that means I have to work more hours. I don't have an inheritance to fall back on."

"Spencer—"

There was nowhere good the conversation could go, nowhere good it ever had. "Tell Alisha I'm happy for both of you. I'll send your kid birthday gifts. That'll have to be good enough."

"Still no for attending our wedding?"

"Are we done? I need to get back to work."

"It's amazing how much you sound like our father."

"He's not *my* father."

"Biologically no, but you inherited his asshole gene."

"Fuck you."

Brett laughed. "Hey, I have the same gene—in spades. I sounded just like you a year ago, but meeting Alisha opened my eyes. It doesn't have to be like this. Family is what we make it, Spencer."

"Good talk, Brett. Goodbye."

Brett sighed. "I'll call you tomorrow."

Don't bother. Spencer hung up. *Brett never gave a shit about seeing me or Mom until Alisha told him he should. He falls in love, and all of a sudden he wants to pretend we're close? It doesn't fucking work that way.*

Love.

All it does is fuck a man's head up.

Spencer finished his beer, reached for another, and groaned as he remembered how that kind of thinking had driven him to step into the simulator. There was someone he needed to see. *Her.*

Hailey was my first. Two virgins. Of course we thought we were in love. I was happy I was finally getting laid. That's all it was. If I met her now, I wouldn't spare her a second look. I've been with women so beautiful I could almost taste the envy of the men around me. I've slept with some so talented they could have taught a course on how to give males multiple orgasms.

It probably wasn't even as good as I remember it. And I can prove it.

Jordan had said he'd loaded the drive with Spencer's old photos. "Run album two." The walls around Spencer were replaced by the college quad setting Jordan had programmed in. He knew Jordan well enough to guess the language he would have written for commands. "Show Hailey Tiverton."

"There are one thousand six hundred seven images detected and fifty-eight videos. Play through or isolate and merge?" a computer voice asked.

"Isolate and merge."

"Location?"

With his heart racing, Spencer said, "Garage."

The grass and college dorm buildings faded away, replaced by a representation of the computer lab he'd built in his mother's garage. Although Spencer knew none of it was real, the experience of literally stepping into a memory was unsettling.

Then Hailey appeared on a stool. Her dark hair was pulled back in a ponytail, and her eyes were just as beautiful and deep blue as he remembered. His heart began to thud wildly in his chest just as it always had when she smiled at him. "Your mom said you skipped dinner, so I brought you a sandwich." She held out a wrapped package, and his memory of that day came back to him in full force. "Put the camera down and eat something." Her eyes twinkled, and she smiled at him as she said, "Or put the camera down and kiss me. Your choice." Her delighted laugh echoed through him, and he remembered exactly what he'd chosen that day. His cock tented his pants in excitement.

Fuck, it was that good.

Her image faded away, and she reappeared in another outfit. This time she had an earnest expression on her face. "I feel silly, but if you think this will help, I'll do it. You know I hate cameras. Don't you dare show this to anyone. And I'd better not end up as an avatar. Unless you make me a kick-ass one. Then I guess I'm okay with it. Really? You need more? You're lucky I love you." She looked toward the entrance of the garage, and a huge smile spread across her face. "Jordan, save me. He's working on that voice-to-face recognition software and filming me again." Her laugh rang out and mixed with his and Jordan's just before the vision faded away. Spencer's chest tightened until he could barely breathe as feelings he'd thought were gone emerged in full force.

The next image of Hailey surprised Spencer. It was from a video project she'd helped him with a month after her father died. He remembered how sad she'd been after it happened, but he didn't remember her looking as shattered as she did in the hologram. There were dark smudges beneath her eyes. She looked significantly thinner than she had in the earlier images. She'd always said she was fine, but she hadn't been. Clearly.

The representation of her in the simulator was so real, it was as if he were in the moment with her, and the pain in her eyes tore through him. "Come meet my brother. You'll love him." He nodded. Of course he would go. Then regret filled him as he watched disappointment darken her eyes. He didn't need to hear his own voice to remember what he'd said. She continued, "Of course. I understand. Maybe another weekend?"

She'd needed me. What the fuck had I been working on that was more important?

He'd always thought their breakup had come out of nowhere, but the beginning of it was right there in her eyes.

No wonder she left me for someone else.

"End album," Spencer had said and strode out of the simulator.

In his apartment, Spencer rubbed a hand over his eyes as if that would clear the images still fresh in his mind. His phone beeped with a message. He checked it, then dropped the phone beside him on the couch. Monica was in town. Usually that meant a no-strings, mind-erasing fuck. She called whenever she was between boyfriends, and they had an understanding that was so easy Spencer never turned her down.

Until tonight.

Seeing Hailey again had left him in a funk. He laughed aloud with self-deprecation. *Seeing her? I didn't actually see her. I saw a video of her.*

The real Hailey wasn't that girl anymore. In fact, she was probably married with children. *Probably to that dick she left me for.*

Still . . . That shit was intense.

That realization changed his view of Jordan's side project. Despite the time, he called his friend and left him a message: "Jordan, your album simulator is fucking genius. You're right. It's going to change the world. Call me."

Chapter Three

A week later, Hailey accepted the hand of the formally dressed driver who'd opened the car door for her. "Thank you, Pete." She slid out and stood on the sidewalk in front of a redbrick office building. He closed the door and said he would park but watch for her.

She'd told Mrs. Westerly she didn't require a driver, but her employer had said that having one would allow Hailey to run errands more efficiently and she'd already hired a very nice man who'd been grateful for the work. Mrs. Westerly had ended all of Hailey's protests when she added, "Should I tell him he doesn't have the job? I'm sure he can find other employment." *She definitely knows how to manipulate someone into agreeing.*

Clutching her purse to her side, Hailey paused before stepping away from the black sedan. *What a week.*

She thought back to her first meeting with Mrs. Westerly and marveled again that she was still employed. It hadn't seemed like she would be when the older woman had asked, "What is your version of why you and my grandson Spencer broke up in college?"

"I'm sorry?" Hailey had stalled as she tried to wrap her head around the ramifications of that unlucky coincidence.

"Answer the question or don't, but don't pretend you didn't understand it," Mrs. Westerly had said curtly.

Hailey felt paranoid for even wondering if what appeared to be an unlucky coincidence was something else, but she'd had to ask. "I had no idea you were related."

"You dated for over a year. In all that time, he never mentioned me?"

"No," Hailey had answered without thinking about how it might come across. She was more concerned that Mrs. Westerly knew any version at all of her time with Spencer. *I probably don't want to know, but . . .* "What did he say about me?"

If possible, Mrs. Westerly looked even less happy. "As little as he said about me."

She'd still been trying to wrap her head around the fact that Mrs. Westerly was Spencer's grandmother. Could something that significant have happened by accident? "Did you know about my relationship with Spencer before you hired me?"

"I found out about it after you had applied. Do you think I would move you into my home without looking into your background?"

Hailey had shivered at that. *She knew* and *she hired me.* "But it didn't have anything to do with why I was hired, did it?"

"Did dating my grandson leave you with a particular skill you think I require in a personal assistant?"

"Of course not," Hailey had responded, feeling foolish. *I'm being stupid. It was a long time ago. A coincidence.*

"Then it's of no consequence to me, is it? Unless, of course, you have feelings toward him that would make either of you uncomfortable should you meet up as a result of your employment here."

"No feelings." Relief had flooded in. *Of course. She wants to make sure it won't be an issue.*

"Good, then you shouldn't mind telling me how it ended between the two of you."

It had been tempting to say that her personal life was none of her business, but something told her Mrs. Westerly wouldn't accept such an answer. *And it's not like I have many options.* "My father died just before my sophomore year. It was a tough time for me, and my relationship with Spencer didn't survive it."

"So it wasn't because you were dating someone else."

Hailey gasped. "Of course not. I left school to move in with my *brother.*" *Hold it together. Maybe she just wants to know how I'd feel about seeing him again.*

An emotion that might have been compassion darkened Mrs. Westerly's eyes. "Ryan was the brother you recently lost?"

"Yes," Hailey had said tightly.

"That must have been devastating." The sincerity in Mrs. Westerly's voice had rung true. "I would trade everything I have and every last breath for one more day with my late husband, Oliver."

Hailey had nodded. On the surface she and Mrs. Westerly had nothing in common, but that afternoon they had connected on an elemental level. Michael had said she was lonely. She'd practically admitted she was afraid to die alone. No matter how strong she looked on the outside, Mrs. Westerly was scared. She just wasn't letting it stop her. *She's a survivor.*

Like me.

It was easier to like her after that. Hailey and Skye had stayed for dinner that first night, and it had actually gone well. Mrs. Westerly definitely had strong opinions and a strict view of how things should be, but there was also a kindness to her.

The rest of the week flew by, a blur of settling Skye into a new schedule with Mrs. Tillsbury, spending most of the day with Mrs. Westerly, then having dinner each night at the main house.

Skye loved visiting with Mrs. Westerly. The staff waited on her as if she were royalty. Her needs were anticipated and fulfilled so seamlessly that Hailey worried it would spoil her. It was difficult to be anything but grateful, though, because Skye looked happier each day.

Even Mrs. Tillsbury had commented on how well Skye seemed to have adjusted to the change. Her therapist said the same. No, Skye wasn't talking yet, but there was a light in her eyes that hadn't been there before. Hailey didn't want to get too hopeful, but the move was beginning to feel like the right choice.

Even if the nature of her job left Hailey feeling conflicted.

There were virtually no duties required of Hailey outside of spending time at the main house and listening to Mrs. Westerly reminisce about her early life. *She really was looking for a companion.* An only child, Mrs. Westerly had spent a lot of time on her own or with her nannies, but she always dreamed of having a large family of her own. She'd only been able to have one child and although he lived close by, she didn't see him often.

There was a palpable sadness in Mrs. Westerly, a feeling that her life had not turned out the way she'd imagined it would. Hailey understood that feeling all too well. She understood loneliness as well.

I wish I could refuse to take money for visiting with her. She shouldn't have to pay anyone to sit with her. I need the money, though—so does Skye. Compassion and pride will have to take a backseat to survival.

"Is everything all right?" the driver asked, likely because she had yet to step away from the vehicle.

"Yes, just trying to remember the office number."

"Two thirty-three, I believe."

"Oh yes," Hailey said and pretended to be relieved he knew. She turned to thank him, but her attention was drawn to a silhouette of a man in a dark suit, standing at his office window several floors up. His features were impossible to distinguish from a distance, but for a heartbeat she would have sworn he was watching her. They connected for a moment in a way that shook her.

Inexplicably, she thought of Spencer. Was he in a similar office somewhere, looking out, thinking of her?

Yeah, right.

According to Mrs. Westerly, he lived in the area and was running a successful tech company now. He was also too busy to visit his grandmother.

She shook her head and looked away from the man in the window. *Same old Spencer.*

At least he got his cake.

An hour later, with a small, gift-wrapped package in hand, Hailey opened the door of the main house herself for the first time since she'd been there. Normally, Michael magically appeared to welcome her. His absence was unsettling. Before stepping into the house, she glanced back at the guesthouse. Mrs. Tillsbury's car was still parked in front, which meant Skye was occupied with her lessons. Hailey checked her phone. No message. If something was wrong, someone would have texted her. She took a few deep breaths.

I refuse to panic every time something is out of the ordinary. Things haven't been easy this year, but that doesn't mean they can't get better. One foot in front of the other. One positive action followed by another. That's how you survive. Right, Ryan? Hailey closed the door behind her with a shaking hand. *And things turn around.*

I just need to believe they can.

The sound of someone racing toward her brought Hailey to full alert again. Michael came to a stop beside her, looking flustered. "Mrs. Westerly means well."

"Means well?"

Before Michael had a chance to answer, Mrs. Westerly's voice carried from the library into the foyer. "Your Latin is rudimentary. Your Spanish is not much better, and dare I say your English could use a good polishing as well. Tell me you at least play an instrument. How do you expect to cultivate a love of learning in Skye when you yourself are ignorant? By the look on your face, I've insulted you. Feel free to refute my assessment, but do try to express yourself with some degree of refinement."

Oh no. No. No. No.

"Or stomp away. Go on, then. That's all the evidence I require that you are ill qualified."

Mrs. Tillsbury burst out of the library, showing relief when she spotted Hailey. "Thank God you're here." She came to a skidding stop next to Michael. "I should have asked you if it was okay to bring Skye to the main house, but she seemed excited by the invitation. Your employer, however, is nasty. I have never been so insulted in my life. If I were you, I would keep your niece as far away from that—that horrible woman as you can."

The sense of mortification Hailey had felt when she'd heard how Mrs. Westerly was speaking to the tutor quickly gave way to defensive anger. "Your concern for Skye's welfare is painfully obvious given your departure without her."

Michael coughed back what sounded like a laugh.

"I was coming out here to call you," the woman said in a huff, then waved her hand around aggressively. "You know, I agreed to drive the extra distance because I felt sorry for your niece, but she needs more help than I can give her."

"That is obvious as well," Hailey said tightly. "We won't be requiring your services after today."

"Trust me, I had no intention of returning," the woman said in an unpleasant tone, and walked out.

Michael stayed beside Hailey rather than rushing over to open the door for her. As soon as Mrs. Tillsbury was out the door, Hailey took a step toward the library.

"Wait," Michael said.

Hailey did only because she needed a moment to choose her words. Without turning toward Michael, Hailey asked, "What was she thinking?" Hailey shook her head. "Mrs. Tillsbury wasn't perfect, but Skye was making progress. She liked her. It's not just about finding a replacement. If the loss of Mrs. Tillsbury sets Skye back . . ." Hailey blinked back tears and raised her chin. "I don't know what will happen."

"Mrs. Westerly only gets involved when she cares."

Whipping her head around to meet Michael's gaze, Hailey said, "I understand that, but we have to be careful. It's about what's best for Skye. How do I make her see that? God, what if I can't make this work?"

Michael walked with her to the door of the library, but stopped her just before they stepped inside. In a low voice, he said, "Don't rush to any decisions. Give her a chance."

Hailey shook her head, but Mrs. Westerly was speaking again, and she listened without moving.

"My mother believed that every lady should know at least two languages besides English," Mrs. Westerly said. "I learned French and Spanish. Which would you want to learn, Skye? I'd love to hear you try French. There's no better excuse to spend a month at my home in Marseille than saying you need to work on your accent. We'd include a trip to Paris and *la tour* Eiffel. I haven't been there since I lost Oliver. It would be good to see it again." There was a pause and then Mrs. Westerly added, "Of course, you can't have any accent unless you speak. Try this: *Je parle français.* 'I speak French.' Come on, we'll make it fun. I'll ask you what you speak and you answer *'Je parle français.'* Just like that. Ready? Even better, I'll ask you in French. It'll be just like we're having our first conversation but in a whole new language. *Quelle langue parlez-vous?* Now you answer, *'Je parle français.'*"

Oh, Mrs. Westerly. Hailey remembered trying to bribe Skye to speak in the beginning. *If only it were that easy.*

"*Je parle Français,*" Skye said in a soft voice, so soft that Hailey was sure she had imagined it. She reached out and gripped Michael's arm to steady herself.

"*Très bien,*" Mrs. Westerly said as if nothing extraordinary had just happened. Hopeful tears filled Hailey's eyes. "Now again, but louder. Imagine we are readying ourselves for a day of shopping in Provence, and we had to procure a driver we've never met before. He doesn't know if we speak French, English, Danish. So he asks, '*Quelle langue parlez-vous?*' What would you say?"

"*Je parle Français,*" Skye said confidently.

Hailey met Michael's eyes and fought the prickling of tears. Mrs. Westerly was doing what no one had yet succeeded at.

"*Excellent!*" Mrs. Westerly exclaimed. "I just had the most amazing idea. What if I teach you French, and you teach your aunt? Imagine how proud she would be of you. Then we could all have a wonderful holiday together. Yes? Perfect." Her tone turned serious. "I don't believe Mrs. Tillsbury is coming back. I didn't say anything that wasn't true, but has her departure upset you? If you want me to apologize to her, I will. Personally, I think you could do much better, but tell me if you would like me to say something to her. I will. For you."

Practically holding her breath so she wouldn't miss a word, Hailey listened for Skye's response. Either she didn't answer or did so quietly that Hailey missed it.

"So you won't miss her? Good." Mrs. Westerly continued, "Your aunt will probably be very upset with me when she hears what I've done, but I didn't like the tone your teacher used with you. You are a very smart child who doesn't need to be spoken down to. Still, I did promise I wouldn't get involved. Don't think you can behave as I do until you are at least seventy-five. I was quite well behaved until then. Mostly. I do need your help, though. What could you say that would make your aunt less cross with me?"

"*Je parle français?*" Skye asked.

Hailey peered into the room and was surprised to see Mrs. Westerly smiling. She didn't appear stern at all in that moment as Skye looked up at her with adoration.

"What if she doesn't speak French? There has to be something you could say that would instantly put her in a good mood so we could all enjoy dinner together."

"I could tell her that I love her."

Oh, baby, I love you, too. Everything else, every worry Hailey had, every fear that had plagued her over the last year, was insignificant in the face of how good it felt to hear Skye's voice again. Hailey hugged an arm across her stomach.

"That might just work. And it's true, which makes it perfect. Is there anything else?"

"I like it here."

"Do you? Do you really?"

"Yes."

"Then that's it. That's what you should say. Tell her that you love her. Tell her you like it here. I'll break it to her that I'll be hiring a replacement for Mrs. Tillsbury. By the way, you should help me choose the next teacher, because we know what we want for you. Then, just in case your aunt is still irritated with me, teach her what you've learned in French, and she'll burst into happy tears."

"I don't want Auntie Hailey to cry."

"Of course you don't, but these would be good tears."

There was a pause, then Skye said, "No, they wouldn't. It's better if I say nothing. Everything I say makes Hailey sad."

Hailey straightened. Her hand left Michael's arm and flew to her mouth in horror. *How could she think that? What have I done? It's my fault she's been silent? Oh my God.*

"Nonsense," Mrs. Westerly said firmly.

"She wasn't sad before she had to take care of me."

"Look at me, Skye. And sit up straight when you do. Your aunt loves you. She loved your parents, too. She worries about you and misses them. If she cries at all, that's the reason. It wasn't fair for you both to lose people you loved, but it happened. You two need to be strong for each other and that means no more hiding. You're too smart of a young lady to act like that."

Oh, Ryan, she almost sounds like you.

Or is that what I'm telling myself because I'm afraid of what will happen if this doesn't work out?

Skye didn't have a response for that, and Hailey almost stepped into the room, but Mrs. Westerly began to speak again.

"Do you know that when I was a little girl, children were told to be silent? Not speaking unless one was spoken to was a sign of good manners. Especially for girls. Our opinions didn't matter. Women fought hard to have a voice. Use yours. Don't let anyone ever silence you, Skye, especially not yourself. And when you have a little girl one day, you give her the same advice."

"I'm going to have a little girl?"

"You may."

"How?"

"How what?"

"How does it happen? How do babies get in bellies?"

"Oh, my, is that the door? Michael, is someone at the door?" Mrs. Westerly called out.

Hailey took that as a cue to step into the library. Skye came running to her. Hailey held out her arms, and Skye ran into them. Silently. Hailey wished she had the therapist on speed dial at that moment. *Don't let me mess this up.* "Mrs. Westerly, I saw Mrs. Tillsbury on the way out, and she was very upset. In fact, she won't be back."

"Really," Mrs. Westerly said with a shrug. "It might have been something I said." She looked pointedly at Skye.

Skye pulled on Hailey's arm until she looked down. There was a pause so long Hailey wondered if Skye would revert to silence. "I love you."

Hailey sank to her knees before her niece. How could anything else matter when Skye was speaking again? "I know you do, honey. I love you, too." Hailey glanced at Mrs. Westerly. "Thank you," she mouthed.

Mrs. Westerly nodded once.

"I might be able to convince Mrs. Tillsbury to come back," Hailey said gently. "If you want me to."

Skye looked back and forth between her aunt and Mrs. Westerly. "I didn't like her. She didn't like *me*. Delinda does."

Hailey felt as if her heart were going to burst from the joy of hearing Skye's voice again. "Her name is Mrs. Westerly." *I can't believe I'm correcting her, but we have to have rules. Don't we?*

"She told me to call her Delinda."

"She's my employer, Skye—"

"Michael," Mrs. Westerly said, interrupting Hailey, "please take Skye to the kitchen for a snack. I'm sure she's ready for one."

Michael waved his arm toward the door dramatically. "With pleasure."

Hailey opened her mouth to protest, but closed it without voicing a word. It was probably better if she had a moment alone with Mrs. Westerly.

Mrs. Westerly called out to Skye as they left, "Skye, do remember to remind Miss Jeanie that the dessert tonight is Jell-O. Perhaps you could help her choose the flavor."

"Strawberry," Skye said with a smile. "Strawberry is my favorite."

Hailey was tempted to rush after her for a hug, but instead she waved and took a deep breath. What was Mrs. Westerly giving Skye that she needed? Treating her as if she were a normal child? Maybe it was time for Hailey to do the same. After Skye left the room, Hailey said, "I heard what you said to her; it was beautiful."

"You're welcome," Mrs. Westerly said, looking pleased with herself.

"Things might have gone very differently. You shouldn't have—"

Mrs. Westerly sighed. "So I'm to be lectured about what *didn't* happen?"

"No, but Skye is *my* responsibility." As soon as the words were out of Hailey's mouth, she regretted them. She crossed the room to sit next to Mrs. Westerly. "I'm sorry. I *am* grateful."

Mrs. Westerly nodded. "Well, at least there is that. Tell me, how was the trip to Braintree?"

"Braintree. Oh." Hailey looked down at the package she'd forgotten was still in her hand. She handed it to Mrs. Westerly. "Fine."

"Nothing out of the ordinary?"

"No, it all went smoothly."

Mrs. Westerly made a face at the package and placed it on the table beside her. "I don't like receiving less than promised."

"The package? Was there supposed to be more than one? Should I go back?"

"Don't get all worked up. The fault isn't yours. I'll call to make sure they'll have everything ready before I send you again."

"If you're sure."

"I am. Plus, tomorrow we should screen potentially suitable instructors for Skye. I've already inquired around and have two who might do nicely."

As if you knew we might need one? "That won't be necessary. I'll call the school department and have someone else sent."

"I'm sorry, Hailey, but I must stand firm on this. For as long as you are under my roof Skye will have the best of everything she needs."

"No."

Mrs. Westerly's mouth rounded in surprise. "What did you say?"

Hailey raised her chin and clasped her hands on her lap. "Please. You're incredibly generous, but I can't accept more from you. It'll only confuse Skye. We may not have much money, but we get by. She'll be happier in the long run if she keeps her feet on the ground."

"Of course," Mrs. Westerly said in a cold tone that would have put most people off, but Hailey was beginning to understand her. She wasn't offended; she was hurt.

"You don't have to give us anything. Skye doesn't need a promise of trips to get her to want to speak French with you. If this job ends for whatever reason, you can still invite us to visit, and we'll come. We like you."

Delinda pressed her lips together in a stern line. She was quiet long enough for Hailey to begin to wonder if she'd said too much.

"Call me Delinda."

What? "I couldn't—"

"I insist."

Addressing anyone as staunchly formal as Mrs. Westerly by her first name felt wrong, but the older woman's expression said she'd accept nothing less. "Delinda."

"Skye may do so as well."

Hailey sighed in resignation of a battle she'd already lost. "Since she already is . . ."

"Tomorrow I'll set up a trust fund for Skye's education. Don't tell me not to. She'll blossom with the right instruction. The trust will carry her straight through college." She raised a hand to silence the protest Hailey was about to make. "Don't let your pride deprive Skye of this opportunity."

Hailey wiped away a tear that had spilled down her cheek. *Am I setting Skye and myself up for a disappointment if I choose to believe that something this good could happen for us?* "Why would you do this?"

Delinda laid her hand over Hailey's. "I have smiled more this past week than I have in years. At my age, that's priceless. A friend of mine told me that if I want a rose garden, I shouldn't plant weeds."

"I don't understand."

"You don't have to. You're the rose."

In his Braintree office, Spencer hung up with the CEO of Incom and stretched. It was a huge win for WorkChat and indicative of how the perception of their simulators was shifting from experimental luxuries to touchstone big-business equipment. He was feeling good about the conversation, but not about much else. Jordan had yet to call him back. That wasn't like him.

"Mr. Westerly?" his secretary said tentatively from the door she'd cracked open.

"What?" Spencer asked impatiently, though his irritation was with himself. He'd let Jordan's simulator screw with his head. He'd even imagined seeing Hailey walk into the building that morning.

Of course it wasn't her, but when the woman had looked up in the direction of his office, he'd thought it was. His gut had clenched, and he'd been tempted to run down to check if it was her.

Idiot.

She made her choice a long time ago.

"Your sister is here."

"Which one?"

Before Lisa had a chance to answer, the door burst open and his youngest sibling, Nicolette, strode in as his secretary hastily shut the door behind her. In her usual jeans and T-shirt, Nicolette looked younger than twenty-five. Over the years a few of his friends had described her as "edgy and sexy." *Once.* Spencer made it clear to all that his little sister was off-limits.

Nicolette tossed her purse in one of the chairs in front of his desk and flopped into the other. "God, I miss you. You're an island of sanity in an ocean of crazy."

Despite his foul mood, Spencer smiled. Nicolette was unapologetically over-the-top. He moved to sit on the corner of his desk. "To what do I owe the pleasure of this visit?"

"You missed quite a dinner at Mom's. Alisha's pregnant."

"I know."

"Are you okay?" Nicolette searched his face.

They'd grown up together, covered for each other more times than he cared to admit. He couldn't lie to her. "I don't know." He ran his hand through his hair. "It's complicated."

"I get it. Even if you didn't love her, it still sucks the way it went down. Mom is confused about why we're not all as happy as she is about it. Next week they're telling Grandmother. Don't make me suffer through that without you."

"She's not *my* grandmother."

"You're lucky."

Spencer crossed his arms over his chest. "'Lucky.'" That wasn't how he felt.

"I envy you. You *know*. I keep thinking I want to find out, and then I waver. I can't decide which would be worse. Do I want a father who didn't care enough to spend any time with me or one who raised me without saying who he really was?"

Spencer had asked himself that same question a hundred times. "I don't believe Mark knew I was his."

"That's worse, isn't it? Doesn't it make you wonder what else Mom lied about?"

"I don't think about it."

"You drink instead."

"Don't knock it until you try it," he joked. Then he added quickly, "Don't actually try it. It doesn't help."

"Then maybe you should slow down."

"Maybe I will."

"You're not the only one who wants to escape. Brett and Alisha are too happy. And they always want to spend time with me. I feel bad, but where was Brett before this year? Because he wasn't in my life. Rachelle loves it, but Alisha is her best friend. They act like I'm choosing to be upset. Why would I choose any of this?" She shook her body like a dog shaking off water. "I needed some brother therapy. Tell me I'm not crazy."

"You're fucking bonkers."

Nicolette stuck her tongue out at him. "Jerk. You're no better. At least I'm not all over the Internet. You need to stop hooking up while drunk with women who tag you in their photos."

"That's the truth." She wasn't saying anything he hadn't told himself.

"Want to get lunch?"

Spencer remembered something Brett had said about family being what a person makes it. *Sometimes* Brett was right. He pushed himself off the desk. "Yeah, I'd like that." They walked out of his office together. He told Lisa to field his calls while he was out, then headed down with Nicolette.

A few minutes later, over sandwiches at a coffee shop across the street, Nicolette said, "I'm thinking about taking an internship with Borderless Photographers. They work with grassroots humanitarian initiatives in almost every country. It would be a chance for me to do something important, and a change of scenery might be good for me— get me out of my head. There are a lot of problems in the world that are a whole lot worse than not knowing who my father is . . . or was."

"You should do it."

Nicolette chewed her lip before saying, "I'd have to leave my job, and traveling like that is expensive. I don't have the savings to get me to the places I'd want to go."

"How much money do you need?"

"Maybe none. Dad offered to pay for everything. Mom said no, of course, but I'm not a child anymore. This isn't about Dad buying me a jet or something completely garish. I'd be volunteering for a non-profit organization that works to make the world a better place. I know Mom thinks money is the root of all evil, but isn't it time we decide for ourselves? I should be able to accept Dad's help, shouldn't I?" She picked up half of her sandwich but put it back down without taking a bite. "On the other hand, he might not even be my father, and maybe I should cut him out of my life like you did."

Spencer pushed his own sandwich away, untouched. He hated seeing Nicolette so confused. "I believe we've already determined I'm not the best role model for anyone. When did you talk to Dad?" He almost corrected himself, but what he called Dereck Westerly didn't matter right then.

"We've spoken a few times since Christmas. I went with Brett to see him. He's lonely. I know it's his fault, but I feel bad for him anyway. Outside of Brett and his mother, he doesn't really have anyone in his life."

"And you feel guilty about considering taking his money?"

"Yes."

Their parents sure had fucked things up for their children. "What does Rachelle say?"

"She thinks the world is a dangerous place, and I should work for the local paper or blog about fashion. My dreams are bigger than that. I know you understand."

"I do."

She laughed nervously. "I should do what you almost did and marry one of my friends for my inheritance."

"No. It was a stupid idea when Rachelle came up with it, and I regret taking it as far as I did."

"Why? It might have worked. I mean, if Brett and Alisha didn't . . . the money would free me, Spencer. I could intern for as long as I wanted—guilt-free."

"Marriage isn't something you should play at. There are consequences you don't expect until you do something that foolhardy. Save your vows for someone you love."

"Love? Since when do you believe in it?"

Caught between what he believed and what his sister needed to hear, he chose to leave her with some hope. "Oh, it's real, but it has a nasty propensity for coming when you're least prepared for it." He thought about Hailey and the look of disappointment in her eyes when she'd asked him to go see her brother with her. Yes, Hailey had left him for someone else, but he hadn't been there for her. "Especially if you're not with the person you should have been."

Nicolette cocked her head to the side. "Is there something you want to talk about? Or someone?"

"No." His gut twisted at the idea of Hailey married to someone else. Was she happy? He wanted to be the kind of man who could be happy for her. "But we're talking about you. You want my opinion? Take Dad's money and stop looking for reasons why you shouldn't. He never gave us anything. For all you know, he's buying his own guilt-free ride. That's what you end up doing when you spend your life making shitty decisions."

Nicolette reached across the table and put her hand on his arm. "I wish I knew what to say that would bring us all back to how we were before. I hate seeing you like this."

"Like what?"

Her eyebrows rose and fell, but she didn't say anything.

"Jordan called me an asshole right before he went MIA, so you may have a point."

Nicolette smiled sympathetically. "Recognizing the problem is half of the solution."

"Thanks, Nik."

"It figures that you're fighting with Jordan. He was the only one I thought I could handle being fake-married to."

"Jordan? The two of you could not be more different, and you can barely stand each other."

"That's why I was going to have you talk him into it. He was perfect. He has his own money, so he wouldn't want in on my inheritance; he doesn't even like me, so there'd be no chance that it could get confusing. It would have been a purely legal arrangement. One he would have done as a favor to you."

"No."

"It's moot now anyway if you're not even talking."

"Hell no."

"Okay, okay. Eat your sandwich. You're getting hangry."

Spencer took a bite and frowned. "Stupidest idea you've ever had. Forget it."

"Whatever you say," Nicolette said with a roll of her eyes.

Chapter Four

After days of intensive interviewing of candidates, Hailey was back in Braintree exchanging the package with a secretary who seemed inappropriately amused by the confusion. Hailey shrugged her reaction off. Nothing was going to ruin her mood that day. She'd left Skye at the main house with her new teacher. Mrs. Holihen was a multilingual retired teacher in her sixties who had not only taught college-level courses on early childhood development, but was also a grandmother. Her easy smile and quick wit were selling points, but Hailey's decision had been made when Delinda had asked her where she imagined herself in a few years. Mrs. Holihen had said, "Hopefully spending more time with my grandchildren and perhaps tutoring on the side. Our goal is for Skye to return to school, isn't it?"

"Yes," Hailey had said.

"I can't imagine how difficult the past year was on her, but children need to be around other children, don't they? They're happiest when they have friends."

"I want that for her," Hailey had said barely above a whisper. She was beginning to believe it was within reach for Skye again.

With a nearly identical gift-wrapped package in her hand, Hailey walked out of the office smiling. *Things are finally turning around.*

"Hailey?" a male voice asked.

Hailey came to an abrupt halt. Her eyes raked over the man. The boy she'd known was gone. His shoulders were broader, his features more defined, but the biggest change was in his eyes. There was a hardness she would have never associated with him. "Spencer?"

"Holy shit, it is you." He stepped closer. The frown on his face was anything but welcoming.

Unexpected desire shot through her. She stepped back. Her body remembered his and craved it with an intensity that scared her. *I should feel nothing after all this time.* "Holy shit. You can say that again."

"What are you doing here?" he asked harshly as he looked her over. There was a boldness to his appraisal that normally would have offended her, but her skin warmed beneath his gaze, and she found it difficult to think straight.

"I—I—I'm picking something up." *Yeah, that's the best I can do. I'm a witty one.* How was it possible that the years away from him hadn't diminished the connection she'd felt? She remembered feeling this same way the first time he'd kissed her. They hadn't taken it further that night, but they'd both wanted to. She'd been with other men since, but none made her feel the way he could with just a look. When she'd said as much to her friends, they told her that she'd romanticized Spencer and used his memory to sabotage her other relationships. *I believed them, but it wasn't that. Whatever else we didn't have, we had this.* "How about you?"

"I own the building."

"Of course you do," she said and took a deep breath. *Delinda, what are you up to now?*

"I was told there was a woman out here asking for me." There was a look in his eyes she recognized. He still wanted her. It was too easy to remember another time when a look like that would have led to them sneaking off to anywhere they could be alone.

"That wasn't me," she said, her voice suddenly husky.

"No?" He didn't look like he believed her.

"No." *Is this a test, Delinda? Am I supposed to prove I don't have a problem with him?* She took another step back. She couldn't do this.

He stepped forward, not taking his eyes off hers. "So you're here by coincidence?"

She clutched the package to her chest. "Yes." A little lie was forgivable in such a situation, wasn't it?

"Come to lunch with me."

Her body clamored to say yes, but it had led her astray before. She'd let this exact feeling once convince her that he cared about her. "Thank you, but no." She went to turn away. He surprised her by closing his hand around her upper arm.

Her heart raced in her chest at the tantalizing image of how he would be now. They'd taught each other the basics. What had he learned since? *Stop.*

He leaned in and his breath tickled her lips. "Are you married?"

She shook her head to clear it. "No, but—"

"Is your boyfriend so jealous that you can't catch up with an old friend?"

"I don't have—"

"Then come to lunch with me."

Saying no and walking away would have been her wisest choice. Part of her remembered how good saying yes to him had been in the past—at least in the beginning. Neither was enough for the woman she'd become. "Why?"

Her question seemed to take him by surprise. "Does there have to be a reason?"

The conversation was going nowhere, and Hailey reminded herself that the only important outcome was one that didn't upset Delinda. "It was nice to see you, Spencer. You seem to be living the life you wanted. I'm happy for you, but I really do have to go."

His grip tightened. "Were you here the other day?"

"Yes."

"I knew it. I saw you enter the building. You looked up at me. Did you know it was me in the window?"

Part of her had. She looked away. "No."

"Liar."

She hated the blush that warmed her cheeks. Lying had never come easy to her, but in this case it was necessary. "I have no reason to lie." *No reason I'll tell you about.*

He leaned in closer and spoke into her ear. "What if I said I'm glad you're here? I've been thinking about you, Sunshine."

His old endearment had tears welling in Hailey's eyes. When they'd first started dating, she used to tease him that he spent too many hours holed up in his garage. He'd joke that he didn't need to go out because the sunshine came to him. She wasn't as swayed by his charm this time around. *This time isn't about what I want, and it's better all around if I don't feel anything.* "Please let go of my arm."

He did. "I understand why you left the way you did. It doesn't matter anymore."

Old anger she'd thought was long gone surfaced. "Did it ever matter to you? Did I? Because I've asked myself that a thousand times—until I stopped caring about the answer. I don't want to do this, Spencer. I don't want to rehash what's over."

With that, she walked away from him and into a conveniently open elevator. Her eyes sought his. He looked as miserable after their exchange as she felt. It was a relief when the doors finally closed and she was swept away from him. She made it to her car on shaky legs.

"Is everything okay?" Pete asked.

It was only then that she realized her cheeks were wet from tears. She wiped them away impatiently. "Yes. Sometimes air-conditioning makes my eyes water."

He nodded politely and opened the rear door to the car. "Where to now?"

She slid in and tried to gather her thoughts. "Back to the house, but would you mind taking the long way?"

"Of course," he said gently before he closed the door.

As they pulled away from the office building, Hailey refused to look back. She kept her eyes on the path ahead, but her mind betrayed her intentions by filling with memories from long ago.

Even as a freshman, Spencer had been well known around campus. He'd gotten there on a football scholarship, but his passion was technology, which made him stand out in both worlds. Gorgeous. Brilliant. Driven. Hailey, with her undecided major and full figure, would have never had the courage to approach him on her own. It had been her study partner, Jordan Cohen, who had introduced them.

The first time they'd met, Spencer had been a muscular giant hunched over a tiny keyboard in his mother's garage, writing code. He looked up, their eyes met and held, and they both smiled. And—just like that—they'd known. Life could be complicated and difficult or as easy and amazing as taking a deep breath and leaping.

Hailey couldn't remember him ever asking her out or ever agreeing to see him. They had simply connected. She'd gone to see one of his games, then he'd invited her to join the team for pizza to celebrate the victory. Afterward he'd taken her back to his damn garage to show her a program he was working on . . . and there, in the mix of all his crazy computers, he'd kissed her.

It had felt more than good, it had felt—right. She'd never believed in soul mates or love at first sight, but their connection was undeniable. He made her smile so much her face hurt. He told her that kissing her was better than the rush of adrenaline that followed successfully executing new code.

They met before classes, started and ended each day to the sound of each other's voices, and tested each other's willpower with kisses that drove them both wild. When he'd admitted he was inexperienced, Hailey handed him her heart and her body. He was the one she'd retained her virginity for. Uncomplicated, mutual lust for each other with no reason to deny themselves the pleasure. She doubted there was a corner of his house or the dorm where they hadn't had sex. And it had been good—so, so good.

Years later, it was too easy to remember the sound of his laugh, the feel of his lips as they grazed her skin. He'd been her first, but he wasn't her last. Her breath shouldn't quicken at the memory of his touch. She shouldn't be able to lick her lips and remember his taste. No one else remained as torturously vivid.

None of that matters, though. I can ask myself what would have happened if my father hadn't died. If I had handled the loss better. If I had given Spencer another chance. So many ifs that don't change a damn thing in the end.

I have Skye. She's what matters.

And Delinda. She wanted me to meet him. Why? To make sure it wouldn't be an issue? I won't let it be.

Things are going too well.

During breakfast that morning Hailey had told her niece she had an errand to run for Delinda. Skye had accepted it without an argument or hesitation. *Every day we're better than the day before.*

Skye had smiled—*smiled.* "So I'll stay with Delinda?"

"Mrs. Holihen will be here for your lessons."

Skye had nodded, then asked, "May I have my lessons at the main house?"

"Oh—I don't know if that's a good idea. I'll take you over there later today."

"Please," Skye had begged and Hailey's heart had clenched in her chest. *She likes her new teacher. She's talking again. How can I say no when she asks me for nothing else?*

"Okay, I'll ask Delinda if you can visit with Mrs. Holihen while I'm out."

"She'll say yes," Skye had said with confidence. "I make her happy."

"Yes, you do."

Skye's expression had turned serious. "Are *you* happy?"

Hailey stood, crossed over to where Skye was sitting, and gave her a long hug. "Oh, honey, I sure am. Do you know that the best day of my life was when you were born and I became an aunt?"

"Really?"

Hailey kissed the top of her head. "Really. I was even in the room when you were born because your mother knew how much I would love you."

Skye's eyes had widened. "Dad told me you were there. He said you cried."

Hearing Skye mention Ryan gave Hailey hope that the worst might really be over. "I did. I knew my life would never be the same—in the best possible way."

Skye had searched her face, then nodded. "I love you, Auntie Hailey."

"I love you, too." Hailey had smiled even as she blinked back tears. "I'll call Delinda right after we get dressed." She checked the time on her phone. "We'd better hurry, though. Want to race? First one fully dressed with hair and teeth brushed gets to do the breakfast dishes."

"Wait. Wait. Wait. Who would want to win that?" Skye had asked with a laugh.

"You used to love to wash the dishes. I was always pulling you out of the sink when you were little."

"I'm not a baby anymore."

"Okay, then loser does the dishes." Feeling more lighthearted than she had in long time, Hailey had posed like a runner at a starting line. "Deal?"

Skye had run off in a flash, and Hailey had smiled all the way through getting dressed. *I can't worry about all the ways this could go wrong. Stay positive. One foot in front of the other. Stay strong and true to yourself and you'll find happiness again. My brother was a very wise man.*

Spencer strode through his secretary's office to his. *What the hell was that? What was I doing?*

He went to the window, but she was gone. *I don't want to look back any more than she does.*

A memory of her boldly kissing him and luring him away from his work by whispering what she wanted to do slammed through him. His cock jerked as his senses flooded with anticipation at the possibility of having her again, tasting those sweet lips, gripping her delicious ass to raise her so he could thrust up into her. *So there's that.*

Jordan.

Spencer pulled out his phone. *This is his fucking fault.*

S: Hailey came to my office today.

Despite the fact that Jordan hadn't answered any of his messages that week, his reply was fast.

J: The Hailey?
S: Yep.
J: How is she?
S: Gorgeous. Single.
J: But?
S: Not interested in me. Couldn't get away from me fast enough.
J: Then she's gotten smarter with age.

S: Fuck you. (He knew Jordan laughed at that.) Hey, I know I've been a dick lately. I found out that my father isn't my father, and it's screwing with my head. When Jordan didn't have a quick answer, Spencer added: My stepfather was my biological father.

J: I know. I'm surprised you didn't.
S: Wtf?
J: You're blond. Mark was blond. Everyone else in your family has dark hair like your mother and her first husband. It was a no-brainer.
S: Thanks for fucking saying something.
J: I thought you knew.

His grandmother had said the same to him. At the time he hadn't believed her, but now he threw back his head and laughed without humor at how stupid he'd been to not see it.

S: I didn't. From now on, just assume I'm dumb as fuck and mention that kind of shit to me.
J: Okay. Then you're probably wrong about Hailey.
S: What?
J: That girl loved you.
S: So much that she broke up with me for someone else.
J: Did she? I don't remember her as the cheating type.
S: I saw her with him.
J: Or you thought you did. You are not exactly Mr. Intuitive.

There was no arguing that, so Spencer didn't. He wasn't introspective by nature, and he'd never found any value in asking people why they did what they did. He wasn't sure anyone even fucking knew.

But if Hailey didn't leave me for someone else—why did she leave? And who was she with that day?

S: I need her phone number.

J: I don't know it.

S: But you know how to get information like that.

J: Look her up on social media. That's how it's done nowadays.

S: I want to call her, not stalk her. Come on, Jordan.

J: Just her number.

Spencer counted in his head. A phone number appeared via text before he got to ten. Jordan was that good.

S: You're amazing.

J: Spencer.

S: Yes?

J: Don't hurt her again . . .

I never, Spencer typed, then paused before sending. *Or did I? Was it me? She asked if I cared, if I'd ever cared. Didn't she know?*

S: I won't.

Chapter Five

A nervous acid churned in Hailey's stomach as soon as she saw several cars parked in Delinda's driveway. She was out of the car and halfway up the stairs of the main house before Pete had time to offer her a hand. The front door opened.

Michael had that anxious look on his face again. "Mrs. Westerly probably should have asked you—"

"Yes, she should have. Who's here? Who is she introducing Skye to?"

Just then a small herd of children squeezed by Michael and burst down the steps. One of them, a boy who looked about Skye's age, stopped right in front of Hailey and called over his shoulder, "False alarm. It's just some lady."

The group turned in unison and stampeded back into the house.

Real panic rose within Hailey. She and the therapist had plans to introduce children back into Skye's life. It had to be done carefully so as not to traumatize her. "Where's Skye?" Hailey asked in a high pitch.

"She's inside," Michael said. "If I might be so bold as to suggest—"

Hailey pushed past Michael. "Please don't tell me what to do or not to do when it comes to my niece. I need to see Skye. Oh my God, this must be overwhelming for her. Delinda has to realize that she can't keep pushing her." Rushing through the house, Hailey called out to her niece again and again. She didn't answer, and Hailey crossed the rest of the foyer in a run.

She spotted Skye darting out the back door with several other children and chasing after them. They looked as if they were playing some sort of tag game in and around a large stone chess set. She called out to her again, but Skye didn't hear her.

"It's good to see her playing with other children, isn't it?" Mrs. Holihen asked as she joined Hailey.

"Yes," Hailey answered automatically, but she was still full of adrenaline and worry. "You should have called me when they arrived."

Mrs. Holihen's mouth rounded in surprise. "I thought you knew."

"I didn't," Hailey said abruptly. Skye turned toward the house, saw her, and waved before joining in another wild race with the children. Her laughter carried across the lawn and confused Hailey even more. Of course she wanted Skye to be happy, but the situation felt out of control. Hailey didn't know if she should be thrilled or angry with Delinda . . . again. "Who are those children?"

"They attend Sterling Waters, a private school, right here in town. They're in camp this time of year, so Mrs. Westerly suggested that meeting them might get Skye interested in attending the school in the fall. How amazing for you to have an employer who is also like a guardian angel for your niece. Their connection is heartwarming."

"Yes, heartwarming," Hailey echoed. *And scary.* "So the camp moved over here for the day? Just like that?"

Mrs. Holihen smiled. "Mrs. Westerly had me call the headmaster yesterday and ask if any second graders would like a quick field trip to her house. I've never seen any faculty fall all over themselves to make something happen. From what I understand, every single parent at that school would love for their child to be friends with Mrs. Westerly's great-grandchild."

"Great-grandchild? You know we're not related to her."

"I do, but it seems that Mrs. Westerly and Skye like pretending you are. From the way doors fly open at the mere mention of her name, I would love it if Mrs. Westerly adopted *me*." Mrs. Holihen's humor was lost on Hailey.

Hailey brought shaking hands to her cheeks. Skye was still laughing and playing with the other children. *Why do I feel like I should grab her and run?*

Is it selfishness? Do I resent that Delinda is succeeding where I failed? No, it's not that.

I'm right to be worried. This is all happening too fast, and it could end. I don't want Skye to get hurt.

Hailey's phone rang in her purse, but she didn't answer it. Her attention was on her niece. She was ready to intervene at the first sign of distress.

"There you are," Delinda said from the doorway. A tall, stocky Italian man who looked to be in his late sixties accompanied her. "Hailey Tiverton, meet one of my dearest friends—Alessandro Andrade."

Hailey held out her hand to shake his.

The man smiled warmly, then pulled her to him for a bone-crushing hug that lifted her off her feet. "Good to meet you." He was a lot stronger than he looked.

Once released, Hailey lowered her hand and caught her breath. "You, too."

Delinda beamed. "You beat the ponies. Skye said she adores them, so I'm having some brought out for her to meet. Two of the girls she is playing with board theirs at a farm in Sterlington. Horses give girls confidence and will provide her a hobby. I'm excited to see the selection today. My riding days are over, but I have many fond memories of my childhood pony, Cinnamon."

"No," Hailey said weakly, then repeated herself in a firmer tone. "No pony."

Delinda turned and looked back toward the front door of the house. "Michael is waving for me to come, so they must be arriving now." Her smile was bright, and she briefly took Hailey's hand in hers. "My heart is racing like it did when I chose my own pony. I didn't think I'd ever feel this excited about anything again. Thank you. I can't wait to see which one she chooses." With that, Delinda turned and walked briskly back into the house.

Momentarily forgetting the older man at her side, Hailey searched the crowd of children for her niece. Skye was standing with another little girl laughing about something, laughing just as joyously as Skye had before her parents had died. Relief battled with self-doubt and guilt.

This isn't our life. It's a dream that could crash and burn on the whim of my employer. I need to put a stop to it.

But how can I when Skye is finally looking like herself again? Do I have a right to take this away from her?

I didn't put that smile on her face. I was the reason she wasn't talking. Was I also the reason she wasn't healing? I keep thinking I know what's best for her, but do I? Maybe I'm doing everything wrong. Ryan, maybe you entrusted your daughter to the wrong person. Hailey wiped a stray tear from her cheek and sniffed loudly. *I'm trying, Ryan. What would you do?*

Alessandro cleared his throat beside her. "Would it help if I spoke to Delinda?"

With a shaky, indrawn breath, Hailey said, "No, but thank you. I'll talk to her."

"She means well."

"I know."

"Delinda has been a second mother to me. It's good to see her excited and happy again."

Watching Skye play, Hailey chose her words carefully. "Delinda is amazingly generous." *I know being here feels good, but this isn't our life. I don't want to deny her a moment of this dream, but what happens if we have to wake up and go home?*

"She likes you, and she doesn't like many people."

Hailey hugged an arm to her stomach. "She said as much, but I don't agree. She has a soft heart under all that tough talk."

Alessandro's voice deepened with emotion. "That she does. I was worried when I heard you were here, but now I understand."

"Really? Sometimes I'm not so sure I do."

Without warning, Hailey flew forward and would have tumbled down the stairs had Alessandro not caught her arm. A flurry of apologetic children encircled them, then rushed down the steps, calling out that there were ponies in the driveway.

Skye ran up the steps and came to a skidding halt in front of Hailey. "Delinda is getting me a pony. A pony, Auntie Hailey. Can you believe it? She said I can take riding lessons." There must have been something in Hailey's expression because Skye's smile wavered. "Please don't say no."

"Ponies need—" *Hell, I've never had a pony, but I know we can't afford one.*

"Delinda said I could."

"Delinda does not make the decisions for our family."

The previously sweet, withdrawn Skye stomped her foot and said, "I'm getting a pony." She glared at Hailey and ran past her into the house.

And just like that, Hailey was thrown a new worry—one worse than the fear that their time there might end suddenly: *Who will we become if we stay?*

How did Skye go from withdrawn and fragile to outspoken and bratty?

Delinda.

No. That's not fair. Coming here was my decision. How it plays out is on me as well. I'll talk to Delinda and explain to her that she absolutely can't make any decisions when it comes to Skye without consulting me.

A month ago I would have done anything, promised anything, just for the chance to hear her voice again. Coming here brought the old Skye back to life.

At what cost? I can't let her begin to think that money equates to happiness. Our family has never obsessed over material things. Ryan wouldn't want his daughter to. No pony.

On the other hand, the pony would give her a connection to the other girls. She has lost so much. How can I even consider taking something else from her?

The aunt in me wants to spoil her and celebrate all the good I've seen in her.

Ryan gave me custody of her, though, because he knew I would love her as if she were my own daughter. I'm a better person because Ryan challenged me to be one. He supported me when I needed him most, but then he made sure I was strong enough to stand on my own. As much as I want Skye to be happy, what am I teaching her if I say yes? How much do we accept from Delinda? Where's the line? "I don't know what to do."

In a deep, sympathetic tone, Alessandro said, "I have one daughter, and she has given me all of these gray hairs." He touched her shoulder gently. "My advice, even though you haven't asked for it, is: Pick your battles. You've already lost this one, but regroup. There's a chance you may win the next."

Shaking her head, Hailey laughed without humor. "I thought I knew what I was doing, but now I wonder if I'm doing anything right."

"I remember that feeling, but it passes. Have faith in yourself. My daughter now has children of her own, and I am able to enjoy watching her fumble through the process. It's not easy for anyone, but love goes a long way to smooth out the mistakes we make."

I just hope my greatest mistake wasn't in coming here. "I know Delinda means well, but—"

"She is as giddy and excited as your niece. You could take that from her, but do you want to?"

The image of Skye stomping her foot returned. She definitely needed to be reined in. *How do I do that without being the killer of all joy?* "Tell me it gets easier."

"It doesn't, but I would do every stage all over again if I could. Come, let's go see which pony you're adding to your family." They started walking, and he asked, "Is your back cold?"

Only when he said it did Hailey realize part of it was. Her hand automatically sought the source. Ice cream—a nice blob of it was smeared into the back of her shirt. "Perfect. Just perfect."

Alessandro chuckled. "Children—a blessing and a bane. Go change, and I'll stall the equine adoption process until you return."

With a nod, Hailey sprinted down the steps and across the lawn to the guesthouse. She rushed to her bedroom and pulled her shirt over her head, then dropped it in the bathtub. She had just finished pulling on a new shirt when her phone rang. *It's probably a zoo calling to announce the delivery of lions or fucking unicorns.*

She answered her phone while striding out of her bedroom. "Hello?"

"Hailey, it's Spencer."

She froze. "Hi." She almost asked him how he got her number, but decided it didn't matter.

"I haven't been able to concentrate since I saw you."

What was the proper response to that? "I'm sorry?" she said in a joking tone.

"Don't be." His voice lowered to a deep purr. "Dinner tomorrow night—six o'clock. Tell me where to pick you up."

"No."

"Thursday, then."

She hesitated. *Yes . . . No. What am I thinking? Of course I can't see him.* "I can't."

"Lunch, then."

She chuckled nervously. Spencer had never lacked in confidence. It was what had drawn her to him in the beginning. If he cared what anyone thought of him, it hadn't been his college classmates.

And in the end—not even me.

After not hearing from him for so long it should have been easy to turn him down, but it wasn't. The boy had become a man who knew what he wanted and, for the moment at least, that appeared to be her. *We always did have bad timing.* "It wasn't the time of day that was the issue."

"There are things we never talked about—things we should have."

Some of her frustration with Delinda and Skye spilled over into her response. "I'm allowed to say no. It doesn't make me a bad person. It doesn't mean that I don't want everyone to be happy. Sometimes no is the right answer. Of course I want to agree to everything. Who wouldn't? But where does it all lead? I can't just throw caution to the wind and fill my life with ponies and ex-boyfriends and think there won't be consequences." She stopped to take a breath and groaned. *Yeah.*

"Consequences?" he asked slowly.

"We don't have anything left to say to each other, Spencer. It's too late." She walked to the front of the guesthouse and watched Skye being led up and down the long driveway on a white pony with a long flowing mane and tail. The exhilaration on her face mirrored Delinda's. "We can't always do what we want and think there won't be a price for it later."

"You asked me if I ever cared about you. I did, Sunshine. I still do."

Tears welled in Hailey's eyes, but she blinked them back. "It wasn't all you, Spencer. When my father died, I kind of crumbled."

"I should have been there for you."

"Maybe you would have been if I'd been able to tell you what I needed, but I didn't know how. All I knew was that I needed to feel safe again."

"Is that why you jumped right into another relationship?"

"I did what?"

"I saw you with him—the guy you left me for. You were all over him."

"What guy?"

"Tall with curly hair and glasses."

"Greg? You saw me with Greg? He was my brother's friend."

Spencer growled. "He looked pretty damn friendly toward you when I saw you with him."

"Honestly, I don't remember. But he did try to cheer me up when I first moved in with Ryan." Like every other man besides Spencer, he'd faded away, unimportant and easily forgotten.

"Did you date him?"

"No, he asked me out, but—" *But I was in love with you and devastated when you didn't come for me.* "So that's why I never heard from you again? You saw me with Greg, and that was it? You were done?"

"You said we were over."

Tears filled Hailey's eyes. "It doesn't matter, I guess."

He sighed harshly. "It does. I was jealous as hell when I saw you with him. The idea of another man touching you made me—still makes me—" He swore. "I thought you had moved on."

The emotion in his voice dissolved the years away. For just a moment she was a young woman hearing her boyfriend open up in a way he never had.

No. He's not mine anymore. I'm not his. We're just two people who had something a long time ago. Love came when neither of us was ready for it. "I went home to be with my brother because I didn't feel like I had anyone else."

He swore again. "Meet me tomorrow."

It would never be the same. Not to mention how dangerous it is to even consider starting something with Spencer while working for his grandmother. "It's hard for me to get away right now. My employer—"

"Lunch. Everyone is allowed one. Tell me where you work, and I'll pick you up."

"No. Don't come here." *Oh, God, why does it feel so good to know he wants to see me?*

"I'm not giving up. Not this time."

Yep, that's why. Spencer 2.0 is everything I liked about the earlier version and more. Saying yes would be so easy, but then what?

Saying no was impossible.

Delinda wasn't the only one who was lonely. Hailey couldn't remember the last time she'd done something for herself. Her social life had come to an abrupt halt when she'd taken Skye in. Meeting Spencer for one lunch didn't need to lead to anything else. *It can't. I'll have to be clear about that.* "One lunch. It wouldn't be a date."

He chuckled softly. "Just two people meeting for old times' sake."

"Yes."

"Do you remember Mangiarelli's Pizza?"

No fair. He'd chosen their old college hangout. "I don't," she lied.

"Really? Luckily, it's on Yelp with directions. I'll see you there at noon."

"Noon," she echoed breathlessly.

"Hailey?"

"Uh-huh?" Her head was spinning.

"I'm glad you said yes. See you tomorrow."

After he hung up, she sat on the couch in the living room and took several deep breaths. *I was going to ask Delinda why she'd sent me to Braintree and arranged for me to meet him, but now I can't. All she'd have to do is ask me one question, and I'd crack and tell her everything.*

What had Alessandro said? "Pick your battles."

Hailey pushed herself off the couch and headed out of the guesthouse and over to the driveway where Delinda and Skye were fawning over an all-white pony. They looked up at her approach, and both expressions became guarded.

The children were standing around in a loose circle, seemingly equally excited about Skye's choice. *I can't say no.*

But I have to say something.

"Skye, come here." Skye looked from the pony to Delinda, beseeching her to intervene. Delinda opened her mouth to say something, but Hailey didn't give her a chance to. "Now, Skye."

Reluctantly, Skye stepped away from the group and over to Hailey. Hailey took her by the hand and led her just far enough away that the others wouldn't hear, then bent down so her face was level with Skye's. "I love you more than you will ever know. I want you to be happy, Skye, but you know your behavior earlier was not appropriate."

Skye glared at her, defensive and angry. Hailey didn't back down even though it broke her heart to see her niece look at her that way. Eventually, Skye blinked and looked down. "I really want the pony, Auntie Hailey."

"I know you do, Skye, but we don't have the money for it."

Skye's shoulders slumped. "Delinda will buy it."

"Look at me, Skye. Delinda's money is not our money. This is not our house. I don't want you to get confused."

Skye glanced over her shoulder at the children who were watching them. When she looked back at Hailey, her eyes were so sad it took everything in Hailey not to burst into tears and hug her. "I understand."

I could be doing this all wrong, Ryan, but I hope not. "Do you, Skye? Because I'm waiting on an apology for the way you spoke to me earlier. We're on the same team, you know, and we always will be."

"I'm sorry." No seven-year-old had probably ever sounded more dejected.

"That's why we'll find a way to afford that pony. You and me. We'll let Delinda buy it for you today, but we'll pay her back. I'll put aside some money, and you'll pick up chores around the house to earn it. It's not going to be easy. We'll need to buy a saddle and brushes, and stabling a pony is probably very expensive. We can only get the pony, Skye, if you agree to work for it."

Wonder returned to Skye's eyes. "You're letting me get her?"

Hailey held out her hand for her niece to shake. "It depends on you. Do we have a deal? Are you willing to work to buy your own pony?"

Skye bypassed the handshake and threw her arms around Hailey. "Thank you. Thank you. Thank you."

"Does she have a name?"

"Clover," Skye said. "You are going to be so happy you let me have her. I'm going to work hard and be good."

She hugged her niece tighter to her. *Imagine that, we both have the same personal goals.* "Ready to introduce me to your new pony?"

"Oh yes!" Skye bounced and took her by the hand, dragging her toward the pony with the same determination Hailey had dragged her away with.

Delinda watched their approach with a carefully blank expression. "Is everything all right?"

"Absolutely." The curious audience made any other response impossible. There would be time later for what she needed to say.

Skye ran her hand along the pony's neck, beneath her mane. "You have to feel right here, Auntie Hailey. She's so soft."

Hailey followed the same path down the pony's mane, and the pony threw up her head and whinnied. "She's beautiful."

"And she's mine." Skye threw her arms around the pony's neck, and Hailey was relieved to see the calmness with which the pony accepted her affection.

Michael announced that more ice cream was being served on the front lawn. The children cheered and bolted away. The woman holding the pony's lead line explained that the pony would be delivered to the barn that evening and they could come by anytime.

Skye looked up at her aunt. "Can I—?"

"Of course." Hailey didn't need to wait for the question to be asked. She'd be lucky if Skye didn't ask to sleep there with the pony.

"May," Delinda corrected firmly. "*May* I."

Confusing Delinda's correction with a request, Skye turned from the pony and threw her arms around Delinda's waist. "Of course you can come with us. Right, Auntie Hailey?"

One glimpse of the hopeful light in Delinda's eyes that mirrored Skye's and Hailey caved. "Would you like to come with us, Delinda?"

Alessandro joined them. With Skye still clinging to her, Delinda blinked a couple of times quickly, then grasped his forearm. "Aren't they perfect?"

Perfect for what? The hair on the back of Hailey's neck rose in sudden apprehension.

Alessandro patted Delinda's hand.

Skye darted off to hug the pony again before it was loaded onto a trailer. While she was out of earshot, Hailey focused on what she'd planned to say. "Delinda, Skye is going to pay you back for the pony. Please allow her to. She's agreed to do extra chores with me to earn the money for it."

"I see no need to have her—"

"I do, and since I'm her guardian and aunt, if I say that's the only way she will get the pony, it's the only way. And if you ever plan another event for her without consulting me, I will have no choice but to give you my resignation and find other employment."

"How dare you—?"

"I dare because no one is more important to me than Skye. I like you, Delinda, and I really need this job, but nothing comes before my niece and what is best for her."

Delinda pressed her lips together in a line, then looked at Alessandro. "It's no wonder she can't keep a job. Do you hear how she talks to me?"

Rather than getting angry with Delinda for the barb, Hailey recognized it as an attempt to avoid addressing the threat. "I'm serious, Delinda."

"I can't imagine how you could have a problem with me wanting her to have friends and getting her excited about going back to school—"

"Promise that you'll ask me before you plan anything else for Skye."

Delinda narrowed her eyes like a petulant child.

Hailey held her breath and raised her chin.

The second standoff of the day ended much as the one with Skye had—Delinda blinked first, then nodded her concession. Alessandro bellowed out a hearty laugh that had Delinda spinning to wag a finger at him. "Don't you dare laugh at me."

His grin was wide and unabashed. "They really *are* perfect, Delinda."

"Hush," Delinda said in a stern voice that did nothing to intimidate Alessandro. Her expression was serious when her eyes met Hailey's. "I promise to consult you before I even consider doing anything nice for you or Skye. Are you happy now?"

She's lashing out because she's hurt. She doesn't have an ulterior motive. She's just a lonely old woman who doesn't know how to connect with people. How awful to be her age, to have all the material things she had, and still not understand how relationships worked.

Hailey took a page from Skye's book and pulled Delinda to her for a tight hug. It was a bit like embracing a plank of wood, but when Hailey stepped back, Delinda looked both flustered and moved by the experience. "Just because I don't agree with how you did it, doesn't mean that I don't appreciate what you did. Thank you for caring about Skye enough to arrange all of this."

Delinda cleared her throat and in a stern tone said, "Hailey, how do you expect that poor woman to be able to load the pony with Skye hanging all over it? Take her to play with the other children before the day ends without her having made any friends at all. I didn't invite that unruly herd here just so they could trample my flowers."

"Of course," Hailey said with a smile. *That tough-as-nails act only makes me want to hug you again.* She walked over to where Skye was promising the pony that she would visit that evening as if it could understand everything she was saying. "Skye, you have company waiting to spend more time with you."

Skye rubbed the pony's nose. "I have to go, Clover, but don't worry. You're my best friend. I'll never leave you, and you'll never leave me. Right, Auntie Hailey?" The uncertainty in her voice gave the question a crushing emotional weight.

Hailey wanted to promise her niece that nothing would ever come between her and Clover. Her heart broke at the realization that she couldn't. Life didn't work that way. Hailey had been about Skye's age when she asked her father why she didn't have a mother. He'd told her the truth, that her mother hadn't wanted to be a mother anymore. At the time, it had hurt Hailey to hear it, but over time she'd understood that lies would have been worse. At least she had the truth. "Ponies are a big responsibility. Remember that you'll have to work to repay Delinda."

Dammit, Delinda. Couldn't you have gotten her a bunny?

"I will," Skye promised, and Hailey hugged her.

Hand in hand, they walked toward where the other children were playing. *Will I ever watch you fumble through raising your own little ones? I hope so. Not about the fumbling part. I hope you do better than I am, but maybe we'll look back and laugh at what right now feels catastrophic.*

After returning Skye to the group, Hailey sat on the stone wall that lined a garden and her mind wandered to Spencer. *I really can't judge Skye for wanting something of her own.*

It took being with other men to realize how unique what I had with Spencer was. Her thoughts wandered back to the simple joy of laughing for hours with him at Mangiarelli's. *We never needed more than each other to be entertained. It was that good.*

Is it a mistake to go back there? I'm not that carefree girl anymore. He's not a football-playing computer geek. What could we be now except for two strangers reminiscing over something that had been good but also too fragile to survive when tested?

He thought I broke up with him for someone else.

I thought he'd never even bothered to come after me.

What did we know?

Maybe Mangiarelli's will be where we forgive not only each other but ourselves.

An image of him leaning over her in the hallway of his office building teased her senses. Her body warmed as she remembered how good it had felt to be near him again. He'd always been attractive, but the boy she'd known had become a man . . . a yummy, confident, sexy man. His eyes were as deliciously dark as she remembered, but his face had stronger lines. He was still built like he could plow across a football field, but there was now a sophistication about him. She'd never imagined him in a suit, but *damn*, he wore it well.

One lunch.

That's it.

We'll talk about the past, have a few laughs, and leave with a sense of closure.

Yes, that's why I'm going. I need . . .

Images of the two of them, pulling off each other's clothing with lustful frenzy, temporarily overwhelmed her. She was there again, arching her naked breasts against his bare, muscular chest. His hands were cupping her ass, lifting her off her feet. She was once again wrapping herself around him, welcoming his cock, begging him to go deeper, harder. The memory shifted, and she was clutching the back of the couch in his garage while he rammed into her from behind. Her body clenched at the hot memory. Yes, they'd had problems, but sex was never one of them. Being with him had always been sinfully, blissfully easy.

Closure.

She shook her head and took a deep breath, glad she was alone.

The next morning could not go by fast enough. Normally Spencer lost track of the time while working on a project, but his eyes kept returning to the clock. He swore when he realized only fifteen minutes had passed since the last time he'd checked the time.

The door of his office flew open and his older sister, Rachelle, strode in, followed by an apologetic Lisa. "I'm sorry, Mr. Westerly. I told her you were busy."

Spencer stood and stretched. He wasn't getting much done, anyway. "It's fine, Lisa. Hold my calls."

"Yes, Mr. Westerly." Lisa closed the door as she left.

With her dark hair pulled back in a ponytail, and dressed in jeans and a flowered blouse, his sister sat in one of the chairs in front of his desk. She and Nicolette had a lot in common, although he doubted either would admit it. Nicolette considered herself the angsty rebel of the family. Rachelle saw herself as a second mother to her younger siblings. The three of them had once been close, but lately their visits were a harbinger of a headache. "What's up, Rach?" *Wait for it. Wait for it.*

"You have to tell Nicolette that she can't take money from Dad. Mom is beside herself."

Spencer moved to the front of his desk and sat back against it. *And they wonder why I don't take their calls.* "Hello, Rachelle. It's nice to see you. Hello, Spencer, it's great to see you, too."

Rachelle sighed impatiently. "Could you be serious for one minute? Everyone is really upset. You shouldn't have gotten involved. You know how Mom feels about Dad's money."

"Whoa," Spencer said as he raised one hand out in front of him. "First, Nicolette asked me for my opinion, and I gave it to her. Second, money is not evil—people are. If Nicolette wants to take her father's guilt money and do something good with it, you and Mom are the ones who should back the fuck off."

Rachelle's mouth rounded in surprise. "Did you just swear at me? Are you okay, Spencer?"

After twelve months of telling himself and everyone else that he was fine, he snapped. "No, I'm not okay. I'm pissed. Every fucking day. But do you know what I'm not doing? I'm not going to visit you at work and ram how I feel down your throat. Nicolette came to me. If that upsets Mom, then she can get over it. She does not get to tell us how we should live our lives anymore. When I think of all the crap she spewed about how keeping our lives simple would make us into better people. Being poor didn't do much for her character, did it? It sure as hell didn't make her honest."

Silence hung heavy in the room.

What he'd said had been a long time coming, but he regretted the way he'd said it. Rachelle had gone pale. Spencer stood and ran a hand through his hair. *I need Dicks Anonymous. Hi. My name is Spencer Westerly. I'm a dick. Not a recovering one; still a dick.* "Sorry, Rach. This is why I'm staying away from the family. You don't need this. I don't want this. I was actually in a good mood before you came." His sister's face crumpled. *Fuck. Even when I'm trying to be nice, I'm an ass.* "I didn't mean that the way it sounded. I meant that today was a good day before—"

Rachelle raised her hands in a plea for him to stop. "I get it." She stood. "I shouldn't have come."

Shit.

He sank into the seat next to the one she'd vacated. "Don't leave. That came out wrong. I should think before I speak."

"Why start now?" she asked in a tone that made him question if there had been a day of his life when he hadn't been an ass. Then she smiled. "I'm just as bad. Sorry. Everything sounded better in my head before I said it."

"I understand that feeling."

She grimaced and sat down next to him. "I wish we could go back to the way we were before."

"It was a lie, Rach," he said bluntly. "I don't want to go back, but we do need to find a way to move forward."

"How do we do that, Spence? How do we piece our family back together?"

He shrugged one shoulder. If he had the answer, he wouldn't have kept it to himself. "I'll try to be less of a miserable prick. It may improve nothing, but I'll give it a shot."

Rachelle smiled again. "You sound serious."

"Sadly, I am."

"What do you need me to do?" she asked quietly.

If ever there were a loaded question . . . He looked across at his sister's earnest expression and laid his hand briefly over hers. "Keep being you. Keep calling. Keep driving me crazy. Someday when I have my shit back together, I'll be grateful for it."

She nodded and blinked a few times quickly. "Join me for lunch?"

The alarm on his phone went off, announcing it was time for him to head out to meet Hailey. He silenced it and stood. "I would, but I have a date."

Rachelle rose to her feet. "A date? During the day? Do you know this one's name?"

He escorted her to the door of his office. "Funny. Yes, I know her name. We used to go out."

"That narrows it down to half the women in the Boston area. Who is she?"

They stopped in front of his secretary's desk. "Lisa, I'm going out to lunch. I may be back today; I may not."

"Yes, Mr. Westerly."

Rachelle linked arms with Spencer as they walked out of the office. "Are you going to tell me or is it a secret?"

"It's not a secret, but I'm not saying anything yet."

Rachelle stopped. "Yet? This sounds promising."

Spencer pressed the call button for the elevator. "It's lunch with an old friend." His mood lifted at the thought of seeing Hailey again.

"An old friend, my ass. I've seen that look on your face before. In college. What was her name?"

Spencer pressed the button again. "Do you expect me to remember all of their names?"

Rachelle rolled her eyes and scratched her head. "As if you looked up from your computer and noticed any of them. Hanna. No. Heather." She snapped her fingers. "Hailey. *She* was the only one who ever put that goofy, smitten expression on your face."

Spencer opened his mouth to deny that he was meeting Hailey, but he'd never lied to Rachelle. "Goofy? Thanks."

"Am I right? Is it her?" They stepped into the elevator together. "Oh, Spencer, be careful. You hid out at my place with what you thought was the flu after you saw her with someone else. You thought you were dying. She broke your heart. We all felt so bad for you."

Spencer groaned as he hit the button for the lobby. The door closed. "You're remembering it worse than it was."

Rachelle made a face, but otherwise didn't dispute his claim. "How did you meet up with her again?"

"She came to see me."

"Out of the blue?"

"Yes."

Rachelle made a disapproving sound.

"Say it," Spencer said impatiently.

Rachelle touched his arm. "Do you think it had anything to do with how you and WorkChat are in the news lately? Mom always said that money attracts people—the wrong kind of people."

"Hailey's not like that." He honestly hadn't considered that possibility. The Hailey he remembered hadn't been materialistic. "And if I ever do need relationship advice, trust me, Mom would be the last person I'll turn to."

Rachelle sighed, and they rode the rest of the way down in silence. "So where are you taking her?"

"Mangiarelli's Pizza."

"Dressed like that? They'll think you're a government health inspector."

"First, they know me. Second, I distinctly remember you lecturing me a few years ago about needing to shed my jeans and T-shirts to look more professional." Proof that there was indeed no pleasing his family.

"Did I?" she asked with a self-conscious smile. "Nicolette says I mother-hen you."

They stepped out into the lobby together, and Spencer studied his sister's expression. By nature he was a task-oriented person. He had enjoyed football for the same reason he enjoyed running his own company: the thrill of plowing through obstacles. He didn't need a crowd to cheer for him, but he did need to make the catch everyone thought was impossible. He didn't need luxuries, but he did need to prove that he could build his own fortune. That kind of drive didn't leave much room for wondering how the people around him felt, but realizing how he'd failed Hailey highlighted the way he was still failing people. Rachelle was smiling, but the smile didn't reach her eyes. The past year had been hard on him, and she looked just as tired as he felt. He pulled her in for a brief hug and said, "Isn't that what big sisters are for?"

She nodded against his chest. When she stepped back, she wiped the corners of her eyes. "I guess."

They walked to the door of his building together, then stood at the entrance. "I'm glad you came by, Rachelle."

"Call me tonight to tell me how it went with Hailey."

"No."

"Or text me."

"Not going to happen."

She put a hand on one hip. "Not knowing is going to drive me crazy."

"A short trip for you."

She smacked his arm. "Jerk."

A step up from dick, I guess. "If I have any news worth sharing with the family, I promise you'll be the first one I tell."

She gave him a long look. "If she breaks your heart again, I may have to kick her ass."

Spencer laughed—Rachelle didn't have a violent bone in her body. Never had. Never would. "I'll be fine." He checked the time on his phone. "Shit, I'm late."

Chapter Six

After three outfit changes and two panicked drive-bys, Hailey parked her car in front of Mangiarelli's. It was better if no one knew she was meeting Spencer. She grabbed her purse off the passenger-side seat and scanned the parking lot. There were no other cars. She looked down at the clock on the dashboard.

Five minutes late.

And he's not here.

There was a slim chance he was inside. Mangiarelli's was within walking distance of their old college. Would he have parked there? Perhaps re-creating even that part of their old visits.

Dressed in a navy pantsuit, Hailey stepped out of her car and entered the restaurant with her head held high. *If he doesn't show, that will be a different kind of closure. I'll know that despite what he says, he really doesn't care.*

Lunch had always been a busy time at the pizzeria, and it still was. Most of the tables were occupied by what looked like college students. She scanned the crowd. Groups of friends. Men. Women. Mixed tables. Some were laughing. Some looked hungover. One couple caught her attention. In the corner booth where she'd spent so many evenings cuddled up to Spencer's side while they both studied was a young woman doing exactly the same with a young man. They looked so comfortable with each other, so blissfully unaware of how little it would take to destroy what they had.

"Sorry I'm late," Spencer said from beside her while his hand came to rest on her lower back.

Hailey gasped and spun, confused by the mix of the past with the present. "Let me guess, you were working on something and almost forgot."

He frowned.

They stood there, looking into each other's eyes without speaking. She waited for him to back down or apologize again.

Instead, he brought a hand up to caress her cheek. "I couldn't sleep last night. This morning dragged on and on. All I could think about was this—" He brushed his lips tenderly over hers.

Whoosh. The crowd around them disappeared until there was only Spencer and the way he made her body hum with need. Her lips parted, and their kiss deepened. He tasted like—coming home.

"Get a room," a female voice called out.

"Or don't," a male voice chimed in. "It might be interesting to see how old people do it."

Spencer raised his head, but his gaze didn't waver from her face. "We're old?"

"To them." The smile that spread across her face felt as natural as breathing. She told herself to keep her defenses up. This was one last, cathartic meeting. Her hand went to her lips. *Goodbye shouldn't feel this good.*

His breath was a hot caress on her cheek. "Are you hungry?"

Oh yes, but not for anything I could have with an audience. Her stomach was churning from nerves rather than hunger. "Not really."

"Me, either." He turned and began to guide her out of the restaurant. "Let's go for a walk."

"Don't go," a male voice called out. "We didn't mean to scare you off."

Spencer turned slowly and Hailey tensed. The Spencer she'd known didn't have a temper, but she realized she didn't know this new Spencer at all. The room quieted as he looked around. He opened his mouth to say something, then closed it without saying a word. A twitch of a smile pulled at his lips before he turned away and began to walk out of the restaurant with her again. Oddly, he looked pleased with himself.

It wasn't until they were walking beneath the shade of the trees of their old campus that Hailey said, "I thought you were going to cut those kids down."

"I almost did. A couple of really good zingers came to mind."

The light humor in his voice put Hailey at ease. They walked, matching their steps naturally. "Really? What was your best?"

He shot her a quick sidelong look. "You shouldn't encourage me."

That's what I keep telling myself, but so far I'm not taking my own advice. "Was it something like: 'I've beaten men twice your size with one hand tied behind my back'?"

He laughed. "Although that's an impressive claim, it probably would have gotten my ass kicked. Boys that age have more testosterone than brains. It wouldn't have scared them."

"Really? Then tell me, wise *old* Spencer, what did you almost say?"

His chest puffed with pride, and he cleared his throat. "'Funny thing about old people—we own shit. When you apply for your next internship, do yourself a favor and don't attach your photo to your résumé. I have a very good memory for faces.' I debated whether or not to mention that I owned my own company, but I thought a vague threat left more to fear."

"Oh, you're good," she said with a chuckle. They walked a little more before she asked, "Why didn't you say it?"

He shrugged. "They were just being stupid." He stopped and turned toward her. There was a look in his eyes that set her heart racing. "And I didn't want you to think I hadn't changed at all."

It was too easy to get lost in those beautiful eyes of his. She struggled to focus on the conversation and not raise herself on tiptoes to kiss him with all the boldness he'd kissed her with. "You wouldn't have threatened them when you were younger, either. You never cared what anyone thought of you."

"That's not true," he said huskily. "I cared what you thought." He looped his arms around her waist and pulled her forward to rest against him. "I still do."

The temptation to give herself over to the heat that sizzled between them was almost too much to resist, but Hailey reminded herself that Skye was more important than how he made her feel. *It's too risky.*

Instead of making her feel better, seeing him again was making the acute loneliness of her present life that much more painful. She pulled herself out of his arms. "I can't do this."

"Talk to me, Hailey."

The irony of his timing was not lost on her. There was a time when she would have given anything for him to utter that request. It was too late, though. "I came for closure."

"Closure?" He ground the word out. "That's what you want?"

She took a step back. "Especially considering what you thought I'd done. I thought we needed it."

He took a step toward her. "So you met me today because you wanted to talk before moving on?"

"Yes," she said, licking her bottom lip as she retreated another step.

"Bullshit." He advanced again.

She tripped over the raised root of a tree and would have fallen backward, but he caught her by her upper arms. He steadied her, but continued to hold her there. Her skin was on fire beneath the strength of his touch, but she tried to sound unaffected. "It's true."

His hands tightened briefly on her arms. "There's only one thing stopping me from believing you." He nipped her bottom lip lightly, and all resolve left Hailey. She melted against him. His arms went around her waist; hers encircled his neck. She arched against him, opening her mouth to the soul-rocking kiss only he could deliver. Other men had tried, but only this man connected with her on a level so intense that circumstance and location ceased to matter. Beneath his touch, there was only hot, all-consuming desire. He raised his head and said huskily, "I don't care about the mistakes we made in the past. We're here now, and we both want the same thing."

She shook her head back and forth slightly. She would have accused him of thinking about only one thing, but she had a hard time imagining much else when he was around. "It's not that easy."

He kissed her again, running his hands up and down her back as he did. Coherent thought scattered. Her hands sought the buttons of his dress shirt even though they were in public. He chuckled, then cupped her face between his hands. "Let's get out of here."

"No." Her refusal sounded half-hearted even to her own ears.

"Whatever you think is more important than this—it's not."

His words seared through the passion. Panicking, she ripped herself out of his arms for a second time. "That's not true. She is."

"She? Who is she?"

Hailey covered her eyes briefly with one hand. The urge to lean on him emotionally was almost as strong as their passion had been. Her friends had fallen to the wayside after Ryan had died. Some had been work friends, and their friendships had dissolved once she no longer had anything in common with them. Others had been put on hold while Hailey reeled beneath the responsibility of becoming an instant parent. Then there'd been the guilt. When her schedule had finally settled somewhat, Hailey had often felt overwhelmed, but admitting it to anyone would have felt like a betrayal—as if she would have been saying she didn't want Skye, when that couldn't be more wrong. Skye was everything she had left in the world. She wiped tears away from her eyes and said, "Coming here was a bad idea. I don't want to make things worse."

"Come here," he said gently and pulled her to his chest. The passion from before took second seat to the comfort she found in his strong arms. "Don't cry."

More tears rolled down her cheeks, wetting the front of his shirt. "I'm sorry, Spencer. I didn't think this through. I just wanted to see you again."

"Shh," he murmured against her hair. "Is seeing me again so bad?"

She sniffed. "You think this is going well?"

He tipped her face up so she'd meet his eyes. Very gently he wiped her tears away with his thumbs. "What's wrong, Hailey?"

Fresh tears poured down her cheeks. She used to believe in happy endings and love being able to conquer all, but then she'd lost and lost again. "It's not just me anymore. I have to make decisions that are best for Skye as well."

"Skye?"

"Ryan's daughter." There was a question in Spencer's eyes that she answered before he voiced it. "My brother. He and his wife died in a car crash."

Spencer's face tightened. "I'm sorry. I know you were very close. When did it happen?"

"About a year ago now."

He wrapped his arms around her again and held her close. "I wish I had known. I would have—"

He stopped, perhaps because he didn't know what he would have done.

Did all old lovers feel a mix of euphoria and heartbreak when they met again? *I can't imagine they do.* She'd run into men she'd slept with before, and none had ever left her feeling gutted and confused. Part of her wanted to run far away from the feelings he brought to the surface.

Another part of her wanted to stay right where she was and pretend that being with him was possible.

Spencer breathed in the scent of her, lust battling with compassion as he held her. He hadn't expected to feel as much for her as he did. Hearing about her brother brought out a protectiveness in him. He wanted to hold her in his arms forever and shelter her from any more loss.

No wonder she looks lost.

Here I am, coming on to her like some horny college student when she needs more than that.

Step up to the plate or go home. He'd never been one to hesitate or second-guess. *Closure or a fresh start. What do I want?* "I'm sorry for your loss. Do you need anything?" He stepped back and took her by the hand.

"No. We're doing okay."

"So you're raising your niece."

"Yes. She's the only family I have left. Ryan entrusted her to me because he knew I would do anything and everything I could for her. I'm not going to lie—seeing you again is confusing, but I'm not in a place where I can do anything about it."

"I like kids." *In theory.*

She dipped her head. "It's not that. It's complicated."

He moved to stand in front of her. "Hailey, whatever this is between us—I've never found it with anyone else. You wouldn't be here if that wasn't true for you as well. Do you really want to walk away a second time?"

"What do you want me to say? That I'll fall into your bed as easily as I did the first time?"

"I don't think we ever did it in my bed. No, wait, there was that one time."

She swatted at him and, for a second, looked as if she might smile. "Everything is still a joke with you."

He ran a hand down one of her arms and took her hand in his. "Not everything. Not you."

She studied their linked hands. She waved her other hand at him. "I know what I should do, but it's so easy to forget when you're around."

"What does that tell you?" He raised her hand to his lips.

"That seeing you is dangerous. I don't have room in my life for another mistake. What I need is a good friend. Someone I could talk to about what I'm doing right and what I'm not. Seeing you again is exciting, but I have responsibilities now. I'm sorry if that's not what you were hoping to hear."

From another woman, the request for friendship might have been the kiss of death for his chance to be with her, but it didn't feel that way with Hailey. He thought about his mother and how many times she'd put what she wanted above the welfare of her children. Hailey's devotion to her niece made her even more beautiful to him, and he hadn't thought that was possible.

"I've been told I'm a good friend." He tipped his head. "But Jordan says I'm a real dick lately."

"Poor Jordan. I doubt you're that bad." Hailey laughed and expelled a shaky breath. "I lost most of my friends after Ryan died. It really shook me when they said I stopped being any fun. One of them told me she would have handled the death of any of her family members better than I did."

"Now that's a dick."

"Yeah," Hailey said with a small smile. "I didn't blame her for jumping ship. My whole life changed in a heartbeat. It went from carefree to all about Skye. Sometimes I still wonder if I've done any of it right. I've done my best, but I don't know if it's good enough."

Spencer didn't know enough about what she'd been through to be able to reassure her with more than platitudes, so he didn't. He caressed her lower back and urged her to walk beside him. "What do you say we go back into Mangiarelli's and show those kids how old people pack in pizza?"

She nodded. "I'd like that."

"And if they start shit with me again, I'll give them the intimidating look I perfected in the boardroom. It shuts down all arguments." He narrowed his eyes, drew his brows together, and waited for her to be impressed.

"That's quite a look you have there."

He arched one eyebrow, maintaining his scowl the best he could. "It says I'm holding in a rage that if unleashed would demolish all around me."

Humor lit her eyes. "Like holding back a bodily function?"

He threw back his head and laughed. "It's effective, anyway."

She laughed, too, leaning against him as she did. "You're still funny."

"You, too." He almost hugged her then, but a hug would lead to kissing, and then perhaps to a place she'd said she wasn't yet ready for. He wanted her in his bed, but he also wanted her in his life. If having both meant waiting, then he'd try not to remember how soft her inner thighs felt against his cheeks or the way she called out his name when she came.

They reentered the pizzeria with less fanfare than expected. He noticed the corner booth was empty and said, "Hey, our old table is free."

She hesitated, then took the seat across from him. "This brings back so many memories."

"We had fun together."

She smoothed her hands over the plastic menu. "In the end it wasn't enough."

He took one of her hands in his. "I don't know if I'm a better man now than I was then, but I want to be."

She laced her fingers through his. "I'd like to think I've become a better person, but betting on me is a gamble, too."

He'd spent the last year hightailing it away from emotional situations, but it was different with Hailey. Jordan had said he hadn't thought Hailey was the type to cheat, and Spencer felt like an ass for ever thinking she had. Hailey had never lied to him.

Trust was something he'd lost in people lately, but he didn't want to be that person. Meeting Hailey again felt like a sign that it was time to let go and start over. "So tell me what you're doing right and what you're doing wrong." There had to be a way to return the smile to her eyes. He waved the waitress over. "And then let's eat. Pizza?"

"Perfect," Hailey said with a warm smile that made him think the second time around might be even better than the first.

Chapter Seven

Hailey took a sip of the soda the waitress had delivered and asked herself why it had been so important to see Spencer. *Is it loneliness and loss that brought me here, or something more? Am I trying to recapture part of the past?*

What was Delinda hoping would come out of us meeting up?

Did she want confirmation that it wouldn't be a problem for her family?

Or was she playing matchmaker?

I wish I knew which outcome ends my employment with her. Is there any way to do this without risking everything? "Promise me something."

"Anything."

"Don't tell anyone about today or that we're talking again. Okay?"

He didn't look happy with her request. "Why not?"

I should just say it now—clear the air. Spencer, I'm working for your grandmother.

Yeah, that would go over well.

What if he has a problem with me being there? Am I willing to accept the consequences when I'm not the one it might hurt the most?

I have to be smart about this. There must be an option that leaves all of us in a better place.

But maybe not one that starts with me blurting everything out. "My employer is very particular. Very. Very. Particular."

"Even about what you do on your own time?"

"She's an older woman with some boundary issues—"

"Then you need to set her straight that your personal life is none of her business."

"It's not that simple." Hailey's mouth dried at the thought she might not be making the right choice. "I can't lose this job."

He leaned forward. "Talk to me."

She needed a shoulder even if the one he was offering was risky to accept. "I had a career up until recently. I'm not irresponsible."

"I know you're not. Things happen."

She searched his face and found no hint of judgment, so she continued. "I was a retail purchaser for DIY Rite, but after Ryan died I took a lot of time off work. I'm not sorry I did. Given a chance to do it over, that's what I would do again in a heartbeat. But it did get me terminated. I told myself that once the dust settled, it would be easy enough to find another position, but that wasn't how it worked out." Hailey paused, uncertain if she could share the story without revealing too much. "I came across this personal assistant opportunity, and it had everything I needed: a place to live, insurance, a good salary. It doesn't matter if I like it or not. We need this."

Spencer laid his hand over hers. "If you need money—"

Hailey shook her head. "It's more complicated than that. Skye had a really hard time after her parents died." Hailey waved a hand in the air. "I know what you're thinking—of course she did. I thought I understood grieving, but before taking this job I was beginning to worry that nothing I did would help her. I was sinking beneath the weight of advice from professionals who kept telling me she was getting better, but I knew she wasn't. She'd become nonverbal, needed to be homeschooled because she didn't want to be around other children, and I felt like I was failing her . . ." Hailey took a deep, calming breath. "Unless you'd seen Skye before and after she met my employer, you wouldn't understand how good the move has been for her. She's talking. She's excited again. If things stay the way they are, I think she'll be returning to school soon. And it's all because the woman I work for has this ability to reach Skye in a way I haven't been able to. She says it, and Skye does it. Just like that. That easily." Hailey winced when she heard resentment sneak into her tone. *I don't want to be that person.* "I'm happy for the change in her. I really am. I don't know what's wrong with me."

He held her gaze. "You wanted to be the one to save Skye."

As horrible as it was to admit, that was a truth she could bare to him. "Yes."

He raised his hand to caress her cheek. "You did."

Hailey shook her head. "I was the reason she stopped talking."

"The death of her parents was the reason."

I'm going to just say it. Get it out of my head. "I heard Skye say she stopped speaking because she thought everything she said made me sad. I never cried in front of her. I always waited until she was in her own bed. I didn't know she could hear me. I knew she needed me to be strong. I thought I had been, but I failed her." *There.*

Spencer stood up and slid into the booth beside her. He put an arm around her and kissed her lightly on the forehead. "You didn't fail anyone. I hate that you went through that alone." He looked as if he wanted to say more but was holding himself back.

Hailey closed her eyes briefly, determined not to cry in front of him again. "The worst of it is over. She's looking more like her old self every day." She opened her eyes but kept them glued to the table. "All I have to do now is not screw it up. It's what I pray for every morning and pretty much what I pray for every night. I just want Skye to be a happy little girl again. I want her to have friends, go to school, come home, and argue with me over things that normal people argue over. I can't afford to lose my job, not just because I need the money, but because I'm afraid of what will happen with Skye if we have to move again."

"She'd survive. She has you."

"That's what I tell myself when I start to panic. I know this job isn't forever, but for now it's the best I can do."

His arm tightened around her. "Hailey . . ."

She shrugged. She didn't want him to feel sorry for her. That wasn't why she'd come. "Enough about me. What about you? How's your life?"

The inner beauty of the woman before him robbed him of his ability to answer immediately. The girl he'd known had grown into a strong and loving person. The depth of her loss and her ongoing struggle to reach her niece made the family issues Spencer had been dealing with seem trivial.

Life had battered Hailey, but it hadn't broken her. She was more cautious, but she wasn't bitter. Unlike him, she wasn't angry and lashing out at those around her.

In truth, she deserved to be with a better man than him. The thought of her with anyone else, though, made his stomach clench painfully. He realized then that she was still waiting for him to answer. "It's good. Busy. I have a virtual reality software company, WorkChat, that's expanding faster than I dared to dream."

She smiled, looking genuinely happy for him. "You got your cake."

"My cake?" At nineteen, he hadn't known to look for hidden layers in the words women used. He'd learned, though, that women sometimes spoke in code—like computers, but it was one they wrote as they went along. Nothing could be assumed. Something Hailey had said to him years earlier came back with unexpected clarity. "What does pie represent to you?"

She didn't answer at first, and he half expected her to say she didn't know what he was talking about. She did, though. He saw it in her eyes.

"Pie is something you could have every week without fanfare. It's a comfort food. A family food. It's what people serve when they gather on a Sunday afternoon."

"And cake?"

"It's a flashy celebration. Layers of intricate frosting designed to impress people."

Ouch. "Back in college, you said you wanted pie, and I wanted cake."

"I *needed* pie." She looked relieved that he'd understood easily. "That's why I moved back to be with my brother. I was falling apart, and I needed the security of being with someone who loved me."

I loved you, he almost said, but he was beginning to wonder if he had known what love was back then. She *had* come second to his goals. He could have gotten her back if he had put aside the program he'd been working on and gone after her. Instead, he'd waited, confident that she'd be there when he finished his work. The more he'd heard about Brett running the family company, the more he needed to prove to himself that he didn't need their father's money. Proving himself had been an obsession back then. An obsession that had taken priority over making up with her. His love had been entitled and shallow.

They looked into each other's eyes for a while.

She deserved so much better than I gave her. "I didn't understand how much you needed me."

"I know."

"But that doesn't mean I didn't care about you."

"I know that now. I didn't at the time."

He leaned forward and almost kissed her, but pulled back just in time. Would an explanation give her more comfort? Sex alone hadn't been enough the first time. "I was obsessed with proving myself that year. My brother, Brett, had just taken over our family's company. It wasn't so much that I wanted it for myself, but I wanted to be considered. When my parents divorced, Rachelle, Nicolette, and I went with Mom. Brett and Eric stayed with our father—or the man I thought was my father."

"So Dereck was your stepfather? I thought he was your father."

There wasn't another person on the planet he would have felt comfortable telling, but this was Hailey. Despite the time they'd been apart, she knew him better than anyone since. "Turns out, Mark was my biological father. I was the result of my mother cheating on her first husband."

"So you were raised by your real father."

"Without either of us knowing. I found out the truth last year."

The shock Spencer expected to see in Hailey's eyes never came. She searched his face as if understanding the extent of how much the news had shaken him. "I remember you talking about Mark. He sounded like an amazing person."

"He was. He never missed one of my games. I don't remember a time when he was too busy to help us with homework or ask about our day at school. I was still in high school when he died. I don't deal well with things like that. I boxed my feelings up and put them aside. It wasn't until I found out who he'd actually been to me that I realized how much I'd lost. It should have made me more understanding about your father . . ."

She smiled gently. "We could probably go around and around about who was the worst, or we could forgive each other and ourselves. I don't want to carry that baggage around anymore, do you?"

"God, no."

"Good, because I'm doing enough shit wrong today to feel bad about what I did yesterday."

He chuckled. "That's a T-shirt motto I'd wear."

Her expression turned serious. "Do you still talk to your dad? The one you thought was your father?"

"No. I wrote him and his whole side of the family off."

"You don't see them at all? Not even the ones you were close to—like any grandparents?"

"All I had on that side was a grandmother." He shuddered. "She's a real pill. I'm okay with never seeing her again."

"I bet she misses you."

"I'm sure she doesn't. She is one coldhearted old lady."

Hailey chewed her bottom lip, then said, "Sometimes people who appear coldhearted are really just scared."

This was the Hailey he remembered. She always saw the best in everyone. Unfortunately, that didn't mean she was right. "You don't know her." The pizza arrived, and a silence hung over them for longer than was comfortable. Spencer picked up a piece. "You know what would make us both feel better?" Since what would really cheer him up wasn't on the menu, he said, "Carbs, cheese, and grease."

She laughed. "What an appetizing description. You'd be awful in marketing."

"I rock at sales, though. I just need to turn on the charm." He flexed his shoulders, then brought the pizza to his mouth and took a bite while imagining every place on her body he'd like to nip. He half closed his eyes, savoring the vision, letting himself remember her taste. From the sweetness of her mouth to the hot heat of her sex. "It's just as good as I remember. Nothing ever compared," he said in husky voice.

A blush warmed her cheeks, and he knew he'd led her thoughts to the same tantalizing place where his had gone. He raised the pizza to her lips. "Try it, then tell me—is it as good now as it was back then?"

Her breath warmed his fingers, and desire flamed in her eyes. "I remember it being really good."

"Me, too. But I bet it would be even better this time around." Her lips parted ever so slightly, and he was so turned on he wanted to toss the pizza aside and take her right there on the table. She licked her bottom lip the way she used to when she was just as hot for him.

"How is everything?" the waitress interrupted, and the mood was broken. "Would either of you like another drink?"

"An ice water," Spencer said in a strangled voice. *For my lap.*

"One for me, too, please," Hailey said.

The waitress walked away, but since she would soon return, Spencer decided to lighten the mood. He placed the pizza slice on a plate and shot her a cocky smile. "See, I could sell pizza."

"He could sell me anything. That was hot," a young woman said from the next table before turning to giggle with her friends.

A male voice boomed across the restaurant. "Spencer Westerly, I heard you were here and had to come out and see for myself. Are you looking to pick up a few hours?" Spencer turned to the man who had bankrolled most of his early technology needs by letting him work for him. Ralph Mangiarelli was still just as round as he was tall with a big smile and dark hair slicked back.

"Not this summer," Spencer said as he rose to accept a backslapping greeting from Ralph. "Just here for a quick meal."

Ralph's attention went to Hailey. "And you brought a beautiful woman with you. She looks familiar to me."

Hailey slid out of the booth to greet Ralph. "I used to eat here all the time when I was in college."

"Did you? Were you two . . ." He paused. Neither Spencer nor Hailey confirmed his suspicion, but that didn't slow Ralph down in the least. "Oh yes. You're the one who broke his heart."

No. No. No. We are not going there. Spencer shook his head.

"I remember you now." He shook a finger at Hailey. "That wasn't very nice. You should have seen him after you left. He sat alone in that booth for months looking like his world had just ended. Sure, he dated other girls"—Ralph frowned at Spencer—"but he never looked happy."

Spencer glanced down at his phone. "Look at the time. I have to get back to the office." He slapped several bills down on the table. "Hailey has to get back as well."

"But you haven't eaten." Ralph called across the restaurant: "Carol, bring a box."

The pizza was boxed quickly. Spencer accepted it as well as another hug from his old employer, then hurried Hailey out to her car.

They stood, pizza between them, next to the driver's door. She moved as if she were about to open it, then turned back. "Were you really that upset after we broke up?"

He could have lied and retained more of his dignity, but if the truth brought her comfort, it was worth being honest. "I was."

"I was, too. You should have asked me about Greg. I would have told you he meant nothing to me."

He shrugged. "I was an idiot."

She smiled sadly. "We both were."

He cupped one side of her face. "Didn't we already forgive ourselves for this?"

"Yes, we did." Her gaze went to his lips, and it took everything in him not to kiss her then.

"Then let's start over."

"As friends," she reminded softly.

"If that's what you want."

A beautiful rosy pink spread up her neck and cheeks. "Okay."

With that, she turned, opened her car door, and slid into the driver's seat. He handed her the pizza box because he was at a loss for what else to do. "I'll call you."

"I'd like that." She closed the door.

He moved to the sidewalk and watched her drive off. The only woman who had ever reduced him to a grinning, lust-filled idiot had just done it again. Then she turned him down and left with his lunch.

And it was amazing—every moment of it.

Chapter Eight

Hailey put the air conditioner on full blast. She was overheating, but it had nothing to do with the temperature of the air. Seeing Spencer again had been a million times more intense than she'd anticipated.

People don't meet up after nearly a decade apart and—bam—feel like that for each other again. That doesn't happen. Does it?

She clenched the steering wheel as she drove. *Holy shit, no wonder I slept with him in college.*

But that doesn't mean I will this time. I'm older, wiser. I understand now that just because something feels good doesn't mean it is good. One good conversation does not make a relationship, or even a friendship.

I have too much to lose to jump into anything.

She stopped at a red light and cursed. *Why did he have to say all the right things? Why couldn't he be the dick he describes himself as? It would have been easy to know what to do then.*

Friends. Who am I kidding? Her thoughts went back to how his kiss had seared through her. One touch. One look. That's all it had ever taken with him, and her body was as eager for him today as it ever had been. Their chemistry was unapologetically primal.

I'm not being honest with myself or him.

I should have told him I'm working for his grandmother—the cold-hearted one he never wants to see again.

As she drove, her thoughts went to the woman she was both grateful for and afraid of displeasing. *What are you really doing, Delinda? Why did you hire me? Was it really a coincidence?*

Her hands tightened again on the steering wheel. *Please, Delinda, please be just a nice, lonely woman who cares about Skye and me.*

Hailey's mind was still racing when she parked in front of the guesthouse at Delinda's. She stopped and breathed in a sigh of relief when she saw Skye and her teacher seated at the kitchen table, working. The talk she'd given Delinda must have sunk in. "How is she doing?"

Mrs. Holihen waved Hailey over to show her the result of Skye's math unit test. "I wish all of my students were as easy to teach as your niece is."

Hailey kissed Skye on the top of her head. "I'm so proud of you."

Skye beamed with pride. "Math is important. Do you know why?"

Hailey could have listed reasons, but she was more interested in what had put that spark in her niece's eyes. "Why?"

"Delinda said people use math to draw the houses they build. You can actually build a house that you *draw*, Auntie Hailey. And if I learn math and draw a really good house, Delinda is going to build it. A house, Auntie Hailey. A real house. For me and you."

Delinda, how do I show you that you don't have to do this? Hailey groaned inwardly. She kept a smile on her face, though. "She means a dollhouse, but I'd love it if you design my dream bathroom. I've always wanted one of those showers that's so big you don't need a door."

"I can do that. It will be perfect. I promise."

"I know it will be." Hailey looked around the guesthouse. "Don't forget that you have chores before you're done for the day. Did you put the dishes away?"

"I did."

"And your bedroom. Did you clean it?"

"Some of it." Skye smiled, reminding Hailey so much of the mischievous child she'd once been.

"Mrs. Holihen, I'm going over to see Delinda. When Skye finishes her work, could you remind her to clean her room before you take her outside? That is, if she wants to go to the barn tonight."

"I do! I'd better get back to work," Skye said cheerfully. "I have carrots for Clover."

Both Hailey and Mrs. Holihen laughed in surprise.

Mrs. Holihen said, "See, easy."

For bribes as big as ponies and houses, yes.

"Auntie Hailey, can Delinda come with us again tonight?"

"We'll see. She might be busy."

"She won't be. Did you see how happy she was when she was brushing Clover? She loves ponies." Skye stopped and tilted her head to one side. "Do you think it's funny that Delinda and I have so much in common? It's like she really is my grandmother."

"But she's not, honey." As soon as the words were out of her mouth Hailey regretted them. Skye's face crumpled, and she turned her back to Hailey. Mrs. Holihen busied herself with rearranging the papers on the table. Trying for a cheerful voice, Hailey said, "I'll see you two when your lessons are finished."

Skye didn't answer her.

Mrs. Holihen looked across at Hailey, her eyes full of sympathy. "I'll bring her over at four. After she cleans her room, I was planning to take her down to the beach for a French lesson."

"That sounds perfect." Hailey stepped forward and went to hug her niece, but Skye pulled away. Hailey dropped down to her knees beside her. "Skye, look at me."

Skye reluctantly turned to face Hailey, but she didn't meet her eyes.

Hailey touched her own chest lightly, then tapped Skye's. "The same team. You and me. Always. Even when we're angry with each other. Nothing changes how much I love you."

Skye raised her eyes. There was a heartbreaking amount of confusion in them. "Why don't you want me to be happy?"

Hailey's heart flipped, and she pushed back the tears that surged to her eyes. *Is that what she really thinks?* "I do. I want you to be happy more than I want anything else in the whole world." She tucked one of Skye's curls behind her ear. "But I don't want to see you get hurt."

"Delinda would never hurt me."

Not on purpose.

Or maybe not at all. She's been so kind to us. What would it hurt to let the two of them go on pretending? So far, doing things my way hasn't worked out that well for any of us.

"You're right. She wouldn't." Hailey straightened and smoothed Skye's hair as she did. "Be good for Mrs. Holihen. I'll see you at the main house later."

"Okay. Then we'll eat with Delinda? And take her to the barn?"

"If that's what she wants—yes."

Skye's smile returned. "It will be."

Hailey wished she were that certain about anyone or anything. *I used to be. There was a time when I trusted myself and other people. Instead of doubting every good thing that comes my way, I should be grateful for how kind Delinda has been to us. Skye used to be as afraid to believe in anything as I am. Look at her now. Who knows, maybe there's even hope for me.*

She nodded to Mrs. Holihen and left so they could get back to work. As she walked over to the main house, she thought back to what Spencer had said about Delinda. His version didn't match the side of Delinda that Hailey had seen.

Yes, she could be cutting.

Yes, she was controlling and had difficulties with boundaries.

But coldhearted? No.

Michael opened the door of the main house. "Welcome back, Miss Hailey."

Hailey had told him several times to just call her Hailey, but Michael took pride in remaining formal. "Thank you, Michael. Is Delinda in the solarium?" It was her favorite afternoon place.

"She is."

"Was she asking for me?"

"Yes, but she seemed quite pleased to hear that you had gone out."

"She did?"

Michael didn't volunteer more.

Once inside the foyer, Hailey hesitated. "Michael, could I ask you a question?"

"Of course."

"Why don't any of Delinda's family visit her?"

Her question rocked Michael back onto his heels. "Her son takes her out to lunch now and then. Her oldest grandson visits her, also."

"I haven't met them, and I've been here for weeks."

"Brett is engaged—getting married at the end of the summer. She recently learned he and Alisha are expecting a baby. It's not a wonder he hasn't been around much."

Why didn't Delinda tell me her good news? "And her other grandchildren? She talks about them a lot, but they don't come by."

Michael cleared his throat. "Every family is different."

"Do you know her grandson Spencer?"

"I have met him many times." Michael adjusted the collar of his dress shirt as if it were suddenly choking him.

"Were they ever close?" Something must have happened to give Spencer that impression of his grandmother. Delinda had spoken of Spencer too many times for Hailey to ever see him as not part of her family.

"It's really not my place to say."

Although that was true, Hailey justified her perseverance by reminding herself that Delinda would not have let that stop her. "I care about both of them, Michael. I just want to understand."

Michael considered her request, then shook his head. "Your questions would be best answered by Mrs. Westerly. I'm sorry."

"Would she tell me the truth if I asked her?"

Michael smiled. "Her truth, yes."

"I was hoping for something a little less subjective."

"Life is subjective, Miss Hailey. From the moment you wake up in the morning to the moment you close your eyes at night, you interpret what happens to you through the lens you choose to use. The challenge is realizing the way you experience any event is not necessarily how the people around you do. The older I get, the more I realize what I once considered lies are really someone else's truths."

Hailey's eyes rounded at his unexpectedly deep response. "Are you saying that it would be a waste of time to ask Delinda anything?"

He gave her arm a pat. "I'm saying that Mrs. Westerly loves her family very much. What is her relationship with them beyond that? I'm not sure you could get two Westerlys to agree, but that doesn't change what I know." He chuckled and started walking. "Did I ever tell you that I studied philosophy in college?"

Hailey almost asked him how he'd gone from college to working as a butler, but she didn't. *How did I go from college to being a paid companion? Life happens.*

As they moved forward, he said, "I've worked for Mrs. Westerly for over thirty years, and I hope to work here twenty years more. When I first started here, I was fresh from a divorce. My son had health problems I couldn't afford. I was desperate. Mrs. Westerly covered his medical bills and never said a word to anyone about it. She paid for him to go to college without him ever knowing the money came from her. He's healthy now, with an impressive job as a broker in New York City. Beautiful wife. Two children I spoil as much as I'm allowed. My son has offered to let me live with them or buy me a place of my own. He doesn't see my employment here the way I do. I wouldn't have a son if it weren't for the generosity of Mrs. Westerly. To her, I'm a butler. To me, she's an angel. A lonely angel. How could I ever leave her?"

Hailey waved a hand at her suddenly misty eyes. With a choked laugh, she said, "Her generosity scares me a little. My biggest concern is Skye and how she'd handle it if we had to leave."

"Then don't leave," Michael said as they arrived at the door of the solarium.

Delinda noticed her and waved her over. "Well, it's about time you returned. How was your lunch?"

Hailey took a seat in one of the overstuffed chairs next to her. "It was nice."

Delinda leaned forward. "Just nice?"

She couldn't know where I was, could she? I didn't tell anyone. I made sure not to use the driver. No, of course she doesn't know. Spencer said they aren't close. "Very nice?"

"Humph." Delinda called out, "Michael, could you bring some tea?"

"Of course," Michael answered from the door.

"Skye wants to know if you'd like to go with us to the barn tonight."

A smile lit Delinda's face. "I would love to. I've ordered a helmet for her along with boots and breeches. She doesn't need a show jacket yet, but when she does, I'll have my tailor fit one to her. I'm not sold on the barn's in-house trainer. A friend of mine works with Olympians—"

"Skye may not want to compete. She may simply want to ride for fun."

"Winning ribbons *is* fun."

"Competition is good, but that's not what's most important."

Delinda pursed her lips, then said, "So you don't believe she could win."

"I didn't say that. I just don't want you to pressure Skye to be someone she isn't."

"So you want me to lower my standards for her? Perhaps if you weren't so willing to expect nothing from her she might have started speaking sooner."

Hailey gasped. "That was cruel, Delinda."

Delinda folded her hands on her lap unapologetically. Michael rolled in a tray of tea and scones, assessed the mood of the room, and made a hasty retreat. "Life is cruel. Step up to the plate, Hailey, and start preparing your niece for it."

Michael's angel also had horns.

Breathe. She throws barbs when she's hurting. "Are you upset with me, Delinda?"

"No. I'm angry with myself. I forgot that I'm not supposed to do anything nice for you or Skye anymore. Should I return the helmet and attire? What about the tea and scones? Too much? Throw them at me if it makes you feel better."

Delinda and Skye actually are a lot alike. The corners of her mouth twitched at the thought. Delinda's expression darkened, and all humor left Hailey. Working for Delinda was as confusing as seeing Spencer had been, but on a totally different level.

They both made her ask the same question: *How do I make you happy without putting aside what I know is important?*

"I want to be able to argue with you," Hailey blurted.

Delinda's eyebrows shot up. "Excuse me?"

Right. Wrong. This is my truth. "I don't want to be afraid that you'll fire me if I don't make you happy every second of the day. I love it here. Skye does, too. But you could let me go at any time. I stay up at night afraid that you'll ask us to leave if I say or do the wrong thing. I don't know what you want from us, but I know what I need from you."

"And that is?"

She needs to hear this. Maybe a little honesty will help her. It worked with Skye. "I need to know that we're on the same team. My father always started our family talks by telling us that he loved us. It made whatever our issues were feel not as bad because our foundation was stable. I like you. I'm grateful for all you've done, but I don't always like the way you talk to me. I don't always agree with what you want to do for Skye. I want to be able to say that. If you're paying me to sit and agree with everything you say, then please stay out of our personal business. But if you want to be part of our lives, then we have to be able to disagree and still be on the same team."

Delinda pursed her lips. "Is this how your generation speaks to their employers?"

There it was, the little dig. *I'm wasting my breath.* "This isn't exactly a conventional job, and maybe that's the problem. If you want to be part of our lives, I need to be able to trust you."

Delinda stood and walked to a bookshelf. She returned with a photo of a handsome man in his forties. She handed the photo to Hailey. "This was my Oliver. He had a big heart just like yours. He loved everyone, and there wasn't a mean bone in his body. He couldn't walk by a person in need and not help them."

Hailey accepted the photo and looked down at the man with dark hair and laughter in his eyes. The profound sadness in Delinda's voice left Hailey unsure of what to say.

Delinda gripped the back of the chair beside her, determined to stand even though she was clearly in pain. "My parents didn't approve of him at first, but I married him anyway. I was so proud of him when he took over my father's company." She took the photo back and seemed to get lost in the past as she looked down at her deceased husband's face. "He wasn't very good at business. It was all new to him. He was a good man, but he wasn't ready for the responsibilities he was given."

"I can't imagine anyone would be ready for such a responsibility."

Delinda shook her head. "He should have been. We should have done more to prepare him. The doctors said he died from an accidental overdose of his heart medication. It wasn't an accident. The company was losing money before my son stepped in. Oliver was desperate, and he felt he'd failed me."

Hailey gasped and covered her mouth with one hand. *Is she saying that Oliver—*

"My son thinks I was oblivious to what was going on, but I knew. Just like I knew Dereck wasn't ready to step into Oliver's shoes like he did. It was almost too much for him as well. He had his father's soft heart. All he wanted was Stephanie, but she made him doubt himself."

And that's why you hated her. It makes sense now.

"I couldn't bear the idea that I might lose Dereck the same way I lost Oliver. So I pushed Dereck to be the man who could succeed where his father had failed. He needed to be stronger to survive. Stephanie saw me as harsh. I could do nothing right when it came to her. Every warning I gave either of them was taken as a criticism." She walked over and replaced the photo in its spot on the shelf. When she returned, her face revealed none of the emotions that must have been raging within her. "I pushed my son because I love him, and it worked. No one won against Dereck. No one. Brett is head of the company now, and nothing shakes him. We raised him strong. No excuses. No second chances. Yes, I push my grandchildren, but only because I know how harsh life can be if one isn't prepared for it."

Hailey got goose bumps listening to Delinda. Her view of life was different, and yet somehow they had the same fears. *I'm also afraid of failing the ones I love.* Hailey placed a hand on Delinda's arm. "I don't know what to say except I'm sorry you lost someone you loved. Have you ever spoken to your family about it?"

"How could I? They barely visit me," Delinda said, her voice just above a whisper.

"I might be able to help you with that." *Did I just say that?*

Delinda's eyes flew to hers. "What do you mean?"

Hailey hesitated. *The solution seems so easy, but who am I to tell her what to do when I can't sort out my own life?*

"Oh, for goodness' sake, have the fortitude to speak your mind," Delinda snapped.

Okay, but this is for your own good. Hailey raised her fingers in a measuring motion. "If you tweak the way you speak to people—just a little bit . . ."

"Now you sound like Brett."

Hailey breathed a sigh of relief. "That's the grandson you're closest to, right? He must know you well."

Delinda's eyes narrowed. "If this is how you are when you're afraid you might lose your job, I cannot imagine how you'll be when you realize I'm too attached to ever fire you."

Wait. Did she just say something nice? "See, that's *kind of* sweet. All you'd have to do is leave off the initial insult, and I would feel all warm and fuzzy toward you."

"Oh, Lord."

"And keep some of your thoughts in your head."

With a sigh, Delinda sat back in her chair. "Anything else?"

"Smile more?"

Delinda glared at Hailey.

Hailey leaned closer and glared back. It all felt so ridiculous that Hailey broke into a laugh and a huge smile spread across her face.

Delinda slowly smiled back.

I wish Spencer could see this side of his grandmother. Blood related or not, they have traits in common.

Hailey's phone dinged with a message. She ignored it because she'd already made the mistake of checking her phone while visiting with Delinda. Apparently, it was poor etiquette.

"Aren't you going to check your message?"

"I'll look at it later."

"It might be important."

"Mrs. Holihen would call if it were."

"There's no one else who might message you?"

Her phone dinged again. "No one that couldn't be answered later."

"Oh, for God's sake, check your messages."

Hailey reacted instinctively to the authority in Delinda's tone. She took out her phone and glanced at it. *Spencer.* Heat rose up her neck. "It's not important."

"Oh, so it's not who you had lunch with. I thought perhaps you'd been out on a date."

Taking a page out of the older woman's book, Hailey said, "For lunch? What a pathetic date that would be."

Delinda tapped her fingers on the arm of her chair. "I suppose it depends on the company."

Does she know? Or is she fishing for confirmation? Would she want me with Spencer?

"It was just lunch with a friend."

"A male friend?"

Hailey tipped her head to the side. "Delinda, you know it's none of your business."

Delinda sighed. "I'm bored. I don't crochet. Hollywood hasn't made a good movie in fifty years. I'm practically housebound . . ."

Oh, please. She lays it on thick. "Where would you like to go? I'll take you somewhere."

"I don't need to go anywhere, but I never had a daughter, so I missed out on talking about dating and lunches out. Humor me. What was your lunch like?"

"He took me out for pizza."

"Pizza?" Delinda exclaimed as if it were a heinous crime. "Oh, dear, no wonder you weren't impressed."

She has to know. Otherwise, why would she be this curious?

Granted, she is curious about every other part of my life that has nothing to do with Spencer.

I could tell her whom I was with.

She just said she likes me too much to fire me.

But should I test it? Now? When things are just beginning to settle?

"Are you planning to see him again?"

Hailey pictured Spencer's smile, his beautiful eyes, and the feel of his strong arms around her. "I think so. Yes."

"I know the perfect designer. I'll have him bring samples tomorrow. I wonder if he is still in London. He vacations in Tuscany if I remember correctly. I'll call Alessandro. He'll know."

"I don't need new clothing."

"You do if he's feeding you pizza."

Hailey burst out laughing. "Delinda, you're so bad."

With a skyward roll of her eyes, Delinda said, "I'm sorry I don't know a nice way to say that you won't get your man if you continue to dress older than I do."

This is her being nice. Hailey laughed until her eyes began to water. "Stop."

"I'm trying. Is there a polite way to tell you that your hair is due for a trim and a treatment, and those fingernails . . . ? I've seen better on Michael's feet."

Hailey laughed harder still, until her sides began to hurt. "Oh my God, Delinda. No. No, there isn't a nice way to say any of it."

"Enough silliness. Let's have a spa day tomorrow. I'll have a foot rub." She waved her hand in a wide circle. "And you can have everything else done."

Gaining control of herself, Hailey dabbed the corners of her eyes. She took a calming breath and agreed if for no other reason than curiosity about what having "everything else done" entailed. "I think I've figured it out," Hailey said suddenly.

"What?"

"Watch and learn." Hailey sat straighter in her chair and clasped her hands on her lap in a mimic of how Delinda often sat. "Hailey, dear, let's pamper ourselves tomorrow." She wasn't one to pat herself on the back, but she was nailing her Delinda impression. "We'll get our nails done, our hair done. I even know a designer. You'd look stunning in anything from his line. What do you say? Will you indulge an old woman? A very, very old woman?"

Delinda nodded a few times slowly, but she was smiling. "I'm not sure you've mastered polite, either."

"We're all a work in progress," Hailey said, feeling more lighthearted than she had in a long time.

Hailey's phone beeped again, not because a new message had come in, but as a reminder that she had one waiting. "Do you mind if I step outside for a moment?"

"Not at all. I have a few phone calls to make for our day tomorrow. Should I plan for Skye to join us? There's no reason she couldn't do her lessons *and* get her nails done."

She's asking? Now there is progress. "I'll speak to Mrs. Holihen. She might be able to fit the lessons around what we have planned."

"Considering what I pay her . . . if she balks at all—"

"Delinda—"

"It's just to make sure we get exactly what we want."

"You're incorrigible."

"That's how I came into the world, and it's likely the way I'll depart it. Now go, answer your friend. Don't say yes to seeing him tomorrow, though. Make him wait until the weekend."

"I have Skye on the weekend."

"I'm sure Mrs. Holihen will come by if I ask her to, or I could watch her myself."

"I'll ask Mrs. Holihen. If I decide to go anywhere."

"Whatever you wish. Go on, now. I'm tired. Being nice is exhausting."

Spencer was back in his office, looking down at his phone like a high school boy waiting for an answer from his crush. He'd made it a lifelong practice to not chase women. There were enough vying for his attention that worrying about which woman he'd end the night with was unnecessary.

Hailey is different.

He'd spent a pathetic amount of time crafting his text to her. It had to be warm without making it seem like he wasn't willing to honor his promise to go slowly.

He'd written: Today was nice.

When no response came back, he regretted not saying more.

It's Spencer.

As soon as he sent it, he groaned. *She knows it's me. I blew my two-line limit on stupid shit. Three unanswered texts spells desperate. All I can do now is fucking wait.*

He sat at his desk and placed his phone in front of him. *She's at work. She might not even know she has a message.*

"What are you doing?" Jordan asked, taking a seat in front of his desk.

Spencer would have put his phone away, but he didn't want to miss her response if she wrote back. "Nothing much. Does this mean you're back?"

"Yeah. I tried to get some stuff done at home, but I ended up watching every season of *Dr. Who* and a disturbing number of reality shows. I was knee-deep in half-empty pizza boxes, and I started to wonder why there were no beer cans. Why would someone like me not wallow in alcohol when he's unhappy? Then I remembered that ass kicking you gave me our junior year when I got drunk instead of working on the coding you'd asked me for, and I started to miss you. You're an asshole, but you're still my best friend."

Spencer pretended to dab away tears. "That's the nicest thing anyone has ever said to me."

"Whatever. You don't look hungover today, which robs me of the opportunity of kicking *your* ass back toward sobriety."

He hadn't thought much about it, but Jordan was right—he hadn't looked at another woman or had a drink since he'd met up with Hailey again. He wanted better than the life he'd fallen into.

"So you really liked my album simulator?" Jordan asked.

"I told you, it's fucking genius. There's nothing on the market that can compete. The way it isolates and creates specific 3-D holograms from merged video is mind-blowing. It's a game changer."

"Thank you. And the volleyball-babe simulator?"

"No."

Jordan laughed. "It was worth a shot. You're probably right about it being a slippery slope to porn. Not that I wouldn't buy the program if someone else made it, but it's not what I want to be remembered for."

"See, sometimes I'm right." Spencer glanced down at his phone.

"Waiting on a call?"

"No."

"Fucking liar."

It was Spencer's turn to laugh. "I had lunch with Hailey today."

"And?"

"And it was good to see her. Really good."

"Tell her I said hello."

"I will. When she answers me."

Jordan sat forward and grabbed Spencer's phone. "That's what you're doing? Sitting here waiting for her to answer a text?"

Spencer was on his feet and around the table in a heartbeat. "Give me the fucking phone."

Jordan read aloud: "Today was nice. It's Spencer." He laughed. "Wow, I thought you had more game than that."

Spencer grabbed his phone back and pocketed it. "She's going through a rough time right now. We're starting off as friends."

"Ouch."

"It's not like that."

"I've been friends with plenty of women, so I'd argue that it's exactly *like that*."

"Fuck you."

"Everything okay?" Brett asked as he strolled in.

"Where's Lisa? I thought I had a secretary who would at least slow the revolving door down."

"He's in a mood," Jordan said as he walked over to shake Brett's hand.

"That's nothing new," Brett said cheerfully.

Jordan returned to his seat and put his feet up on the corner of Spencer's desk. "A woman he likes just kicked him to the friend zone."

Brett grimaced in sympathy. "That's rough."

"She didn't kick me anywhere. I told you, she has a lot on her plate, so we're taking it slowly."

"Is she married?" Brett asked.

"No," Spencer said impatiently.

"He's not even sure she'll answer his text. That's as slow as it gets."

"You know who misses you, Jordan? Your office. You should go see it," Spencer spit out.

"Is this a party someone forgot to invite me to?" Nicolette asked as she entered the room. "I didn't see Lisa at her desk, so I figured it was okay to come right in." She nodded at her brother. "Brett." She smiled when she saw Jordan. "Hi, Jordan."

Jordan dropped his feet to the floor as he stood, looking flustered. "Nicolette."

"I hope I'm not interrupting anything," Nicolette said, gauging their expressions.

"No, everyone was just leaving," Spencer said.

"I wasn't going anywhere," Jordan said.

"I just got here," Brett supplied.

Spencer slapped his forehead before going over to hug Nicolette in greeting. "Or they were staying. I've lost control of my office."

"I'm so sorry," Lisa said breathlessly from the doorway. "I stepped away for a moment to use the ladies' room."

"It's fine," Spencer growled.

Jordan nodded at Lisa. "Hey, Lisa, what do you tell a guy when you don't want to date him, but you know he likes you?"

Lisa went three shades of red. "That I just want to be his friend?"

Spencer threw up his hands. "You need to leave. All of you. Now. Some of us actually work."

"By 'work' he means he wants to sit at his desk and stare at his phone until she answers his text."

"She?" Nicolette asked. "Are you dating someone, Spencer?"

This might drive me back to drinking. "Thank you, Lisa. We'll talk later." Lisa closed the door behind her as she left. "I'm not dating anyone. Jordan is being an ass. Which I probably deserve, but let's move on. Brett, did you need something?"

"Just dropping by to see how you're doing."

"Wouldn't want to miss an opportunity to play the doting big brother," Nicolette said under her breath, but everyone heard her. Her cheeks turned pink when she realized how far her voice had carried.

Brett's face tensed, but he said nothing. He looked genuinely hurt by her comment.

Jordan looked away.

For the first time, Spencer felt sorry for Brett. "It's not that we don't appreciate it, Brett; we're just not used to it."

After a long moment, Brett said, "Well, get used to it, because we're family, and I'm not going anywhere."

"Why would you? You got everything you wanted," Nicolette said. "Guilt-free."

Jordan said, "I can come back later."

Spencer put up an arm to block him. "Oh no. You wanted to stay."

The ding of an incoming message echoed in the awkward silence. Spencer fumbled for his phone.

"Is it Hailey?" Jordan asked.

Brett stepped closer. "Hailey?"

"Do I know her?" Nicolette leaned in.

I had fun, too. Spencer was about to reply when he told himself that doing so would make it seem like he'd been waiting for her response. He stood there, frozen.

Jordan answered, "Hailey from college." When Nicolette didn't immediately recognize the name, Jordan put his hand over his heart and feigned agony. *"Hailey."*

"Now I remember her. The one who used to hang out with you guys in the garage all the time." Nicolette peered over to see what Hailey had written.

Spencer turned away and walked back to his desk.

Jordan shrugged. "I read the first message. She probably answered, 'Hi, it's Hailey.' So far their dialogue isn't exactly earth-shattering."

"We should go," Brett said, waving them toward the door.

"Are you kidding?" Nicolette sat down in front of Spencer's desk. "Do you know how many of my dates Spencer interrogated? I distinctly remember him giving Todd Manx a lecture on why birth control wouldn't be necessary because if I missed curfew he would remove his genitalia. I'm not going anywhere."

"That's hard-core," Jordan said, sitting on the arm of Nicolette's chair.

"I was serious," Spencer said. And just because the last thing he needed was to see his best friend get his heart broken by his little sister, he added, "You don't mess with a man's sister."

Nicolette rolled her eyes.

Jordan swallowed hard and stood up.

Brett stayed where he was, halfway to the door. Spencer didn't like seeing his normally confident brother looking unsure of himself. *I could throw him a bone. I am trying to be less of a dick.* "Brett, what do you think I should say back? She said, 'I had fun, too.'"

"Ask her to dinner," Brett suggested as he walked over to stand with them.

"That's unimaginative," Nicolette said.

"Ask her to go in the simulator with you," Jordan suggested.

"That's creepy," Nicolette countered.

"Have you already been on a date?" Brett asked.

"I took her to Mangiarelli's for lunch today."

Jordan chuckled. "Now that you have money, you sure know how to throw it around. Did you order a whole pizza or just a slice?"

"None of you are helpful," Spencer said with a sigh.

S: Meet me tonight.

H: I can't tonight.

S: Tomorrow then.

H: I have plans already.

"She doesn't want to see me."

"Ask her why," Jordan said.

Nicolette slapped his thigh. "He can't ask her why she doesn't want to see him. What is she saying?"

Feeling about as ridiculous as a man could when he was sitting at his desk reading text messages to his family, Spencer asked exactly that. "I don't get it. We had a real connection. I felt it."

"I feel the same way every time I look at a centerfold." Jordan sighed. "Then I remind myself they're just one-dimensional, anyway."

Nicolette slapped his leg again. "You're such a dork."

Brett took another step closer. "Wait."

"For what?" Spencer asked.

"Just wait," Brett said.

The longer they all just stared at each other, the more Spencer wished he hadn't told them anything. Just when he was getting ready to wrap up all the fun, another message came in.

H: I could get a babysitter for Saturday.

"She could get a babysitter for Saturday," Spencer announced triumphantly.

"She has a child?" Brett asked.

"She has custody of her niece."

Brett went to stand beside his desk. "Tell her you'll pick her up at noon. Close the deal."

Spencer did, but then frowned when he saw her response. "She says she wants to meet me somewhere."

"That's not a good sign," Jordan said.

"It's because of her boss. She was telling me about the situation. The woman is a control freak with no boundaries. I hate the idea of Hailey working for someone like that. She wouldn't even tell me her employer's name. Jordan, can you find out where she works? You know, hack into something and just check if she's safe there."

Nicolette waved a hand in the air. "You think that would be respecting boundaries? I can't believe you would ask Jordan to do something like that. I mean, that's stalking."

"Yeah," Jordan said. "I'm offended that you'd even think I'd get involved in something like that."

Really, Jordan? Like you haven't done a complete social background investigation of every woman you've ever dated.

Brett said, "You could always help her find a new job."

"I could." He let the idea sink in and repeated more emphatically, "*I could*. I have a friend who owns a chain of department stores, and he owes me a favor. I'm sure he'd hire her."

"I'd look into it," Brett said firmly.

"After you ask her if she wants you to," Nicolette corrected.

Jordan pointed toward the phone. "For now, you might want to just answer her."

Brett said, "I have a two-hundred-fifty-two-foot yacht sitting in Boston Harbor."

Jordan added, "I have a motorcycle. Sure, it's not two hundred feet, but it instantly gets her wrapped around you and holding on."

Shaking her head, Nicolette said, "Seriously?" She waited, but none of the men in the room had a response to that. She threw up her hands in surrender. "Of the two, I'd choose the motorcycle. It's less pretentious. Take her for a picnic in Plymouth or on the Cape. Friends go for walks on the beach. And the beach can be romantic."

Oh no, don't get Jordan started.

"You like the beach?" Jordan asked.

Spencer sent him a look that shut him down. "The beach sounds good." He texted the question to Hailey and waited. "She said yes," he announced. "Looks like I'll be borrowing your motorcycle, Jordan."

"That's fine. You can pick it up Friday."

Spencer looked at each of them. "I don't know about any of you, but I actually do have work waiting for me."

Brett nodded. "Will we see you at Mom's on Sunday?"

"Please," Nicolette templed her hands in mock prayer.

"I don't know," Spencer replied, hedging. He might have met his family quota for the week. Especially if Sunday became an extension of this.

Jordan said, "This has been fun. I suppose I should try to get something done today."

Nicolette stood. "I'll walk out with you. I have a question for you, Jordan."

Spencer leaned over his desk. "Nicolette—"

Jordan looked back and forth between brother and sister.

"I wasn't going to ask him that," Nicolette protested. She walked out in a huff. Jordan followed.

Brett lingered. "What are you afraid Nicolette is going to ask Jordan?"

"You know how siblings are. You do something stupid, and instead of watching and learning, they want to try it themselves."

"What?"

"If Jordan gets engaged to her, I'll fucking kill him."

Chapter Nine

On Saturday morning, after leaving Skye happily hunting through rocky tide pools for crustaceans with Mrs. Holihen, Hailey drove her own car toward a nearby beach to meet Spencer. Although she'd told him she only wanted to be friends, the spa day with Delinda had left her feeling young and beautiful. She hadn't realized how little attention she'd given herself until Skye said she looked like a princess in the designer dresses she'd tried on. It was a day Hailey would hold dear in her memories, because it had simply been fun. No pressure. No guilt. Just a lot of laughter and silliness as Delinda looked on with a smile. *We all needed that.*

Although Hailey had refused to let Delinda buy her a whole new wardrobe, she had accepted the cotton summer dress she was wearing and one slip dress by another designer that fit her to perfection.

It hadn't seemed right to put such an expensive summer dress over a bathing suit, but that was what she'd gotten it for. She'd chosen a peach bikini to wear beneath it. In a pinch, the bathing suit could pass for underclothing and the dress would be appropriate for most restaurants.

When she pulled into the parking lot, she noticed a man sitting on a motorcycle. Although she was excited to see Spencer, she couldn't look away from those powerful jean-clad legs and the muscular back that the man's white T-shirt lovingly clung to. Hailey had never been one to gawk at men, but this one was perfection, the kind that inspires sculptures. *I'd sculpt that. And I'm not even a sculptor.*

He turned, removed his helmet, and waved in her direction. *Spencer?* Hailey accidentally blew the horn of her car as she rushed to pretend she was gathering up her purse.

I thought he looked good in a suit, but holy crap. How could any woman be just friends with that?

He hung the helmet on the handlebar and walked over. Hailey opened her car door and went to get out, but realized she hadn't undone her seat belt.

"Need help?" The smile he shot her was wickedly tempting as he smoothly reached over her to release the clasp. Instead of immediately withdrawing, though, he lingered, his face just above hers. He filled her view and her senses, bringing back an onslaught of intimate memories. Lust might not be enough to build a relationship, but damn it felt good.

"Thank you," she said in a strangled voice.

She didn't need to ask if he was experiencing the same hot and wild desire that was surging through her. It was there in his eyes and in the prominent bulge in the front of his jeans.

"God, you look good, Sunshine."

She took a shaky breath. It would have been so easy to lean forward for a kiss or to run her hands over the powerful expanse of his chest. "Thanks. I wouldn't have worn a dress if I had known you rode a bike."

"The dress was a good choice. The bike is Jordan's." The boyish smile he gave her nearly melted her away. "He said it would improve my image. I've spent too much time in suits lately." He withdrew from the car and offered her a hand.

"I'm sure it's more fun out of them." She groaned inwardly at her phrasing. "I mean, hanging out in something more casual."

His smile widened, but he thankfully let her slipup slide. She really did want things to be different this time. Rushing into sex the first time hadn't given them anything to build on. It had given them a false sense of knowing each other and had made everything too easy. And then too hard.

Friendship, whether or not it leads to something else, is where we need to start.

I just wish my body agreed with me. She placed her hand in his and swung her legs out while pushing back images of what he'd look like without his suit or those jeans on. *There should be support groups for people who have been celibate for over a year. I want to do the right thing, but it's not easy when I can't remember the last time wrong felt this good.*

"Did you bring a bathing suit?" He nodded toward the beach bag she'd forgotten on the passenger seat.

"I'm wearing it, but I should bring my towel and sunblock." She turned and bent into the car to retrieve it. When she turned back around with the bag slung over her shoulder, she noticed his expression had changed. The smile was gone, and naked hunger raged in his eyes. *Just how much did I flash him?*

They stood face-to-face simply breathing each other in. His hunger fired her own until there was no denying the effect they were having on each other. As much for her benefit as his, she said, "Back in college we had no responsibilities. There was no one who could be hurt by us getting together. It's different now."

"I know." His nostrils flared slightly.

As hard as it was to say, Hailey felt she had to. "There are things I should tell you before we go further."

He raised a finger to her lips and placed it over them gently. "Later. For now, let's find a spot on the beach, strip down, and jump into that still-cold Atlantic water. Trust me, I'll be able to think more clearly if we do."

Hailey smiled against his finger and stopped just short of kissing it. He lowered his hand as if understanding how close she was to losing her battle for self-control. "I could use a swim as well."

They walked hand in hand onto the beach and scored a prime spot near the shore. They spread out two towels and secured them with their shoes. Hailey's mouth went dry with anticipation when Spencer's hands went to the sides of his shirt. With one swift move he had it up and over his head. She stood there, frozen, as his hands went to unclasp his jeans, then raised her eyes to his.

"When you look at me like that all I can think about is fucking you," he growled.

"Sorry," she said, because a more coherent response was impossible.

His laugh was deep and sexy. "Don't be. I'm not." He stepped out of his jeans, tossed them onto the towel, and straightened. "But I need a quick swim because it's harder for a man to hide how he's feeling."

No, don't look. Don't do it. Her eyes wandered down his broad chest, over his flat stomach, and halted at the obvious tenting of his swim trunks. *Oh, God. If we weren't in public, I would sink to my knees and welcome him back with my mouth.*

This is bad.

She pulled her dress up and over her head and tossed it on top of his jeans. *I need the cold swim as much as he does.* "Race you in." She took off at a run, splashing her way to deeper water.

"You're on," he said from close behind her, crashing through the waves as well.

The water was up to her chest before she stopped. He swung her around and up, surprising her, but also making her laugh.

"You won," he said, sliding her down the front of him and standing her back up. "But it feels like I did."

The cold water wasn't as effective as he'd hoped. She put her hands on his shoulders to steady herself, then pushed slightly off him. "This is harder than I thought." She groaned when his eyebrows rose in response. "I mean more difficult."

The laugh he let out was infectious. "For me, too, on both counts."

It was too easy to smile with him, too easy to forget how much time had passed since they'd been together. Exciting, but equally scary. *I'm usually sensible. I've always worked hard and made decisions I've been proud of. My father once said, "Easy rule of thumb: if you can't look me in the eye and say you did it, chances are it's not something you should be doing."*

I'm glad you're not here now, Dad. I wouldn't want to attempt explaining Spencer to you or to Ryan. I had an excuse when I leapt into his arms the first time: I was young.

What would be my excuse now? That I'm lonely?

That's why I'm willing to risk losing my job? Uprooting Skye again? For sex? Really? I'm not better than that?

"We're not going to be able to do this, are we? Be friends, I mean." She heard the disappointment in her own voice.

Spencer's smile was wry. "The beach might have been a bad idea."

Her lips twisted in a matching smile. "Yeah."

"It is a beautiful day, though. It would be a shame not to enjoy it."

"We could set some ground rules. Like no touching."

"No touching," he repeated slowly. "Because you don't like it when I touch you?"

She could have lied, but that was something they'd never done with each other. "Because I like it too much."

He sucked in a breath audibly. "You're not making this easy, Hailey."

"I'm trying to be honest."

"Your honesty makes it pretty damn hard to remember why we're trying to be friends."

Hailey watched the waves crash against the shore and disappear. Being with Spencer had been like that. Beautiful. Simple. Gone as soon as it hit resistance. A night or two in his arms wasn't worth reliving losing him or risking the progress Skye had made. "I need more than what we had, Spencer."

"What does 'more' mean?"

"I'm not sure."

"Then how do we move forward?"

Hailey wrapped her arms around herself. *Wasn't this how I lost him the first time? Because I didn't know what I wanted? Because by the time I figured it out I couldn't articulate it?* "I need something I can trust. Something solid."

Spencer was old enough to have heard something similar from a variety of women. It wasn't unusual for them to want more than he offered because normally he offered nothing beyond sex. He'd never had a problem issuing an ultimatum: *take me as I am or take a hike.*

He couldn't imagine saying that to Hailey. In fact, when she looked at him with those big eyes of hers, he regretted being the kind of man who'd ever said it. Unlike the man he'd been for too long, she wasn't in it for the thrill of the game. She was honest, even with her desire, and it touched him as deeply now as it had when they had been young virgins learning each other's bodies together. With them it might not always have been good, but it had always been real.

Another man might have said exactly what she wanted to hear and not meant it, but that was another thing he could never do to her. "You need pie."

She smiled at his reference, and he tried to ignore the way the waves seemed to caress her breasts each time they washed over them. "I guess I do. What about you?"

Not an easy question. I do love cake. What man doesn't? At work. In bed. I've never been one to turn down a good piece of cake.

But has it made me happy?

Her smile wavered the longer he took to respond. He didn't want to rush and say more than he meant. "I've never tried it."

"Never?"

He frowned. "We're still talking on a deeper level, right? Because I'm getting confused and a little hungry with all the pastry talk."

"Hungry? Are you serious?" He liked how his joke returned a smile to her face.

He shrugged. He wasn't in a place where he could give her the answers she was looking for, so it was better to lighten the mood. "I'm not that complicated. Feed me—"

She raised a hand toward him and said, "Stop right there." But she was still smiling.

His grin widened. "I see you've become wise to the ways of men."

"You, anyway," she said lightly.

"I like to make you laugh. It's my second favorite thing to do to you."

Her chest and cheeks turned an adorable pink. "Rule two: easy on the innuendos."

He rounded his eyes and touched his chest, feigning surprise. "Me? Have you heard yourself?"

"I have. Sorry." She laughed and the sound sent his heart beating wildly in his chest.

She was relaxing with him, so he kept the banter up. "It's understandable." He flexed an arm for her. "What woman could be around all this and not have those thoughts?"

"Wow, that's a healthy-sized ego you have there," she said and splashed him.

He almost joked about what he had in an even larger size, but that would have broken rule number two. He could have pulled her to him and kissed her soundly, if not for rule one. *Why did I agree to these rules?*

Oh, yeah, because it's Hailey.

And she matters.

In the end, Spencer's body succumbed to the chill of the water and he felt safe in suggesting, "Want to get out and go for a walk down the beach?"

"I've always loved that."

He frowned as they made their way back to shore. "I don't remember us ever going to the beach together."

"Unless you count Mangiarelli's, campus, or your garage, we didn't actually go anywhere."

Shit. We didn't. "Why did you date me?" he asked, turning to face her once they were both clear of the water.

She touched his arm gently. "I didn't care where we were. I just enjoyed being with you."

She was breaking rule one, but he wasn't about to say it. "It was the same for me. I don't remember ever having a bad time with you."

Her hand fell away. "We didn't have to work on it at all. Do you think that's why it didn't last?"

He didn't know, so he took a step to start off their walk. She matched her pace to his. "Maybe, or maybe we were just too young to know what the hell we were doing."

She nodded. "It's funny. Back then I thought I had all the answers, now I second-guess so much of what I do."

"You've been through a lot."

"So have you, but you didn't let it stop you. You took your dreams from back then and made them a reality. That has to be amazing."

She is amazing. How she makes me feel is amazing, too. "Sometimes. Other times I wonder why it doesn't matter as much as I thought it would. Part of me needed to prove to myself that I could do anything Brett could do. I proved it. My company will soon be as successful as his. I did it on my own, without the family's money. So in a way I beat Brett, but it doesn't feel how I thought it would. When he comes to see me, he looks disappointed. I don't know why he even comes around. It's not like either of us enjoys his visits."

They walked along the shore together for several minutes, then Hailey said, "Maybe he's not disappointed in you. Maybe he's disappointed in himself."

"Brett? That's unlikely."

"It's easy to write someone off and walk away. That's what we did to each other. I didn't ask what was important to you. I didn't think about what you might be going through. I focused on my experiences only. It stopped me from really knowing you. How well do you actually know Brett?"

Spencer paused and looked out over the water. He could have told her he'd been just as self-centered the first time around, but she knew it. He couldn't go back and fix the past, but he could try to make more of the present. Hailey was pushing him to face issues he'd spent a lifetime denying he cared about. Honesty was long overdue. "I don't. Not on any level that matters."

"Then my next question is—do you want to?"

He found that he wanted to share how he felt with Hailey. Was it because they'd once come to each other, naked and unsure, and guided each other along? Did a bond like that endure? "He came to my office this week, and when I saw the way my little sister . . . Do you remember Nicolette?"

"I do."

"Anyway, she didn't sugarcoat what she thought of him and kept giving him these little digs."

"And you felt bad for him."

"Yeah, I did. Which is surprising because, all my life, he's been cutting me down, telling me what I was doing wrong. Nothing I did was good enough."

"Just like your grandmother."

"Exactly like my grandmother." He paused and looked down at her. "Did I tell you about her?"

"No," she said hastily. "It's just a guess. You said she's coldhearted."

They started walking again. "She is. They're very similar. Put the man I thought was my real father in the same room with them and you'd have a trifecta of judgment."

They'd reached a part of the beach that was deserted and rocky. Hailey stopped, picked up a stone, and threw it in the water. "That's so sad."

Great, how did I get her to sleep with me? I depressed her until she gave in out of pity. He pushed his feelings back into the box he kept them in. "Really, what is family except a huge time-suck, anyway?"

She spun on him then with unexpected anger in her eyes. "Do you honestly feel that way?"

He rocked back onto his heels in the face of her challenge. This was a new side of her. The easygoing girl he'd once fallen for now had an edge. He had a feeling that if he said yes it would bring a swift end to their time together.

The bullshit I tell myself isn't enough for her.

"No, I don't, but telling myself that makes the shitshow of my family bearable."

An awkward silence followed.

She sat on a large rock and pulled her legs up protectively in front of her. "Sorry. I didn't mean to react like that. I'm not judging you, but it's hard for me to hear you talk that way. You have a big family. They make you angry. They drive you nuts, but you could work it out if you wanted to. You have the luxury of being with any of them if you choose. I can never have even a bad day with Ryan again."

Spencer sat beside her and put his arm around her shoulders. *Screw the rules. This isn't about sex.* "Did my family send you? Because you've got me ready to call every last one of them and apologize."

She tensed beneath his arm. "Of course they didn't."

"I was joking."

Her expression remained strained. "I know."

Is it my arm? Am I crossing a line? He removed it and shifted to break the contact between their bodies.

They sat for a while without speaking, looking out over the water. The view got Spencer thinking about how he could incorporate it into his next themed virtual office program. "I want to show you what I do. Let's shower, get something to eat, and I'll take you to my office."

"I should get back. I hate to leave Skye for too long on a day when I don't have to."

"Of course." In an attempt to mask his disappointment, he ended up sounding impatient.

She searched his face and said, "She takes up a lot of my time. And that's the way it should be. She and I are a package deal. I wouldn't want to be with anyone who saw her as less than the blessing she is."

Was that what drove my mother to divorce her first husband? Did he resent me? The love in Hailey's voice when she defended Skye sparked yearning in him that had nothing to do with lust. People spoke about loyalty and commitment, but Hailey *lived* that virtue. She could have been resentful of how easily he'd believed the worst of her, but she wasn't like that. She was the kind of woman a man could picture building a life with if he were ready to take such a step.

He offered her a hand to help her back to her feet. She took it. They stood there, hand in hand, in a moment outside of time. He could have kissed her then and she might have let him, but he held himself in check. Yes, his body went haywire whenever she stood too close, but he wasn't a boy anymore. He didn't have to let his desires rule him.

As he looked down into her trusting eyes, he asked himself where he wanted this to go. The answer came to him without hesitation. *Whether we last for a week or a lifetime, I don't want her to regret giving us a second chance. I want her to be happy.*

He'd forged his place in the tech industry by being a problem solver, an obstacle remover. He couldn't bring her father or her brother back. His experience with children was extremely limited, so he didn't feel qualified to advise her on anything when it came to her niece. Her employment situation, however, was another story. He would find her the perfect job, one that would ease the worry in her eyes.

Doors were about to fly open for Hailey.

Some of his thoughts must have shone on his face because Hailey looked uncomfortable beneath his sustained attention. "You are my favorite view, beautiful inside and out. I forgot how good it feels just to look at you." He gave her hand a gentle squeeze before releasing it. "I hope saying so doesn't break any of our rules."

She shook her head slowly as if she'd been as lost in him as he'd been in her. Her voice was husky and sexy as hell when she said, "No. That's okay."

He nodded toward where they'd left their towels and deliberately kept the return conversation light. The perfection of the weather and the day made it easy to talk about nothing in particular and still smile through it.

Too soon, they were shaking the sand out of their clothes and putting them back on. Hailey smoothed the material of her dress over her hips and said, "I was so excited about getting this dress, and I didn't even wear it that long."

Spencer stepped into his jeans but halted before securing them. Tongue in cheek, he said, "I won't say it. I can't say it."

She made a face at him, then put her hands on her hips. "You might as well. I'm curious."

"Nope, I'm abiding by our rules."

"Just spit it out."

He let his grin shine. "A dress that doesn't stay on long? That's always been my favorite kind."

She laughed and smacked his arm playfully.

Being with her shouldn't feel as good as it had the first time around, but it did. In many ways, it was even better.

God, I hope I don't fuck it up a second time.

Chapter Ten

That night, after tucking Skye in bed, Hailey took the remaining craft supplies off the kitchen table in the guesthouse and tucked them away in a cabinet. When she finished, she sat down with the four freshly painted sets of wooden nesting dolls. Each said something about its creator.

Delinda chose to draw cats of various colors. She'd chosen a traditional style, and the result rivaled the quality of any Hailey had ever seen in a store.

Michael attempted to paint *Star Wars* characters with hilarious results. They all ended up looking vaguely like who he said they were. Everyone had fun guessing, and he didn't seem to mind when they guessed wrong.

Hailey found a design for robots that made Skye laugh, so she did her best to re-create them. They weren't perfect, but Skye was playing with them even before they'd dried and that was good enough for Hailey.

Skye had stared at her unpainted wooden dolls for a long time before snapping her fingers and saying, "I'll do it by age. Delinda, you're the oldest, so you'll be the biggest." She'd looked at Hailey, then

Michael. "Then Michael, right? Or are you older than he is, Auntie Hailey?"

Hailey had ruffled her hair. "I'll get you for that."

Skye was already choosing her paint while she answered, "Bring it on."

Delinda's delighted laugh surprised them all. "Oh, Hailey, we're in trouble."

With a cheeky smile, Skye had replied, "You're the ones who wanted me to speak—"

"Yes, we did, and hearing you joke again makes me so happy."

Skye had looked up from painting, suddenly serious. "I make you *happy*, Auntie Hailey?"

"You do, sweetie. Happy. Sad. On our best days and our worst day—I'm always grateful for you."

Skye had held up the tiniest of her nesting dolls. It was still blank. "If you ever have a baby of your own, will you love me more because you knew me first? Or will you love it more than me because it will really be yours?"

Michael had cleared his throat.

Delinda had remained surprisingly silent.

Hailey had stood, then bent down so she was eye to eye with her niece. "There is no more or less when it comes to love. I love you, and if I ever have a baby I will love it, too."

"What if you don't have enough love?"

Not caring that they still had an audience, Hailey pulled Skye in for a hug. "When you look up at the stars, can you see them all?"

"No," Skye said softly.

"But you know there's more of them than you can see, right?"

"Yeah, everyone knows that."

"Well, that's what your father would have told you about love if he were here. He and your mom loved you more than you could ever measure. I love you the same way. And if I ever do have a baby, that's what I hope you'll feel because it doesn't matter how we came together—we're family."

Skye had looked across at Delinda. "I changed my mind. I hope she has a baby. I hope she has a hundred babies. I want a big family."

"Easy there, Tiger." Hailey laughed. "I'm a long way from getting married and thinking about babies."

"The important thing is that Skye would be okay if you did meet someone," Delinda had asserted.

Hailey was beginning to think Delinda might be hoping something would develop between her and Spencer. If she was, Hailey wasn't sure how she felt about that. On one hand, it was sweet and could be taken as a compliment. On the other hand, not everything worked out the way people hoped and it was pressure Hailey wasn't prepared for.

Alone in the guesthouse kitchen, Hailey picked up Skye's tiny piece that now had a face and a baby bottle drawn on its side. She didn't dream about having a baby of her own—not anymore. Any desire she'd ever had had taken a backseat, along with so much else, as Hailey had gone into survival mode.

Things are finally stable. Shouldn't that be enough for me?

Her phone buzzed with a text message. You up?

Spencer.

H: Yes.
S: Busy?

She could have said yes. She could have also said she was too tired to talk, but the truth was she wanted to hear his voice before she went to bed. No, Skye is asleep.

Her phone rang and she answered it on the first ring. "Hey," he said in a deep tone that always sent her heart racing.

"Hey, yourself."

"How was your day?" he asked even though he'd spent the day with her.

"Better than expected."

"Mine, too. What did you end up doing with Skye?"

Her gut reaction was to wonder if he was asking to be polite or if he really cared. *I'll never find my way back to happy if I second-guess everything everyone says.* "We had craft night."

"What did you make?"

"Russian nesting dolls."

"And here I was picturing finger paint and Play-Doh."

She laughed. "Skye's seven and she's bright. She likes a challenge."

"Me, too."

A flush warmed Hailey's cheeks, and she closed her hand around the baby nesting doll she was still holding. At any other time in her life flirting with him would have been exciting. There was too much to consider to let go and enjoy it now. "If it were as simple as just you and me—"

"I know, but I won't pretend I'm not interested in more. You and I have always been real with each other."

Now. I have to tell him now. "Spencer, there's something you need to know."

"Auntie Hailey? Who are you talking to?" Skye asked from the kitchen doorway.

"A friend," Hailey answered quickly. "Go back to bed."

Skye walked into the kitchen instead and sat down next to Hailey. "Is it a boy?"

"I shouldn't have called so late," Spencer said.

"It's okay." Hailey tried to keep a stern face as she said, "Even if my phone rings, she knows she should be in bed."

"What's his name?" Skye asked. It was hard to be upset with her when she propped her face up on her hands and smiled.

"Skye, I'm having an adult conversation—"

"Is he your *boyfriend*?"

Spencer laughed. "She sounds terrified of you."

Yeah. I'm still working out a few things. "Skye Hannah Tiverton, get your butt out of this kitchen and back in bed."

Skye stood with a huff. "Fine, but we'll talk about this tomorrow. If you want to date someone, I want to meet him. What if I don't like him?"

"I'm not dating anyone." Hailey sighed. "I'm not talking about this right now. Bed."

I did push her to start speaking again. She remembered her sister-in-law, Erin, once joking about how excited she'd been for Skye to start walking until she realized how fast that meant she could get into trouble. *I finally get why that's so painfully funny.*

"Will you read me a story? You know I can't fall asleep without one."

That had started with Ryan. He'd always said it was his favorite time of day with her. "I'll be there in a minute."

"Can you read the part where he meets the lion?" Skye asked at the door.

"Yes. Go." Hailey nodded, and Skye scooted out of the room. "I need to go so I can tuck her back in bed. Looks like I'll be reading *Billy and the Lion* for a third time tonight."

"That was my favorite series when I was her age."

Hailey's breath caught in her throat. Was that why Delinda had given Skye the book? Because she knew children in general loved it or because she wants—*No, now I'm starting to sound paranoid.* "I'll have to look for more of them. She can't get enough of it." Which Hailey had taken as a good sign since before that book Skye had only wanted to hear stories her father had read to her.

"I looked up to Billy like a superhero, but better. He didn't have powers, but he saved that lion from everything imaginable. Whenever

I was afraid of something, I reminded myself that a scrawny kid could save a lion if he was brave enough."

"And look what you accomplished with that philosophy." *Had Delinda instilled confidence in him?* If so, things couldn't have always been bad between them.

She could hear the smile in his voice when he said, "All thanks to Billy. Who knew?"

Delinda did. There has to be a way to bring the two of them back together.

"Auntie Hailey?" Skye called out from her bedroom.

"Coming. Good night, Spencer," Hailey said reluctantly. Being with Spencer had always been good, but this time there was more.

"Hailey?"

"Yes?"

"Tomorrow morning I will be sitting next to my phone asking myself if I should call you. We've always been honest with each other. Do you want me to?"

Hailey blinked several times before answering. He wasn't asking to sleep with her. He wasn't pushing to meet Skye. He just wanted to talk. Did she have to deny herself even that? "I do."

"Then I will. Good night, Hailey."

Hailey hung up and went into Skye's room. There were aspects of Spencer that hadn't changed over time. Even when they'd both been inexperienced, it had been good because he'd asked her what she liked. *He did care back then. He cares now.*

I wish that made any of this easier.

"Auntie Hailey, are you okay?"

"What? Oh yes." Composing herself, Hailey climbed up onto Skye's bed and sat down beside her. "I'm not reading the whole book. It's late."

"Just a few pages," Skye said as she snuggled against Hailey's side. "Start where Billy gets lost."

"Please."

"Please start where Billy gets lost."

Hailey hugged her. "Okay, but just to the end of the chapter."

"Unless you want to read more. I'd be okay with that."

Looking down into her niece's pleading eyes, Hailey felt her resolve crumble. What was more important than this? "What if I start from the beginning and we see how far we get?"

Skye snuggled closer. "Keep reading even if I close my eyes. Promise?"

"I promise." Hailey gave Skye a kiss on the forehead and reached for the book. As she started to read a story she practically knew by heart now, her mind wandered back to Spencer. He was also not a stranger to loss. When she came to the part of the story where Billy came across a roaring lion in a net, she wondered who had read the story to Spencer when he was Skye's age.

Had they connected with the story, also? A timid lion, trapped and dangerous but impossible to walk away from. Complicated, just like life.

Skye fell asleep halfway through the book, but Hailey stayed and finished it. She tucked it beneath the pillow before climbing down. Before she turned off the light, she looked up at where Skye was sleeping.

I'm not afraid anymore, Skye. We can do this.

Monday morning Spencer smiled at his secretary as he walked past her desk. He hummed as he answered his e-mails and planned for his meetings. He felt good—better than he had in a long, long time.

He was still smiling when Lisa knocked on his door. "There's a Mr. Kyees here to see you."

"Send him in."

Spencer stood and met his old college friend halfway. They shook hands vigorously. "Thanks for coming by, Kyle."

"You said it was important."

Spencer motioned for Kyle to sit. "It is." Spencer could have gone to Kyle's office, but he'd learned early that the one with the desk had the perceived power. He implemented the technique in business, but he'd learned it from his family. Want control of a situation? Be the one who summons, not the one who is summoned.

"Is it about the next update? I heard it was on schedule."

"This is a personal matter."

Kyle took a seat. "One that couldn't be handled over the phone? It must be important."

"It is." Spencer stood in front of his desk. "Do you have any openings in your purchasing department?"

"I might. I'd have to check with that department. Why?"

Perfect. Spencer folded his arms across his chest. "There's someone I want you to hire. The position not only has to pay well, but you need to keep all mention of me out of it. I want her to think she got the job on her own."

Chapter Eleven

Later that week, Hailey was sitting in the wooden bleachers of a large indoor arena, watching Skye take her second riding lesson. Delinda had wanted to come, but Hailey had convinced her to give Skye a chance to decide for herself if she liked the barn's instructor. Although both Delinda and Skye had been disappointed, Hailey was trusting her instincts on this one.

Going along with whatever Delinda wanted was easier, but Hailey wanted more for Skye. Skye needed to be confident enough to choose her own path—even if it ended up not being one that Delinda approved of. That kind of strength could only come from having time apart as well as together.

None of that conversation had been easy to have with Delinda. Especially considering that Skye had just been accepted to Sterling Waters, the private school many of the children at the barn attended. Skye had even expressed excitement about attending that school in the fall. There weren't words to describe how good it felt to watch Skye making friends, being silly, and acting like a kid again. It was beyond anything Hailey had dared dream for. Hailey's gratitude made her want to help Delinda. Like the roaring lion in Skye's book, Delinda lashed out when she was afraid.

Another reason to maintain some boundaries with her and Skye. It was a rescue mission that wasn't without risk. People, even those a person thought they knew, could disappoint.

Like Spencer.

Hailey had made the mistake of looking him up on social media. Although he hadn't posted them, there were endless photos of him partying with so many women she'd had to stop scrolling because it sickened her. The Spencer she'd known wasn't a playboy. The man he was presenting himself as didn't seem to be either, but evidence of the other side of him was plentiful.

Which was the real Spencer?

If she hadn't seen the photos online, she'd think he was a sweetheart. He called her every morning simply to say he hoped she had a good day. He sent her a text or two during the day that never failed to make her laugh. Each evening, after Skye was asleep, he called and they talked for hours.

He seems to genuinely want to get to know me.

Or am I just a challenge?

She pushed that particular thought back and focused on how much she loved when he spoke about his day, the projects he was working on, and his family. She wondered what he'd think if she told him Delinda described them all almost exactly the way he did. They both saw Nicolette as a little lost and somewhat of a rebel. They both worried about Rachelle since she tended to internalize the pain and confusion of those around her. Eric, the well-known actor in the family, was too absent from the mix, always off in Europe re-creating himself. The only real discrepancy was Brett. To Delinda, he was the kindest, most caring of them all. Spencer saw him as condescending and overbearing. *The truth is probably somewhere in the middle.*

And it's not stopping my heart from opening to him again.

Hailey hadn't realized how much she'd missed simply having someone to talk to. It was freeing. When he'd first asked about Ryan and his wife, Erin, Hailey was afraid that talking about them would make her sad, but she discovered the opposite was true. Memories of their kindness brought her comfort. While talking about them, she realized how much they were still here. *I'm not alone. They're the lens I see the world through. That's how we all live on.*

Will Skye one day see me the same way? I hope so.

After nearly a week of opening up to each other, Hailey was conflicted. She and Spencer had shared so much, but there were definitely topics they were both avoiding. He was evasive when she asked him about his social life, and she wasn't ready to tell him about her work situation.

Am I a coward for not simply telling him? I thought I was past letting my fears stop me. What am I waiting for? Do I think an easier option is going to drop out of the sky?

Hailey's phone vibrated in her pocket. She took it out. The number wasn't one she recognized. Telemarketer? She kept her voice low and said, "Hello?"

"Miss Tiverton?"

"Yes, that's me."

"My name is Kyle Kyees, CEO of SmartKart."

The CEO of an international department store chain is calling me? Me? This has to be a scam. "How nice to speak with you, Mr. Kyees. How's business?"

"Up in the US, improving in parts of Asia, and losing ground in Europe, but that's not why I called."

No actual business owner would ever divulge that kind of information. It was either a scam or someone's idea of a joke. "Happy to hear about the US, sorry about Europe. I'm sure you'll figure it out. Goodbye."

"Wait. You haven't yet heard the reason for my call. I came across your résumé on a Boston job site. I have an opening for a full-time executive purchaser for my New England stores. If you're interested, the job is yours." He quoted a salary that was double her income with Delinda, and it came with benefits.

It sounded too perfect. "Don't you need to interview me first?"

"No need. I've checked your references. You come highly recommended."

"From DIY Rite?" Although she'd worked there for years in the purchasing department, she didn't leave on the best of terms. They'd resented the amount of family leave she needed to take during Skye's initial transition to living with her. Although they'd muddied the water with other claims, Hailey knew the real reason they fired her had been because of the amount of time she needed to take off. Hailey had even understood because the time that went into setting up a support system for Skye had been extensive. *Highly recommended? I don't think so.*

"And other sources. I'll admit I don't usually get personally involved with most of our hires, but my offer stands."

Hailey chewed her thumbnail. Could something like this happen? And if it could, was it even something she wanted? She and Delinda had found a workable balance. She didn't want to leave any more than Skye would want to.

Making my own money might make things even better with Delinda. I could show her that we don't need to be paid to be with her. With that kind of salary, I could afford Skye's tuition and Clover's board, and have enough left to pay rent if Delinda agrees to let us stay in her guesthouse.

That is, unless this is someone's idea of a sick joke.

"Could I have some time to think about it?"

"I'll give you a week. Take this number. It's for the Human Resources department. They'll be able to answer any questions you might have about the role."

Hailey wrote the number down on a piece of paper in her purse. *Holy shit, this sounds legit.* "Would I contact them with my decision?"

"Yes, they'll have all the paperwork."

"And you don't need to meet me first?"

"I can schedule an interview if it would make you feel better, but I'm very busy."

"Oh no. It's not necessary. Thank you."

"We look forward to having you join us, Miss Tiverton." He hung up, and Hailey sat there with her mouth wide open for several minutes.

She sought out Skye and the instructor. The lesson was still going on uneventfully.

All those résumés I blanketed Boston with finally paid off. An executive purchaser for SmartKart? Oh my God. Finally, I did something right.

She looked back at her phone. She was bursting with excitement, but whom could she call? *Spencer.*

He picked up on the first ring. "Hey, Sunshine."

"Are you sitting?" she asked in a rush.

"I am."

"You are not going to believe who I just got off the phone with. I'd have you try to guess, but you'd never be able to. I never would have expected him to call me. I mean, I'm still not entirely sure the call was legit, but I'm going to look into it. Or maybe you could help me?"

"Slow down," Spencer said with a chuckle. "Why don't you start by telling me who called you?"

"The CEO of SmartKart. The *CEO*. That's what makes it unbelievable, but the way my life is going lately, maybe anything is possible. He offered me a job."

"That's great."

"It's not great, Spencer, it's an answer to my prayers. Last year I kept wondering if anyone was even listening upstairs, but I guess I was waitlisted because this could not have come at a more perfect time. I don't want to get too excited, though, before I figure out if it was just a prank."

"I'm sure it wasn't."

"He gave me a number to call. It's supposedly to their Human Resources department. Oh my God, Spencer. Can this really be happening?"

"I'm not surprised to hear it is. Your luck is turning around."

"It sure is." She wiped a happy tear from her cheek. "Every part of my life is coming together. I'd started to lose faith that it ever would be this good again. If I gave you the number, would you be able to tell if it's the real deal or not?"

"Absolutely."

She read it off to him.

He said, "Hang on. I'm going to put you on hold for one minute while I check it out."

"Thank you, Spencer." She barely breathed while waiting for him to return.

"I made a call. That's the real number to SmartKart's HR department, and my friend said it sounds legit."

Hailey was so excited she was light-headed. "I can't believe it. I can't believe this sort of good really happens."

"So you're obviously taking the job."

"I think so," Hailey said. *Delinda won't take this well, but I'll find a way to convince her that it's for the best for all of us. We'll still be part of her life.*

"You just said it was the answer to your prayers."

"I know. And it is. I just need to think about how I'm going to tell my present employer. I don't want to hurt her feelings."

"You're a good person, Hailey Tiverton, but you have to do what's best for you."

"Yes, but she has been so good to me and Skye. I'm not saying I won't take the job, I'm just saying I need time to think it all through. I have a week to decide. The only way I'll do this is if I'm sure it'll be the best choice for all of us."

"All of us?" Spencer asked in a deep tone.

"I'll need to know if it involves travel. I can't take the job if it does. That wouldn't work well with Skye."

"Ah yes."

She almost added him to the equation, but it was too early. Their shared history gave their relationship a depth that otherwise wouldn't have been there. She had to remind herself that they weren't picking up where they left off. *We're not even dating yet—we're friends.* "I have a week to find out more about the job before I decide."

"That's smart. You can come to me, too, if there's anything else you need to know. I have a good network of people. If I don't know the answer, they might."

Warmth spread through Hailey. He was giving her exactly what she hadn't known how to ask for the first time. "Thank you for being there for me, Spencer. I can't tell you how much it means to me."

"I want this for you, Hailey. I want you to be happy."

She smiled. "I want the same for you."

Coming back into each other's lives can't be an accident—not when it's this good.

Hailey looked up and realized the instructor was waving her over. "I have to go. Skye just finished her second riding lesson."

"How did she do?"

"She's still smiling, so I'd say well."

"I read an article about equine therapy this week. Horses are a good confidence builder for children."

The idea that he might be reading up on things that mattered to her and Skye was touching. "Did you have a pony when you were little?"

"No, we couldn't afford one. How about you?"

"Same," Hailey said automatically as she made her way toward where Skye was standing with Clover and her instructor. She couldn't wrap her head around how half of Spencer's family had been raised with money while the younger siblings had been left without, but she didn't have time to delve into it then. "I have to run."

"Talk to you later, Sunshine."

Hailey hung up, smiling. Her conversation with Spencer was temporarily overshadowed by Skye's enthusiastic retelling of everything she'd learned that day. The instructor's next student was waiting in the wings, so Hailey and Skye took Clover to an aisle to untack him and brush him down and then to a field outside the barn to graze for a few minutes. Another girl about Skye's age was already out there with her pony. It didn't take more than a moment for the two girls to start talking. There was a twinkle in Skye's eyes, a bubbling enthusiasm in her voice that drew people to her—just as it once had.

She's back, Ryan. Skye's really back. Hailey looked on with gratitude welling within her. *We did it.*

"Your sister, Rachelle, is on hold," Lisa said from the doorway of Spencer's office. "Would you like me to tell her that you're in a meeting?"

With a smile left over from his conversation with Hailey, Spencer closed out the program he was working on. "No, I have a minute."

"You do?" Lisa said, then looked mortified that she'd revealed her surprise. "I'll put her through."

"Thanks, Lisa."

Lisa left with an odd expression on her face. Spencer didn't care if his change in attitude confused her. Life was beginning to make sense to him again, and the relief was immense—like a weight had been lifted from him. Spencer picked up his office phone when it rang, stood, and stretched. "Hey, Rachelle."

"Sorry to call you at work."

"It's fine. What's up?"

"I wanted to thank you for coming to Mom's on Sunday."

Normally he would have taken her comment as a dig about the many times he'd refused to go. Instead, he remembered what Hailey had said about how she would give anything for even a bad day with her brother. *It's time to let some shit go.* "It was good to see everyone."

"We shouldn't have grilled you about Hailey. Who you date is actually none of our business."

True, and in the past he might have agreed with her, but he didn't this time. "You ask because you care; I get it. I'd probably do the same."

Rachelle's tone lightened. "Wait, you sound happy."

"Is that so shocking?"

"Yes. We're talking, and you sound like you're still in a good mood. What have you done with Spencer?"

He chuckled even though he was aware of the serious undertone to her joke. "I told you all I needed was time."

"Time, huh? So this has nothing to do with Hailey?"

"It might." He caught his reflection in the windowpane and liked what he saw. He'd never understood men who linked their happiness to that of their mate, but nothing he'd done with WorkChat ever made him feel as good as getting that job for Hailey. Her excitement had become his.

"I feel bad about what I said about her, Spencer. I was just worried about you."

"We're good, Rach. Don't give it another thought. I'm not going to."

"When do we get to meet her?"

"You've already met her."

"*This* decade."

"I told you—we're taking it slow. Are you teaching summer school?"

"Not this year. I'm taking a college course instead. Why?"

"You busy this afternoon?"

"No."

"I was thinking about texting Brett to see how busy his day is. We could try for a late lunch."

"He'd love that. Let's do it."

After hanging up with his sister, Spencer returned to his desk and finished writing the code for a glitch he'd noticed in Jordan's album simulator. He sent it to Jordan and returned to a mailbox of e-mails.

He swore as he realized he'd almost forgot to contact Brett.

S: Want to meet for lunch?
B: Yes, but Alisha and I have a sonogram at noon.
S: How about after? Bring her. Rachelle plans to join.
B: Sounds good. We can meet in the middle.
S: Yes.

I'm beginning to think we can.

Chapter Twelve

Saturday evening, still hungry after devouring a high-priced meal of minuscule proportions, Hailey took a sip of wine while letting her eyes wander over Spencer's chiseled features. *He is too damn good-looking.* She was glad she'd chosen to wear the second dress Delinda bought for her, a formfitting, knee-length emerald frock with spaghetti straps, because otherwise she would have felt dowdy next to him. He'd casually thrown a jacket over a button-down shirt and gray slacks, and somehow he looked as if he could model the outfit. Some people looked good in anything.

And nothing.

Oh yes, she remembered too well what was under his clothing.

Hailey tore her gaze from his and glanced around. More than one woman was shamelessly trying to catch his attention despite the fact that he was with someone. Handsome, confident, and in the news for making a name in the tech industry—Spencer could have probably left the restaurant with half the women in the place.

And according to Instagram he already has.

"What would you like to do after dinner? I've never planned a non-date." All it took was for him to look up with that boyish grin for Hailey to forget about everyone else in the room.

"I told Mrs. Holihen I'd be back by ten."

"That gives us a few hours." His smile was easy and warm. "It's entirely up to you how we spend them. I set up a couple of contingency plans, but you can suggest something entirely different."

"Contingency plans?"

"I like to be prepared."

She leaned forward. "This I need to hear. How does Spencer Westerly prepare for a night out with a woman?"

"Normally I just buy condoms and keep hydrated."

She rolled her eyes skyward. "Charming." He wasn't pretending he hadn't been with anyone else. A lot of people go through wild stages. *Maybe I'm worried about nothing.*

"This isn't a date, though, so I took a different approach."

"I'm afraid to ask what that was."

He sat back, looking incredibly proud of himself. "I booked a helicopter tour of Boston, arranged a private harbor cruise on a yacht, and bought out Steve's mini-golf in Mendon, in case you want to stay local."

"You did all that? Seriously?"

His eyes burned with the same hunger she was fighting. "I want you to see that this time would be different."

Whoosh. She could hardly breathe. *It already is. This time is frighteningly perfect—the kind of perfect that is too good to be true. Nothing this good happens in real life, and if it does, there is always a catch.* She grasped for a joke. "All that and no condom."

"Oh, I brought some." His smile turned lusty.

"'Some'?" she croaked. *No. Traitorous mind, don't go there.*

He took her hand in his. "Full disclosure. I felt guilty when I stuffed them in my pocket, but that guilt wore off. They have a long shelf life, and I didn't expect to tell you I had them. I figured if you came across them on your own, we were probably doing something that would require them."

Hailey imagined him having that very internal debate and burst out laughing. *I want to believe in this, Spencer.* His smile widened. Being with him was that easy. "Did you hydrate?"

He raised his glass of water with his other hand.

She laughed again. "Do I dare ask what it does?"

"Any athlete will tell you that performance is improved by maintaining optimal health conditions."

"Athlete? Isn't that a stretch?"

He wiggled his eyebrows. "I've learned a few things along the way."

She had the feeling that if she asked, he would have volunteered to show her. Instead, she blushed and glanced away. She wasn't ready to take that next step with him. "I'll take your word for it."

His fingers laced with hers. "So what do you want to do?"

She considered the options he'd listed, but they were his attempt to make up for what he thought he'd done wrong the first time. She hadn't needed fancy dates then, and she didn't yearn for them now. "I'd like to see your office. The other day you offered to show me what you do, but I didn't have time to see it. I have time now."

He looked momentarily torn, like a child being offered a chance to do something he felt he shouldn't. "Are you sure?"

"Absolutely. I spent enough hours with you while you came up with concepts. I'd love to see what you moved on to."

"All right, then." Spencer called their waiter over and paid the bill. There was something magical about how he didn't spare a glance at the other women in the room as they left. Before they were even at the car, he started describing how he'd solved the bandwidth problems. As they sped toward Braintree, he summarized the turning points that had brought him to where he and his company were today.

Hailey's head was spinning from the terms he was using. She didn't understand the difference between virtual reality headsets and the holographic AI processor that formed the cornerstone of his programs. Parts of what he was saying were so full of technical terminology, it was as if he was speaking another language.

And Hailey loved it.

His excitement was infectious. This was the Spencer she remembered, the reason she'd once been content to sit with him as he wrote code. The passion he brought to the process made it like watching a gifted painter. She was excited to finally see his masterpiece.

He parked in front of his building and practically dragged her by the hand through the foyer and up to his office. Intense. Driven. Boldly innovative. The Spencer she'd once loved was still in there, and she was falling for him all over again.

It wasn't until he and Hailey were standing in front of the simulator that Spencer realized he had traded all semblance of coolness for exuberant geekiness. When she'd said she wanted to see his work, a switch in him had flipped, and he was reasonably certain he hadn't stopped talking since they left the restaurant. *I have all the finesse of a toddler.*

But WorkChat is a large part of who I am. Everything has always come second to this dream.

Even Hailey.

It wasn't something he was proud of, but there was no rewriting history. Given a second chance to go back and do it over, he wasn't sure he could have done it differently. He would have wanted to. He wished he'd been more aware of her needs. But could he have put her before his dreams? Not back then.

Will letting her experience WorkChat help her understand why I needed to get here or remind her that I chose it over her?

He looked at her, trying to gauge her mood. "It doesn't look like much from the outside." Spencer typed a code into the security pad, and the door swung open. Without any programs running, it wasn't much more than a large empty closet. He shrugged. "It gets better."

She stepped inside without hesitation and looked around. "Do things come out of the wall?"

"They do. It's one of the limiting aspects of each simulator. In order for a person to be able to sit on a holographic chair, a physical object must be present. In the beginning, the physical supports are designed around the program. However, once the simulator has reached capacity for retractable physical supports, programs have to be tailored to match the simulator."

"I think I understand," she said slowly, then pointed to the vents. "Does that spit out water like a 4-D movie theater?"

"Something like that. A good amount of brain research went into our design. So much of what we see is actually a filtered view our brain processes from an overwhelming amount of stimuli. We see, hear, feel what our brain decides is necessary for survival. What we can't see, our brain often fills in. Sometimes what's left out of a simulation is what makes it most believable. Name a place you'd like to go. I might have a simulation for it."

"Oh, I don't know."

"Anywhere."

"Today or in the past?"

"Would you want to go back in time?"

She wrinkled her nose. "That's a complicated question. I wouldn't want to go back if it cost me what's in my life now. But it would be interesting to see if anything was as I remember it."

A younger Spencer would have plowed forward and shown her his projects, but Jordan's program fit what she was wishing for. Hopefully, his friend hadn't made any obscene additions to it. "There is a way you can, at least within the confines of my recorded life. Jordan took my old photo albums and created something you might enjoy. Stand close to me and try not to touch the walls."

She smiled. "Is that what you tell everyone you bring here?"

"Usually anyone who makes it this far has signed a nondisclosure contract and has put down a substantial deposit. I've never brought a date here." The pleasure that shone on her face filled him with warmth he wasn't sure how to label. "Luckily, you're a friend."

Her smile wavered, and he regretted the stupid joke. "That's right. Lucky me," she said.

He wanted to say something to reassure her, but the rules they were following were hers. Not that he'd done well with keeping his hands off her or avoiding suggestive innuendos. He had, however, done his best to honor her request that they begin again as friends. "You might feel slightly disoriented for a moment, but it passes. Ready?"

"Ready."

"Run photo album two. College quad background only. No isolation." He put his arm around her waist to steady her if she needed it. The bland walls filled with scenery from their old college campus.

"Oh my God," she exclaimed, gripping his side with one hand. She looked around in wonder. "It's so real."

"It gets better. Walk with me. The simulator was designed for one user. If you stay in step with me, the computer should read us as one and maintain the integrity of our location in space." He took a step, initiating the floor to begin moving. She stumbled at first, but clung to him before matching her steps to his.

"Is this a photo or a video? How are we able to walk through it?"

"It's actually a synthesis of every photo and video I have of the college campus. The computer meshes it all together and fills in what's missing. Your memory or expectation of what should be there does the rest."

"Wow. Just wow."

They walked to where the images began to blur. "Jordan and I are debating if we should sync the program with media feed from the Internet. Doing so would eliminate the limitations of the experience, but it would introduce outside images into what is otherwise a memory database."

They turned and began to walk back across the quad. "So you took all of these images?"

"I did."

"How do you call up a picture of something specific?"

"What would you want to see?"

"Jordan?" she asked.

"Show Jordan Cohen."

"There are three hundred two photos. Play through or isolate and merge?" the computer asked.

Hailey's pace slowed. Spencer adjusted his stride to match. "That's an interesting voice," she said.

"We call her Riley."

"Riley." She shook her head. "Sorry. For a second there I thought—"

How could I have forgotten? Shit. "You're not crazy. Riley utilizes artificial intelligence to expand the voice samples from our database. When I designed the software, your voice was what I had the largest sample of. Essentially, she guesses at how you would say any new word she's introduced to, based on regional speech patterns."

"That's—that's—"

"Incredibly romantic or creepy?"

Her smile returned. "Somewhere in between. My face isn't on a robot anywhere in this building, is it?"

"No," he said with a laugh. When she continued to look uncertain, he added, "I swear." Then he thought of a caveat to his declaration. "Unless Jordan is working on something he hasn't told me about."

Hailey stopped walking completely and turned to look up at him. "I draw the line at robots."

"I'll tell Jordan."

She smiled.

He did the same.

She placed a hand on one of her hips and said, "Show Spencer Westerly."

"There are two thousand one hundred photos and seven videos. Play through or merge and isolate?" the computer prompted.

"You don't want to see—"

"Yes, I do," Hailey said with an impish smile. "Play through."

The walls around them filled with one-dimensional images of a young Spencer in diapers. Each image remained for three seconds before being replaced by another, showing him ever-increasingly older. He was about to prompt the playthrough to end, but she was clutching his arm and exclaiming with each new image that was displayed something along the lines of "That is so adorable. Look at that. Aww."

I was kind of a cute kid.

"Are those braces? You had an awkward phase? I love it."

"End playthrough." She was laughing, and he gave in to an undeniable urge, wrapping his arms around her waist and pulling her to him. "I'm glad you find my pain amusing. That was a long year," he growled into her ear.

She arched back to smile up at him. "Year? Cry me a river. I had a late growth spurt. Most of my teen years I endured being asked whose little sister I was when I was hanging out with my friends."

He would have found that image amusing if his entire body wasn't overheating. The feel of her against him made picturing anything besides kissing her impossible. *No, I won't ruin this. I promised I wouldn't rush her.*

She must have sensed, or perhaps physically felt, the direction his thoughts had shifted to, because she stepped out of his arms. "What else does it do?"

Pretty much that. Oh, the album program.

"It can create a hologram of a person if enough images exist to complete one."

"Show Spencer Westerly," she said softly.

Again?

"There are two thousand one hundred photos and seven videos. Play through or merge and isolate?" the computer prompted.

"Merge and isolate," she guessed correctly, reminding him of something she'd always done that had impressed him. She wasn't a gamer, nor did she claim to know anything about coding programs, but she could intuitively navigate them. In fact, if she'd struggled with part of a program, he knew it required an overhaul.

"Location?" the computer asked.

"Garage," she said.

Her request floored him in that it was identical to his search for her. Was she seeking what he had been?

The walls of the room became the walls of the garage. A three-dimensional image of Spencer appeared in a seated position. He was working so intently he didn't notice the arrival of whoever was filming him.

His image turned, and his face transformed completely. If either of them had ever doubted how he'd felt about her back then, it was right there on his face—pure, unrestrained adoration. "Hey, Sunshine. Want to see what I'm working on?"

The program skipped her response and went to his. His eyes darkened, and he turned off the computer behind him. "On second thought, it can wait. Come here."

Spencer remembered exactly what had followed.

"End merge and isolate," she said quickly, revealing that she did as well.

His image faded from the garage.

The only sound in the simulator was their heavy breathing. He would have taken her then, but he had enough regrets when it came to her. Their next step would come at her request.

"End garage," she said, and he nearly groaned aloud.

I'm a grown man. I'll survive.

Maybe.

He was acutely aware of every breath she took, every shift of her weight. The subtle scent of her shampoo was sexier than any perfume.

"Wow," she said in a shaken voice.

"You can say that again." There wasn't an inch of her he wasn't hungry to taste. *If she gave me the option, where would I start? Her mouth is heaven. But that neck. It doesn't really matter where I start because I'd work my way down . . .*

"I've tried to convince myself over the years that it wasn't as good as I remember, but it was." There was a look in her eyes he hadn't expected. It was conflicted and sad, reminding him of the first time she'd walked away. "Maybe thinking we can re-create that is a mistake."

Is she saying what I think she's saying?

A defensive wall rose within him that he'd thought had washed away after seeing her again. "No one is forcing you to be with me. You want to go? Go. I don't fucking need you."

Hailey took another step back. "That's not very nice."

"I never said I was nice."

She held his eyes for a long moment. "Who are you, Spencer? I looked you up online. I don't know that man."

Shaking his head in disgust, Spencer spat, "Does it matter? You've already made your choice."

Instead of leaving as he expected, she put her hands on her hips and glared at him. "You'd like that, wouldn't you? If I stormed away, you could blame me again. Just like the first time."

"You're the one who left me."

"Because you were just as thickheaded then as you are now."

They stood there, both breathing heavily, in a sexually charged standoff.

He ran a hand through his hair in frustration. "I'm doing the best I can. If that isn't good enough—"

"Don't go there. Don't take the easy way out. I'm trying to tell you that I'm scared. You. This. The whole thing scares the shit out of me. I need to know if it's real."

"What do you want me to say, Hailey?"

She stepped toward him and laid a hand on his chest. "All I need is an honest answer. If I agree to give this a second chance, which Spencer would it be with?"

Chapter Thirteen

As an awkward silence dragged on, Hailey cursed herself for essentially vomiting her fears at his feet. "I'm sorry. That's not a fair question."

He held his hand over hers, where it lay on his chest. "Maybe not, but I've asked myself the same thing."

"And?" She held her breath and waited.

"Partying didn't fix anything. Avoiding my family didn't work, either. I thought if everyone left me alone long enough, I'd feel better. No such luck. Lately I've been talking to my family again. I thought I had my shit together, but I don't know."

"You're talking to your family again?" *Maybe now is the time to tell him about Delinda.*

His smile was gentle. "Some of them. What you said was a wake-up call for me." He raised her hand to his mouth and kissed her palm. "I didn't mean what I said about not needing you."

His face lowered until his lips were just above hers, but the kiss she expected didn't come. His breath was a tickle.

I can tell him later.

"Run secluded beach three," Spencer said.

The scenery changed around them, but Hailey didn't care. Her body was humming with a craving only he could satisfy. A moment dragged into two. Memories marched like hot lava through any reservations she still had. This was Spencer, her Spencer, and deciding to give herself over to him felt as natural as breathing. She licked her bottom lip and tipped her head back while her eyes fluttered closed. *Oh yes.*

Still no kiss came.

She opened her eyes again. Desire was there in his heated gaze, but his hands hadn't moved. One still held hers; the other was sadly at his side. "What's wrong?" she asked, feeling foolish yet hungry to feel his mouth on hers.

"Nothing," he said in a tight tone.

"I ruined it for us, didn't I? I complicated what could have been simple." She went to move away from him, but he pulled her flush against him, a move that made his level of excitement deliciously obvious.

His hand came up to hold her chin, raising it so her eyes met his. "No, you made me want to do it right this time. I don't want to rush you. If anyone is ruining this, it's me, because all I can think about is how much I want to fuck you. Right here. Right now. On a conference table with the sound of waves crashing in the background. I want to hear you come while the two of us free-fall through clouds. That's what I want. What I don't know is if I can be here, kiss you, and stop without taking us both there."

This was the Spencer she knew—the one she'd never stopped loving. No hiding. No games. Honest. Real. "I want to go there with you," she said.

He groaned. "Are you sure?"

A smart woman knew a simple action could get a message across faster than any words could. She ran one hand down his flat stomach and caressed the hard bulge in his trousers. "Don't make me beg," she said in a low tone she hoped was sexy. "Unless you're into that now."

With a growl, he gathered her closer and kissed her. There was no hesitation in his claiming. His tongue slid between her lips and sought hers, hot and demanding. He lifted his head briefly and pulled the hem of her dress over her hips in one strong move. "I'll show you what I'm into." His next kiss was more playful, nipping at her lips before his tongue dipped inside her mouth again.

She'd wrapped her arms around his neck but lowered them just to allow him to slide the straps of her dress off. He efficiently unclasped her black lace bra and dropped it to the floor. "Add conference table. No chairs," he said.

All while kissing her, he lifted her and seated her on the edge of a smooth surface that had the appearance of a long table. He hooked a finger beneath each side of her panties. She shifted her weight so he could slide them off.

"I want you so much it hurts," he growled as he kissed his way down her neck. Her dress bunched around her waist, and her feet, still in the heels she'd worn, dangled several inches off the floor.

Frantic to feel him, Hailey slid his jacket off, pulled his shirt from his trousers, and began to feverishly unbutton it. He moved his attentive mouth to one of her breasts, and her hands went to the table behind her to brace herself as she arched, heat searing through her.

As young lovers, they had been novices in the art of lovemaking; Spencer had obviously learned some new tricks. He teased her nipples, one then the other, with his tongue and teeth. He warmed them with his hot breath before starting again. Each pause made Hailey anticipate the next touch more.

His hands adored her, caressing her long legs, her arms, every inch of her.

She was already writhing, already wet and ready for him when he parted her labia with his fingers. He kissed his way back to her mouth as his fingers worked their magic on her clit. She wanted to hold him, caress him, bring him the kind of pleasure he was bringing her, but she was positioned for him to helplessly devour.

He thrust a finger inside her, then another, while his tongue claimed hers. He pumped slowly with his thumb, leisurely circling her clit each time. Heat built up within her, and she spread her legs wider for him, moaning her pleasure into his mouth.

He withdrew his fingers, and she watched him undoing his belt and trousers. She shivered with need at the sound of a condom wrapper ripping open. In a heartbeat he was kissing her again, cupping her ass with his hands and lifting her slightly off the table.

His first thrust was deep and sure. Hailey threw back her head and exclaimed, "Yes. Oh, God, yes."

He withdrew, then drove into her again with the same power. She came as soon as his pace increased, clenching around his big cock and crying out his name. He didn't break stride, continuing to pound into her. His strong hands gripped her ass, holding her in place even as she returned from heaven.

He stepped back, bringing her forward off the table and wrapping her legs around his waist. Hailey gripped his shoulders for support as he kissed her deeply while moving his cock slowly in and out of her. The way he filled her was divine, and she buried her hands in his hair as they kissed with the passion of lovers reunited.

He lowered her feet to the floor and withdrew. Lost to mindless need, she moved against him, begging him wordlessly not to end it too soon.

"Turn around," he said as he spun her.

She turned eagerly, relieved it wasn't over, and placed her hands on the edge of the table. Her high heels lifted her ass for him. One of his hands went to her hip. His other caressed the exposed length of her back, over the curve of her ass, down one of her legs, before taking hold of her other hip.

She closed her eyes with molten hunger as he teased her with just the tip. She moved back against him, needing more. When he plunged into her, she cried, "Oh yes. Oh yes."

His hand snaked up her back and fisted around her hair, pulling her head slightly back. "Open your eyes," he commanded.

She did, willing to do whatever he asked as long as he didn't stop. He was rough without hurting. Forceful without forcing. Nothing he demanded was more than she wanted to give.

"Retract table. Run free fall," he said, and the beach beneath Hailey's feet morphed to an aerial view of Earth. A strong wind rushed upward as the clouds flew by. It was enough to convince Hailey's body that it was falling, and adrenaline rushed through her as Spencer continued to take her from behind. Deeper and deeper he plunged as she gave herself over to the experience. Hot desire mixed with a whisper of fear, taking Hailey to a whole new level of euphoria.

"You're fucking incredible," he said as he increased his speed.

She was beyond words. Overwhelmed by him and the simulator, she came with an uninhibited, animalistic cry of release. He thrust into her with an answering growl, climaxing together as the program reset to the peaceful beach.

She sagged forward, bracing herself with her hands on her knees. He withdrew and turned her, pulling her to his bare chest. She snuggled against him even as she playfully reprimanded him. "You're lucky I'm not afraid of heights."

He kissed her tenderly before answering, "I knew you wouldn't be, but I'll admit I wasn't thinking clearly." He removed his condom and tied it off, then staggered, readjusting his pants. "Next time I'll at least get us out of our clothes."

Hailey glanced at the dress that was still around her waist and his still-unzipped trousers. "Nah," she said playfully. It wasn't the first time they'd had half-dressed sex, and she hoped it wouldn't be the last.

He cupped one of her breasts, gently circling her nipple with his thumb. "This wasn't as good as it was back then—it was better."

She half closed her eyes in pleasure. "Wait till I show you what *I've* learned."

His thumb paused, and he pulled her tight against him. "I don't like imagining you with another man."

"At least they're not all on my Instagram feed," she countered sassily. The years they'd been apart couldn't be wished away. How they dealt with them was just another part they would have to figure out.

"Touché," he said and kissed her again. A slow, lusty smile spread across his face. "Come back to my place, and I'll see if you learned as much as you think you did."

"What time is it?" She stepped back, pulled the hem of her dress down, and bent to retrieve her bra from the floor of the simulator.

He picked up his jacket and took out his phone. Hailey paused to watch the rippling muscles of his back as he did. There was humor in his eyes when they met hers, as if he knew exactly what watching him was doing to her. He glanced down at his phone and swore. "Time for you to get back unless you want to call your babysitter and ask her to stay over."

"I can't," she said as she fastened her bra and pulled the top of her dress back into place. She turned her back to him as she'd done many times before. "Zip, please."

He did, then retrieved her panties from the floor and held them out to her. "You don't want to leave these here." She stepped into them as he finished zipping himself.

"You might want to get that as well." She nodded toward the condom he'd dropped to the floor.

He opened the door of the simulator and disposed of it in the trash near his secretary's desk. Before walking away, he frowned, took a blank piece of paper off her desk, crumpled it up, and tossed it in the trash on top of the condom.

When their eyes met, Hailey felt like they truly were back in college disposing of the evidence of their wild encounters. "Do you remember when Ralph went on vacation and left you the keys to the restaurant?"

He laughed. "How could I forget? It really *was* our booth after that week."

She laughed along with him. "It sure was. I couldn't look him in the eye for weeks."

Spencer closed the simulator door and put an arm around Hailey as they walked through the office toward the elevator. "I couldn't sit there without a hard-on for about as long."

They both glanced back at the simulator at the same time, then met each other's eyes again, and the air sizzled with sexual energy. "Are you thinking what I'm thinking?" Hailey asked.

The flush that spread up his neck hinted he might be. "It wouldn't take me long to write that program. All we would need is enough footage of the booth." He shook his head and chuckled. "Now I want a private simulator. How am I going to explain that to Jordan?"

They walked toward the elevator together. "It was just a thought."

"A fucking amazing thought," he said before pulling her into the elevator and kissing her deeply as the doors closed. They hit the ground all too soon.

Conversation was comfortable and easy as they left the building and climbed into his car. They had just pulled into traffic when he glanced at her quickly and asked, "Any regrets?"

"About tonight?" she asked.

"About any of this."

"No, but I need—" *Time to think. This is what I want, but is it what's best for Skye? Is it selfish to even consider something like this when she's finally doing better? I need to take the job at SmartKart. It'll free me to tell him everything. If I do it right, Delinda will see she doesn't have to pay for companions. We'll stay in the guesthouse, and Skye and I won't lose either one of them.*

Spencer placed a hand on one of her thighs. "What do you need?"

"Patience," she said automatically. "We need to move forward slowly."

"Because of Skye," he said, rather than asked.

"She's a big part of it." She turned his hand over and linked her fingers with his. "I'll introduce you, but not yet."

"In case we don't make it."

Hailey's heart clenched in her chest. She didn't want to lie to him. "She's lost so much. I won't be the reason for more loss in her life, not if I can help it." She stared down at their linked hands for a few moments before saying, "I've decided to take the job with SmartKart."

"Fantastic. It sounds like a good move for you."

"I hope so. I have to admit I'm a little nervous about telling my present employer, but mostly because she has been so good to us."

"You're doing it because it's what's best for you and your family. She'll have to understand that."

"I think she will."

Before long they pulled up beside Hailey's parked car. Spencer undid his seat belt and leaned toward Hailey. She met the kiss halfway. The passion that flared between them was intense and instant. He raised his head, his breath as ragged as hers. "Tonight shouldn't end this way. You should fall asleep in my arms."

She traced the line of his strong jaw. "We'll get there." *I hope.*

His eyes darkened. "You are incredible." He kissed her briefly.

"I don't know about that, but it's nice to hear." Leaving wasn't as easy as Hailey made it sound, but she knew she had to. "I should go."

"How does your week look?"

Hailey gathered up her purse. "Before I make any plans, I want to talk to SmartKart. They may need me to do something. I also don't want to stay out very late. It's summer, but Skye still takes lessons every day."

He shot her a crooked smile. "So I should plan on Saturday."

"Probably," she said with a nod. "And I'll meet you somewhere."

"You sure know how to keep me humble," he joked.

"That's not my intention—"

"I know," he said, cutting her off with a quick kiss before leaning across her to open her door. "Fuck, this isn't easy."

His face was mere inches from hers. She wanted one more kiss yet felt dangerously close to giving in to the part of her that wanted to stay. "Spencer—"

"Go," he said as he straightened away from her.

Hailey stepped out of his car and walked over to hers. She looked back at him as she opened her door. *He's as scared as I am.*

Is that better or worse than our first time around?

Spencer watched Hailey drive off and folded his arms across his chest. Being with her had him all tied up in knots emotionally. The sex had been phenomenal, better than he'd expected, and he'd gone in with some pretty fucking good memories of being with her.

Strong and loyal.

Funny, intelligent, and sexy as hell.

She deserves better than the man I am today. He didn't normally turn to others for advice, but he almost lost her this night. He needed to figure some shit out, and evidently that wasn't something he was succeeding at alone. He called someone he knew would give it to him straight. "Jordan, I need your advice on something."

"Don't worry, I already erased the video feed from tonight," Jordan said. "I was working on a program remotely when I noticed someone had accessed the simulator after hours. I watched a few minutes because, honestly, it's hilarious to see you that smitten with a woman, but then clothing started flying off, and I hit 'Delete.'"

Leaning against the side of his car, Spencer covered his eyes and groaned. "I didn't even think that it might be recording us."

"I can't imagine what else might have been on your mind," Jordan said dryly.

Spencer shook his head. "Thanks for deleting it. I have a demo scheduled for the Chinese company next week. That would not have been good."

Jordan laughed. "It would have been karma for calling my realistic portrayal of a day at the beach a gateway to porn. You threw that gate open and ran through it naked."

"Are you done?"

"I hope you sanitized the room."

"Anything else?"

"Now will you let me add private access codes?"

"No, but I'm ready to authorize in-home models. We talked about making them more accessible to the public. Maybe now is the time to design personal-use models."

"You argued it wasn't feasible and there would be no market for it. I wonder what changed your mind. Hmmm. A real mystery."

"Yeah. Okay. Fine. Back to why I called. I think I'm losing my mind. I'm not even dating Hailey, but tonight I thought she was calling it off and I lost my shit."

"What did you do?" Jordan asked quietly.

"I told her I didn't need her. You should have heard me. I was a real dick. Why would I do that? I want to be with her. What the fuck is my problem?"

"Are those rhetorical questions or are you actually asking me?"

"This isn't like me."

"Well—"

"Or this is exactly who I am—who I'll always be? There's no going back, is there?"

Jordan groaned. "I'm not a therapist or a psychic, but I do think you have the power to stop being an asshole."

Not fun to hear but not wrong, either. "If it were that easy, I wouldn't still be saying stupid shit, would I?"

"Yeah. It might be too late for you. All that's left is to wait it out and die alone."

"I don't know why I thought talking to you would help."

"Hey, I'm not the one you have a problem with. Talk to someone you do. It might help."

"I went to see my mother."

"Maybe she's not the one you're most angry with."

Maybe not. There were two people he refused to speak to because the idea of even seeing them again made him sick. Dereck and Delinda— two people he'd once thought were family. He couldn't imagine going to see either one of them or what he'd say if he did.

When Spencer didn't say anything, Jordan added, "What are you going to do?"

"I don't know. Take it slow, I guess. What else can I do?"

Chapter Fourteen

Sunday afternoon, in the shade of a huge oak tree, Hailey reclined on a cushioned lawn chair next to Delinda and tried not to think about why Spencer hadn't texted or called her yet that day. She didn't want to believe he was the type to bolt after he got what he wanted, but it would fit with his online reputation.

Either way, we're going to be okay because we have to be. Skye and her new friend, Kim, were sitting on the lawn playing with a litter of fluffy Yorkshire terrier puppies.

"We're not getting a dog," Hailey said between sips of lemonade. "We don't have the time or room for one. Especially now that we spend so many nights at the barn."

Delinda fanned her face with the information sheet the breeder had handed her. "These are teacups. The mother was six pounds. The father was barely five. People carry them around in their purses. How much trouble could one be?"

"Skye doesn't need a dog, Delinda."

"They aren't for her." Delinda waved the breeder over and pointed to one of the puppies flopped at Skye's side. The woman scooped it up and brought it over to Hailey.

Hailey refused to look at it. "No, thank you."

"Is it a male or female?" Delinda asked.

"Female," the breeder answered, offering her to Delinda.

Delinda put the puppy on her lap. It wiggled joyfully, almost falling off. "How big do you think she'll get?"

"She's the runt of the litter, so I'd guess four or five pounds."

"Hailey, what do you think of her?"

Is she considering one for herself? Now I feel bad for thinking she was setting me up again. Hailey checked the puppy out. "She's beautiful." *Adorable, actually.* The most adorable ball of fur Hailey had ever seen.

"Help me decide," Delinda said, handing the puppy to Hailey. "Do you think she has a good personality?"

Unlike the other puppies that were jumping and yipping at the girls, this one snuggled right up against Hailey's chest and wiggled its little tail joyfully. "She has my vote."

"She chose this one," Delinda said to the breeder.

"Me? I don't want a dog," Hailey said. She went to remove the puppy from her chest until it protested and squirmed to stay with her. "I'm not a dog person," she added half-heartedly. Panic began to set in. She wanted to talk about the job she was about to accept, not argue over another of Delinda's heavy-handed gifts.

With a wave of her hand, Delinda requested a moment alone with Hailey. "Do you know who loves Yorkies?"

"People with time for them?" Hailey asked, cursing herself for not being stronger and simply handing the puppy back to the breeder. That was the only way to win with Delinda. A softer approach was as good as giving her permission.

"Michael. His ex-wife has never been particularly kind to him, but she's getting remarried and is being quite nasty as of late."

"I didn't know."

"Michael doesn't talk about his personal life, but sometimes I hear him on the phone with his children. He needs something to cheer him up."

"So you're getting him a puppy without asking if he wants one?" A sweet gesture, but still wrong.

Delinda's chin rose in the haughty way it often did. "No, I'm getting you a puppy. It just happens to be the breed he adores. Over the years he has inquired about getting a dog, but I've always considered them filthy little creatures who had no place inside a home."

"Which is why you want it in the guesthouse."

Delinda sighed. "You have the subtlety of a train wreck, Hailey. Must I spell it all out for you?"

Me? Not subtle? Look who's talking. "If you want me to go along with it, yes."

"If you get the puppy, and it ends up being too much for you to care for, whom would you turn to for help with it?" She rolled her eyes skyward. "And please don't say me."

"Michael."

"If you ask him to spend time with the puppy, he'll get attached to it. Especially if you tell him you don't really want it. He'll feel sorry for it and start sneaking it into the main house. I wouldn't be surprised if he tries to win me over to the idea that I need a dog. I'll tell him he can have it as long as it doesn't make a mess. He'll be proud of himself and feel that he saved it. There, Michael will have the dog he wants and his pride will remain intact. Isn't that far better than telling him we're getting him a puppy to cheer him up?"

Hailey worried when Delinda's way started to make sense. "You've overlooked one problem with your plan."

"Really?" Delinda asked as if there were no possibility of that happening.

"Skye. If that puppy comes home with us, do you really think it's not staying?"

"She understands that it's meant for Michael."

Hailey's hand stilled on the puppy. She didn't like the idea of Delinda having secrets with Skye. "You told her about your plan?"

Bringing a hand up to her chest in restrained outrage, Delinda said, "Of course I did. I'm not cruel. Do you honestly think I'd give a puppy to a child only to take it away?"

"You don't know if she'll fall in love with it and change her mind."

"That, my dear, is what I call an acceptable unintended outcome. I weighed the risks and decided they were worth it. Worst case, Skye has a new puppy that Michael adores visiting with, and you're irritated with me. You'll be upset for a bit, but it will pass. I've gotten used to your moods."

"Delinda, we talked about this. You're not supposed to give us anything unless you and I have talked it out first."

"Aha, but this is not a gift for you or Skye. Loophole."

Hailey lifted the puppy so she could look into its eyes and joked, "Are you sure you can handle us, little one? This is our norm."

"Are you unhappy here, Hailey?"

"No, not at all." Hailey lowered the puppy. "But that doesn't mean I approve."

"Yes. Yes, but will you help me get Michael the pet he has always wanted?"

"I don't like that you spoke to Skye about this before you spoke to me."

Delinda waved a finger at where Skye and her friend were all smiles, their laps full of puppies while they chatted. "I feel awful about how much it upset her."

"That's not the point and you know it."

"I'd say it's the only point with any value."

I'm not going to change her mind. "There's something else we need to discuss."

"Your date yesterday? How did it go?"

"It was very nice, thank you, but that's not what I want to talk with you about."

"Oh, dear, this sounds serious. Your forehead is doing that double wrinkle it does when you get yourself all worked up."

"Delinda, I've been offered a job at SmartKart as a buyer. I plan to take it."

The older woman gasped.

Hailey rushed to add, "The salary is good enough that I'll be able to afford to pay you rent as well as afford Skye's school and Clover's board. That is, if you'll still want us here. Nothing has to change. I'll still spend time with you; you just won't be paying me a salary. We'll be friends."

"I didn't realize you were looking for a job."

"I wasn't. This one came to me. It's too perfect to pass up, though. It comes with benefits and a good salary, and it's a job I'd enjoy. Not that I don't enjoy working for you. I do. It's just that there would be room for advancement. Please don't be upset."

Delinda fanned her face for a moment, then smiled. "Upset? I'm happy for you, of course. What kind of hours will you be working?"

"Nothing crazy or I won't take the job. There are still some unknowns, but I didn't want to move forward without telling you."

"I appreciate that," Delinda said. "And, of course, the guesthouse is yours for as long as you'd like to stay in it."

Hailey touched Delinda's arm gently. "We're not going anywhere."

Not looking at Hailey, Delinda said, "You must do what's best for you. I understand."

"It's just a job. We're not leaving. You're stuck with us, Delinda."

Delinda expelled a half laugh and met Hailey's eyes. "And you call me stubborn."

They both watched the children in quiet contemplation before Hailey asked, "Are you okay?"

"Of course," Delinda said with a smile. "As I said, I'm happy for you." She looked down at the puppy. "I see now why you were so sure you wouldn't have time for her. Don't feel you need to take her. I'll find another way to cheer Michael up."

"No, no. We'll make it work," Hailey found herself saying urgently as her eyes filled with tears. She didn't realize until then how much Delinda had started to feel like family. The idea of hurting her was unacceptable and losing her felt just as scary.

"Oh, please, don't start. I'm not upset with you."

"It's just that I want to make sure you know this doesn't change anything."

Delinda gave her hand a pat. "Of course it doesn't, Hailey. As you said, we'll make it work."

Later that night, Hailey unsuccessfully tried to put the still-nameless puppy to bed in a crate. It cried long and hard enough that Hailey found herself comforting it in her arms as one would an infant. "Is this how you worm your way into people's purses? Don't give me those cute eyes. It's blatant manipulation, and you know it." *Which means you'll fit in perfectly here.*

She'd just shifted the puppy in her arms when her cell phone rang. "Hey, Sunshine," Spencer said in a deeper-than-normal voice, which made her wonder if he was in his bed already. "How was your day?"

Better now. "Good."

"Are you okay? With us, I mean. You said you wanted to go slowly, and I should have respected that."

"I'm fine, Spencer. It was probably unrealistic to think we could do the friendship thing. We never could keep our hands off each other."

She pictured him smiling when he said, "That's for sure." They were quiet for a moment, then he asked, "How is everything else?"

"I told my employer that I'm taking the job at SmartKart."

"And?"

"She seemed okay with it. Not happy, but okay."

"That's good. Does that mean you can finally tell me who you work for?"

Hailey tensed, and the puppy squirmed in her arms. "I'd rather save that conversation for when I see you next."

"You worry me when you talk about her. I picture you locked up in some tower."

"It's nothing like that, just complicated." She tried to put the puppy down, but didn't when it whimpered in protest. "Like why I'll probably be sleeping with a puppy tonight when I'm not even a dog person."

"When did you get a puppy?"

"It's a long story—one that will make sense when I tell you everything else." Hailey yawned. "Sorry, I'm beat. Skye talked me into taking a riding lesson this morning. It's harder than I thought. Do you ride?"

"I used to when I was a kid. Mark took all of us to a park that had trail rides. I'm not sure you could actually call that riding. The horses knew what to do more than we did."

"That's my kind of riding," Hailey said with a smile. "My father took Ryan and me on something similar. I loved it."

"I did, too. Mark had a way of making everything fun."

"You must miss him very much."

"I didn't realize how much until recently."

"He would have been proud of the man you've become."

"I'd like to think so."

"I know so. Nothing stops you. You go after what you want, and you get it." Her cheeks warmed as she remembered just what he'd gone after in the simulator and how much she'd enjoyed giving it to him.

He seemed to sense where her thoughts had wandered. "Why are we waiting until later in the week to see each other?"

Hailey laughed and made a joke because it was easier than the truth. "To give you time to think of something as exciting as simulator sex."

"Challenge accepted."

"I was joking—"

"No backpedaling. I've got this."

"Good night, Spencer."

"Good night, Sunshine."

Hailey hung up the phone and hugged the puppy to her as she walked toward her bedroom. *I can't judge you for not wanting to be alone in your crate. I tell myself I'm okay with being on my own, then I talk to Spencer and I can't help but want more.*

Hailey slid beneath the sheets on her bed and put the puppy on top of them near her feet. She'd barely laid her head down on the pillow when she felt the puppy scramble up to snuggle into her side. "You've got the right attitude. Life doesn't just hand us what we want. We have to go after it—believing that the outcome we want is possible."

She closed her eyes while lightly petting the puppy's head. "Hope. That's what I'll call you. Everyone needs it in their life. Skye. Me. Spencer. Delinda. Even Michael. Don't worry, little Hope, you're exactly where you need to be."

Late the next day, Spencer was having a hard time concentrating during an excruciatingly long staff meeting. Work had always been his sanctuary, but lately his thoughts were pulled elsewhere.

Saturday felt like a lifetime away. *I've never been good at waiting.*

"We'll move ahead on a timeline they're comfortable with," Jordan said to the team seated around the conference table.

From now on call me Mr. Nice Guy.

One young man raised his hand. "Is the simulator broken? Is that why we're meeting in person?"

"No," Jordan answered. "I wanted to remove all distractions." He looked over at Spencer. "But I guess it's not a matter of location."

"Everything is set for the Chinese presentation," Spencer assured him.

"That's good, but we're discussing WelTune and the order they submitted over the weekend."

"Sorry, missed that part."

Jordan turned to the team. "We're done for today. Get out there and start this ball rolling." Once they were alone, Jordan dropped into a chair beside Spencer. "Okay, what's wrong?"

"Nothing. I'm good."

"Really?"

"I'm taking your advice and going slow."

Spencer's phone rang. He almost ignored it, but took it out to check the caller ID. "It's Hailey." He answered without hesitation. "Hey, Sunshine."

"Do you have a minute?" she asked in a small, tight voice.

"Sure," Spencer said. "What's wrong?"

"I screwed up."

"How? Talk to me."

"I didn't get the job at SmartKart. I called today to tell them I was accepting it, and they told me the position had been filled."

"Who did you speak to?"

"HR. They were quite clear."

"You didn't speak to Kyle Kyees?"

"No."

"Then it's probably a clerical error. I bet the next call you get is them saying they were mistaken." *Especially after I rip Kyle a new one.*

"I shouldn't let myself get upset about this. I mean, I already have a job anyway. It's just that this one seemed like the answer to sorting everything out. I thought it would make things better for everyone. I shouldn't have said anything to my present employer before checking that the position was still open. I'm such an idiot."

"No, you're not. I have a good feeling about this. It sounds like your folder didn't make it on someone's desk. An easy fix."

"You think so? I'm sorry to call you at work with this."

"You can always call me, Hailey. Always."

Her voice shook as she spoke. "You don't know how much it means to me to hear you say that."

"Where are you? Just tell me, and I'll be on my way over." Funny how priorities could quickly change. Hailey wasn't an interruption. There was nothing at WorkChat more important than knowing she was okay.

"No. You can't come here. I'm still at work. Oh, I hate this. If I get a babysitter, would you meet me tonight?"

"You have to ask?" When she didn't answer right away, he said, "What time?"

"Seven o'clock? Where we met last time."

"I'll be there."

Immediately after Hailey hung up, Spencer made a call. As soon as it went through, Spencer said, "Kyle, someone in your HR department dropped the ball. I need you to clue them in to the fact that you're hiring Hailey Tiverton."

"Spencer, I meant to call you earlier."

"Now there's no need. First, assure me that you'll have this immediately resolved, then we can address your question."

"Hailey Tiverton, or rather the job we offered her, was what I wanted to discuss with you. That position has unfortunately been filled."

"This is a joke, right?"

"I wish it were."

"What changed?"

"Nothing. I thought we had an opening for a buyer, but we're already overstaffed in that department."

"Wait, are you overstaffed or did you just fill the position we spoke about?"

"Shit. There is no job here for your girlfriend."

"Then—I repeat—what changed? We had an agreement."

"I know."

"But?"

"I—you—sometimes—"

"Fucking spit it out."

"You're putting me in an awkward position."

"It'll go from awkward to painful if we have to have this conversation in person."

Jordan waved a hand in front of Spencer to catch his attention. "Is that Kyle Kyees? Ask him if he is still meeting with Darion Galloway in Sydney next month."

"The billionaire real estate agent, Darion Galloway?" Spencer asked. "The one responsible for the success of the last three chain stores that tried to break into that market? I think I did hear he might not be able to make that meeting."

"Spencer, come on. I hate to do this, but I don't have a choice. Not even if it kills that connection," Kyle said.

"What the fuck?" Spencer mouthed silently to Jordan while putting Kyle on speakerphone. Maybe Jordan could figure out what the hell had changed Kyle's mind. "You sound scared."

"Not scared. Realistically cautious."

"Of what? I asked you to hire a woman I know. How is that a problem?"

Jordan shrugged, looking as confused as Spencer was.

"Listen, as much as I'd like to help you, I'm not getting between two feuding Westerlys."

"Two Westerlys? What are you talking about? Did someone from my family tell you not to hire Hailey?"

"That's messed up," Jordan said loud enough for Kyle to hear.

"I've already said more than I should have."

"Who? Who told you not to hire her?"

"I shouldn't tell you, but what the hell? You *have* been good to me over the years, and you should know. Your grandmother called me and told me to make the job disappear."

How does she know about Hailey? "Why would she care if you employed a friend of mine?"

"I didn't ask. I didn't want to know. It's bad enough to be on her radar. Your grandmother has more connections than the Pope. Frankly, she scares me a hell of a lot more than you do. If I were you, I'd apologize to your grandmother, because you won't find many willing to go up against her if she blackballs you, too."

Beyond speechless with anger, Spencer hung up. *Delinda blocked Hailey from getting a job. Why?* He turned on his heel and strode toward the door.

"Where are you going?" Jordan asked in a worried tone as he rushed after Spencer.

Only one reason made sense to Spencer. "If Delinda is trying to get my attention, she has it now."

Jordan was at his side as Spencer stormed down the hallway. "None of this makes sense. What is she hoping to gain?"

Spencer stopped, asked himself the same question, and the answer had come like a punch. "She needs to win. It's all a game to her. She hates that I didn't accept her apology. She can't handle not being in control. She tried having Brett plead her case. She went as far as to become chummy with my mother. Why? We never had a good relationship. I'm not even fucking related to her. It's past time to tell her to stay the hell out of my life."

"Give yourself some time to cool off first," Jordan cautioned in the parking lot as Spencer reached his car.

Spencer ripped his car door open. "You don't understand. She didn't just fuck with me this time; she went after Hailey. No way. No fucking way."

"Don't do anything stupid."

Too furious to care that Jordan looked like he might be sick, Spencer peeled out of his parking spot and sped toward the mansion by the sea he'd sworn he'd never step foot in again.

Chapter Fifteen

Hailey was in the guesthouse, checking in on Skye's lesson, when she heard a squeal of tires in the driveway and rushed to the window. Her heart leapt to her throat when she realized it was Spencer's car. He parked in front of the main house and took the steps two at a time. Even from a distance she could tell he was furious.

"Please keep Skye here," Hailey said in a hurry.

"What's the matter, Auntie Hailey?" Skye asked.

Hailey forced a smile. "Nothing, sweetie, I just remembered that Delinda asked me to be there for some business she's conducting. It's all really boring adult stuff. Mrs. Holihen, if she finishes her lessons early, maybe you could take her to the park?"

"That sounds like a wonderful plan," Mrs. Holihen said before tapping the table to bring Skye's attention back to the paper they were working on.

Hailey walked as casually as she could to their door and down the steps. As soon as she knew she was out of view of the guesthouse, she sprinted the rest of the way. Spencer was already inside. Hailey wasn't surprised that Michael didn't open the door. He would be in the wings making sure Delinda was okay.

Does he know? Is that why he's here?

Hailey sped to the door of the solarium, but didn't enter. Spencer's visit might have nothing to do with her. If that were the case, then waiting to tell him later when they were alone might still be the best option.

"You've gone too far this time," Spencer's voice thundered.

"Would you like some tea, Spencer? It calms the nerves," Delinda answered, not sounding at all intimidated by his anger.

"No, I don't want any fucking tea."

"Watch your language."

"What a hypocrite you are. You think *I'm* poorly behaved? What would you call being petty enough to block an innocent woman from getting a job? That's a new low for you, Delinda."

Delinda blocked me from working at SmartKart? Oh, Delinda.

"If you calm yourself, perhaps we could discuss it like two civilized people," Delinda said in her haughty defensive tone.

"There is nothing to discuss. I don't care what you thought you would gain by using Hailey as a pawn, but she is off-limits to you. If I hear you so much as say her name to anyone else—"

"What? What will do you, Spencer? This entire conversation is ridiculous. Instead of coming in and threatening me, perhaps you should ask me why—"

"I know why, Delinda. You can't lose, and you don't care who you have to hurt to win. What is it you feel like you lost when I walked away? Was it your pride that took a hit? Did your old cronies suggest you should have been able to bring me back under your control? It'll never happen. The only reason I was ever nice to you was because it was important to my mother. I don't give a shit about you or—"

"Stop," Hailey said, stepping into the room. "Both of you—stop."

In a few long strides, Spencer was at Hailey's side. "What are you doing here?"

Oh, God. "I work for your grandmother."

He shook his head as if warding off a blow. "What do you mean you work for her?"

When she put her hand on his forearm, Hailey felt the tension raging through him. *I wanted to do this in a much better way.* "She's the employer I told you about, the one who has been so good to Skye and me."

He blinked a few times slowly. "You're living here? With Delinda?"

"Yes."

He spun and stood protectively in front of Hailey. "Get your stuff, Hailey. Get Skye. We're leaving."

Hailey looked from Delinda's carefully composed face to Spencer's tight and flushed one. "No," she said softly.

"Yes," Spencer countered. "I'll explain it to you when we're alone, but you're going to have to trust me on this. You can't stay here."

"I'm not leaving," Hailey said in a firmer voice. "I won't uproot Skye before I understand what's going on." She looked across at Delinda. "Delinda has been good to us."

Spencer put his arm around her waist. "She wants you to think that, Hailey. She is a manipulative liar. She wants you to believe she cares about you. She doesn't. She's been using you to get to me. It makes me sick to see how far you're willing to go, Delinda. She has a child, for God's sake."

All color left Delinda's face. "I would never do anything to harm Skye."

"You'll never be given the chance to prove that. We're leaving. All of us," Spencer said.

Hailey planted her feet when Spencer urged her to walk off with him. "Spencer, she loves you. Give her a chance to speak."

He frowned down at her. "Why are you defending her?"

Hailey glanced over at Delinda. She was trying to hide it, but she was hurting. "Because I've gotten to know her, and she would never—"

"You don't know what she's capable of." His frown darkened. "Why didn't you tell me you were working for her? What is this all about?"

She hated the doubt in his eyes. "I was going to explain it all to you tonight."

He stepped back from her. "Explain away. I thought I'd had my fill of lies, but I'm honestly curious. What were you going to tell me?"

"I've never lied to you."

He held her gaze and waited.

"This isn't what you think. It's a coincidence. Or, I like to think, a nudge from Ryan. I didn't know she was your grandmother when I took the job, and she didn't know about us until after she'd interviewed me. I know that sounds crazy, but it's true."

"I don't believe in coincidences," Spencer said in a tight voice.

"Well, do you believe me?" She put a hand on one hip.

"Yes, but that's more of a reason for you to leave with me now." His arm was protectively back around her waist. "You see the good in everyone, but this time it's not there. She duped you. Tell her, Delinda. Look her right in the eye and tell her the truth, if someone like you even knows how to."

Delinda's eyes narrowed, and she looked down.

No. Hailey shook her head vehemently and went to kneel beside Delinda's chair. "I'm the one who found the ad. I'm the one who called you. Tell him."

Delinda refused to meet her gaze.

Hailey took Delinda's hand in hers. "I know why you blocked me from getting the SmartKart job. You were afraid I would leave you. What you need to see, Delinda, is that what you do to keep people with you is actually what drives them away. I've seen the good in you. No one could change our lives as much as you have and not be a good person. Don't shut Spencer out. He won't ever see the loving side of you if you let your pride stop you from showing it to him. Tell him you missed him. Tell him you're sorry. Show him the real you."

Delinda's lips pressed together in a straight line, then she said, "Ask him why you were offered that job in the first place. Are you as honest as you think everyone around you should be, Spencer? Are you?"

Hailey stood and slowly turned toward Spencer. It was his turn to look guilty. "Did you get me the job at SmartKart?"

Confusion and anger blazed in Spencer's eyes. "You said you felt trapped in your job. I wanted to help you."

Hailey's emotions roller-coastered. She looked down at Delinda. "I did feel trapped but taking the job at SmartKart would have changed that. We weren't going anywhere. Skye and I were still going to be here with you. Did you know about us before the interview? How? You need to be honest with me, Delinda."

Looking like a child who was cornered into admitting a wrongdoing, Delinda said, "I might have learned your name from his mother. She told me you were the only woman Spencer ever loved." She glared at both of them. "Was it so wrong to give you a chance to get it right?"

"But I found the ad. It was on the seat next to me on the bus." Hailey's chest constricted painfully. "Did you have someone put it there?"

"I only did what I thought was the best for both of you."

Hailey swayed on her feet. "I feel so stupid. I knew it was too easy, too convenient, but I wanted to believe Ryan was somehow looking out for us. All this time, I felt like I was being guided, and I was."

Spencer put a hand on her lower back. "You were manipulated, Hailey—that's what she does. I wish I could spare you from the truth, but you need to see her for who she really is."

Delinda rose to her feet. "If you weren't so stubborn, Spencer, I wouldn't have had to—"

"Don't put this on me," Spencer growled.

"It is your fault. You won't forgive me for being the one who told you that Dereck wasn't your biological father. I've said I'm sorry. I'm eighty-one. Are you waiting for me to die before you forgive me?"

"Enough," Hailey said in a tone that shocked Spencer and Delinda into silence. "You're both right, and you're both so wrong I can't begin to sort it out. Delinda, I'm grateful for all you've done for Skye, but I am so disappointed in you right now I can hardly look at you. You're being childish and spiteful when you should be apologetic and comforting. Spencer, the way you're attacking Delinda is just wrong. She's old and scared she might die without you in her life. Is there no compassion in you? She didn't make your mother have an affair. She's not the one who lied to you about who your father was. You're both hurting, but this is wrong."

They each took a step toward Hailey, but she raised her hands in the air. "I don't want to leave here, Delinda. We both know how hard Skye will take it, but if the two of you can't resolve this, I will. It's unhealthy. Spencer, I would love to say that your problems with Delinda are none of my business, but I refuse to bring this hate into my life—or Skye's. You're better than this. Or you're not and you're right—I see good where there is none. I'm going back to the guesthouse. Don't follow me. Either of you."

Hailey walked out of the solarium with her head held high but her heart breaking. Tears freely flowed down her cheeks. She didn't try to conceal them from Michael when he came to open the door for her.

"No matter what happens next, you said what they needed to hear and you said it from a place of love. It's up to them now."

Hailey nodded and wiped at her cheeks. "I don't want to leave, Michael, but even if it hurts Skye in the short run, it might be better for her in the long run. What I saw in there wasn't love."

Michael stood with the door open. "Don't give up hope just yet."

His words echoed in her as she walked back to the guesthouse. Thankfully, Mrs. Holihen had already left with Skye, which meant it was perfectly okay for Hailey to flop down on her bed and have a good cry. She was just about to do that when a whimper from the other room caught her attention.

Hope beckoned.

Hailey opened the crate, let her out the back door to relieve herself, then picked her up for a snuggle. "How do you feel about moving?"

Hope buried her face in the nook of Hailey's arm.

"Yeah, me, too. But you know what, Hope? You're a Tiverton now, and we're survivors. Every decision we make teaches Skye something. I could have left with Spencer. I love him . . . I do. Even when he makes me so angry, I could slap him. He's upset, and he has a reason to be, but guess what? Life sucks sometimes. Look at you: you just lost your whole damn family because we thought you were cute. But what are you going to do? Bite me? Bite everyone around you? Would that bring them back? No."

Hope looked up at Hailey with big sad eyes.

"See, it's depressing when you look at life that way, isn't it? It's why I can't go there with them. I don't want their anger. A drowning person pulls others down with them. I'm a swimmer, Hope."

Pawing at Hailey's chest, Hope whimpered again.

"Of course we may end up alone at the end of this, but I refuse to let that decide my path. Skye and I will make a life for ourselves—here or somewhere else. And we'll be okay. Tivertons don't give up. We don't let fear win."

Hope twirled in a circle on Hailey's lap and yapped happily.

"Exactly."

Spencer stood absolutely still for several moments after Hailey rushed from the room. He'd almost raced after her, but she was quite clear about how she felt about that.

When Delinda spoke, Spencer realized she was standing beside him. "Did she just break up with both of us?"

He didn't find her joke funny, but it was accurate. Without looking away from the doorway, he said, "I believe she did."

"I've never been spoken to that way."

"Nor have I."

"I may have deserved it."

"You definitely did."

"You couldn't have chosen a less outspoken woman to fall in love with?"

"I wouldn't change a thing about her." Spencer glanced at Delinda. His anger toward her was overshadowed by how disappointed he was in himself for acting the way he had. Hailey had been right to remove herself from the situation. "Not that she'd say the same about me."

"It's probably all that drinking. You're functioning on fewer brain cells."

"Is it impossible for you to say anything nice?"

"Maybe I would if you weren't always scowling at me like I'm the villain in a fairy tale."

"When something looks like a duck, walks like a duck, quacks—"

"And I'm the one who's not nice?"

She has a point, but while we're being honest . . . "We wouldn't be here if you had just accepted that I don't want you in my life."

She was quiet for a moment. When she spoke it was in a softer tone than he'd ever heard her use. "I won't ever accept that. I don't care what blood runs in your veins; you're my grandson. You were from the first day I held you in my arms." She cleared her throat.

Spencer's head snapped around so he could gauge her expression. She looked serious and unusually vulnerable. "I don't have a single memory of you that doesn't include you either humiliating my mother or harshly critiquing me or my siblings."

"Then you've forgotten the time you spent here before your parents divorced. You used to sit beside me on that very couch, and I'd read story after story to you."

"I don't remember that." Even as he said it, memories of sitting with her and asking her to read to him returned. He could almost hear her roaring like a lion and feigning the voice of Billy. "How did we get from there to here?"

"I was angry with your mother, and I didn't hide it."

"I remember that, too."

"I thought she was the worst possible choice my son could have made, and they would never last. I wish I had been wrong."

Spencer sighed. "Your son was no saint. In a way it was a relief when I discovered he wasn't my father."

"Dereck loves you. He just doesn't know how to express it."

"I've heard that before. Rachelle loves to say that about Brett. It's okay. We're not children anymore. We don't need to all get along."

"Is that why you won't go to Brett's wedding, because you think he doesn't care about you?"

Before now he would have ended this conversation prior to this point, but Hailey's words kept circling back to him. He never again wanted to see her look at him the way she had just before she walked out. If that meant staying and talking things out with Delinda, he would do it. For Hailey. "Actions speak louder than words. Brett chose to not be part of our lives."

"There's so much you don't know." She sat down, and he found himself sitting across from her a moment later. She looked tired, and he was tempted to say they could speak another time, but that would have meant he would need to return, and he wasn't sure that would happen. He could work to let his anger go, but welcome her into his life?

"You would have loved my Oliver. He was a lot like Mark. Family was everything to him. He never stayed upset with anyone. It was his warm heart that I fell in love with first, but it was that softness in him that took him from me."

Spencer didn't know what to think at first when a woman who had always held herself above everyone opened up in a very human way. She told him the truth about how her husband had died and how it had put great pressure on her son. She unapologetically described how she'd tried to toughen Dereck up because she feared if she didn't, she might lose him, also. By the time she brought up Brett, Spencer already saw the pattern that had shaped his brother's personality. He'd spent a good portion of his life envying Brett, but he saw then that he'd actually had the better childhood. Spencer's had been full of love and laughter. Brett had been raised by two emotionally stunted adults. Was it any wonder he couldn't express himself?

Delinda continued, "Dereck may not have known how to be with you when you were living with your actual father, but that doesn't mean he didn't care about you. Your mother didn't want you or your sisters to take anything from us. I doubt Dereck ever told her about Oliver. In her mind, it was greed that ruined her marriage. She wanted to raise you away from that. You never went without anything you needed, though. Dereck made sure of that. He and Brett were quite crafty when it came to finding ways to take care of all of you without her knowing. Do you remember when Mark wanted to spend the last of his life at home? His insurance wouldn't pay for it. Dereck made sure it happened, and he paid for it."

"Why would any man pay for nursing the man who stole his wife?"

"Because my son still loves your mother, just like he loves all of her children. How could he not? You are part of her. And Mark was good to you. Dereck didn't hate him. He did what he could for him, and then later Brett took on the responsibility of watching out for all of you when he took over the company. Do you know he has people on his staff whose sole job is to make sure you get any loan you apply for? Every scholarship you were denied, then received—that was Brett. Tell me, does that sound like a brother who doesn't love you?"

Spencer took a moment to digest that claim. There had been times in his life, more than he cared to remember, when something had come through after it had looked like it wouldn't. He'd always prided himself on having done everything without the help of his family's money, so it was unsettling to discover he received boosts along the way.

There was a slim chance the entire story was bullshit, that Delinda had made it up. The Spencer who'd stormed into her house a short time ago would have accused her of exactly that. He would have stood up, told her to keep her lies, and walked out. He didn't want to be that man. It wasn't how he'd been raised. It wasn't who he was in his heart. He looked at Delinda and asked himself who she would be to him if he let his anger go.

"Okay, there's no blood, so that's a good sign," Brett said from the doorway. His fiancée, a woman who had briefly been Spencer's as well, stood at his side.

"They look calm," Alisha said as they walked into the room together.

"Brett," Delinda said with a smile. "What are you doing here?"

"Jordan called and said I needed to get here ASAP."

"Whatever for?" Delinda asked innocently.

Alisha looked back and forth between Spencer and Delinda. "Are you okay, Spencer?"

You know, my brother chose well. Alisha always felt like a sister, and now she'll be one. "I am. We're talking things out."

"I'm glad," Alisha said.

"And it's going well?" Brett's eyebrows rose to his hairline.

Nicolette and Rachelle burst into the room. Nicolette rushed to Spencer's side. "Are you okay, Spencer?"

"I'm fine," Spencer assured her, not completely flattered to see how women seemed more worried about him than the old lady sitting across from him.

Nicolette sat down on the chair beside him. "Jordan said he's never seen you so angry."

I'm going to have to speak to Jordan about loose lips. "It's all good."

Nicolette glared at Delinda. "Is she making you say that? Does she have Hailey locked in the basement or something?"

Rachelle touched her sister's shoulder. "So dramatic. Of course she doesn't. Right, Brett?"

Delinda placed a hand on her chest. "First of all, I'm offended that you'd think me capable of such a thing. Second, if I did have someone locked up somewhere, I wouldn't require Brett's permission to do it."

Brett raised a hand. "She's joking. Delinda, you know they don't get your sense of humor."

For the first time in his life Spencer felt like he was on the right side of that inside comment. He winked at Delinda. "It wouldn't be the basement. It would be the dungeon. She has to have one. And it wouldn't be Hailey. We never see Delinda with a man. Maybe that's where she keeps them."

Delinda's cheeks turned red. "I do not have one of those lewd rooms."

Spencer couldn't resist. "I wasn't even thinking that, but now we all know what you've been reading."

Delinda was spared from responding by the arrival of Stephanie and Dereck.

"Don't tell me," Spencer said, "Jordan called you."

His mother avoided looking at Dereck. "Actually, Rachelle told me you were here."

"Brett called me," Dereck said gruffly.

The idea of his family gathering to save him from Delinda, or vice versa, was suddenly pathetically amusing. "We're fine. We're just talking."

"You are?" Stephanie asked.

Dereck said, "That's—"

"Unexpected," Stephanie supplied the word for him.

"Yes," Dereck said. "Wonderfully unexpected."

Brett walked over to stand beside where Spencer was seated. "So everything is fine?"

"Not everything," Spencer said grudgingly.

Delinda pinched an inch of air. "I might have meddled in Spencer's private life a little bit."

"Might have?" Spencer frowned. "Hailey lives with you."

"Technically, she lives in my guesthouse."

"What did you do, Mom?" Dereck asked as he took a seat next to her.

Delinda pointed at Spencer. "She's just as upset with him as she is with me."

Brett and Alisha stepped closer. Brett asked her, "What did you do?"

"Oh, for goodness' sake, do we have to rehash everything I did wrong, or could we focus on what I've done right? Spencer and Hailey were back together before he started yelling at me in front of her."

The anger that would normally have surfaced in response to Delinda's deflection didn't. She was childlike in some ways, but not malicious. And unfortunately, she had a point. "She's right. I handled the situation poorly."

Alisha looked around. "Where is Hailey? Is she okay?"

"She's back at the guesthouse," Spencer said.

Brett asked, "Then why are you still here?"

"It's complicated," Spencer said, running a hand through his hair in frustration.

Dereck surprised everyone by sitting down across from Spencer and leaning forward, elbows on knees. "Do you love her, Spencer?"

"I do." It was surreal to be discussing anything of significance with the man he'd once thought was his father.

"Then get your ass over there," Brett said.

Dereck shook his head. "No, you're right; it's not that easy. You need to know that you can make her happy. Sometimes loving a woman means knowing when to let her go."

Stephanie crossed the room and sat beside her ex-husband. "And moving on the best you can."

Dereck took her hand in his and gave it a visible squeeze. "And all you can do is hope you made the right choice."

The mood of the group was quickly taking a downward turn. Alisha dipped under Brett's arm to hug Spencer. "You *are* what she needs. I grew up with you. You have a good heart beneath all that anger. Hailey's been through a rough time. She needs a rock, and you can be that for her. She's going to want someone who can love her niece as much as she does. You would do that. You know what that looks like. Mark loved all of us that way. He didn't need a label or a blood test. He was simply there for us, helping us with our homework, making us laugh when we were sad, cheering us on even when we struck out. You could be that to Skye." She looked over at Dereck and Stephanie, then placed her hand on her small baby bump. "I'm not wasting another moment on the past. From now on, all of my energy is going into making the future everything I know it can be. Ask yourself what kind of life you want—then go out and make it happen."

Brett kissed Alisha on the temple and hugged her to his side. "What she said."

Spencer surged to his feet. "You're right. I know how to do this."

"You do," Alisha said with a proud smile.

Spencer stopped in front of Brett. "Is there still an opening for a groomsman in your wedding party?"

"There is," Brett said before smiling down at Alisha. "I told you I could talk him into attending our wedding."

"You? I had nothing to do with it?" Alisha swatted his arm playfully.

Spencer watched the two of them and found himself smiling along. Alisha brought out a warmer side of Brett that Spencer hadn't realized was there. She'd become a bridge between him and his family.

"Alisha," Spencer said.

"Yes?" she responded, reluctantly pulling her attention away from Brett.

"Thank you. For everything. For saying you'd marry me. For being smart enough not to. For trying to make things better for me by speaking to Delinda. It didn't work out the way any of us had planned, but I believe it worked out the way it was supposed to. I've always considered you a sister. I'm glad my brother is making it legal."

Alisha wiped the corners of her eyes. "Thank you, Spencer."

He noticed Delinda watching them. Her face was set in an expression he'd once read as displeasure, but he was beginning to think it was all bravado. "Could we speak privately?"

"Of course."

Brett raised a hand toward the door. "Let's give them a moment."

"The garden is beautiful this time of year," Stephanie added.

Dereck fell into step with her as they walked out of the solarium. Nicolette and Rachelle left with more reluctance, but followed the rest of them out.

When they were alone, Spencer went to sit beside Delinda. "Why did you bring Hailey here?"

"Stephanie told me about her. I told you, I thought you and Hailey deserved a chance to get it right."

"You went to great lengths to make it happen. It was more than that."

Delinda didn't look as if she would answer at first. "What more could there be?"

He leaned forward and looked directly into her eyes. "You tell me. What was your endgame?"

"You wouldn't forgive me. What was I supposed to do? Sit back and accept never seeing you again?" Delinda folded her hands on her lap and squared her shoulders. "Love is supposed to heal all wounds—"

"Don't you mean time?"

Her eyes shone with emotion. "I don't have *time*. That's the point. I won't be here forever, Spencer. I have done many things in my life that I regret, but none more than telling you about Dereck the way I did. I thought you knew, but that's no excuse. I haven't slept well since that night. I hoped if you fell in love with the right woman, she might bring you back to us."

Spencer sat back and folded his arms across his chest. "So you hired Hailey and arranged for us to meet."

"Yes."

"That's—"

"Brilliant," Delinda cut in.

"Machiavellian. You used her. How do you think she feels about that?"

Delinda deflated a little at his accusation. "Not good, I imagine."

In the quiet that followed, Spencer weighed the wrong of what she'd done against the outcome. "Hailey said her niece is talking again, and she credits you."

"Skye is a remarkable little girl. All I did was nudge her."

"You were lucky it worked out that way. What you did wasn't right, Delinda."

Delinda's chin rose. "It wasn't all wrong, either."

He stood. "No, it wasn't all wrong, but I don't know what the hell to say to her to make this right. Where do I even begin?"

Delinda pushed out of her chair and stood beside him. "Tell her you love her."

He nodded and turned to walk away. She halted him with a hand on his arm. "I am sorry, Spencer—more sorry than you'll ever know. And I do love you."

Suddenly there was nothing intimidating about Delinda at all. She looked almost frail and sincere in her need to be forgiven. Her fear of being left behind reached past years of anger and questions and touched his heart. He knew exactly how it felt to desperately want to be part of something yet have no idea how to be. He opened his arms to her.

She hesitated, then stepped into his embrace. She was so small he wondered how she could intimidate anyone. When she stepped back, she looked up at him with her usual stern expression, and said, "Quit stalling and go after Hailey. Don't you dare come back without her. Remember, Westerlys don't give up."

"I'm not—" Spencer started to say that he wasn't a Westerly, but stopped mid-sentence. He saw his family through the solarium window. From his quiet mother to a still-angry Nicolette, from a worried Rachelle to a supportive Brett and Alisha—*our family is what we make it.* His gaze settled on Dereck, who was standing off to one side of his mother, looking as lost as Brett once had. "I am a Westerly."

She nodded in approval. "Yes, you are."

A warmth filled him that he'd waited a lifetime for. Things hadn't always been bad between them, and the early days were becoming easier to remember. "Hailey isn't going anywhere."

"Michael," Delinda called out, then issued instructions to her butler in a tone too soft for Spencer to hear. Michael returned moments later with a small box that he handed to Delinda before once again leaving.

She opened the box and took out an antique round diamond ring that had to be at least five karats. "You may need this. It was my husband's grandmother's ring—your great-great-grandmother's. Hailey will say the diamond is too big, but tell her this story when she does . . ."

Chapter Sixteen

In the kitchen, with Hope in hand, Hailey froze when she heard Spencer at the door. It wasn't that she didn't want to see him. She wanted nothing more than to throw open the door, jump into his arms, and let their passion chase away her doubts.

Life didn't work that way.

"Hailey?"

She walked over to the door but didn't open it. "Go away, Spencer."

"I'm not going anywhere until we talk."

She put Hope down, then placed a hand against the inside of the door. Opening it would be so easy. Forgetting the scene back at the main house wouldn't be. *We were all wrong. Delinda manipulated me. I wasn't honest with Spencer, and he wasn't honest with me. We all thought we knew what was best and look where it brought us—here we are crashing against the shore again.*

It was all too good to be real . . .

"The person you should be talking to is Delinda. She's obviously willing to do anything to get your attention."

"What she did was wrong, Hailey. I'm not defending her choices, but I understand her motivation now."

"I don't. I thought I did, but I don't know anything anymore."

"Open the door, Hailey. This is an impossible conversation this way."

"No. I want to, but I have zero confidence in my judgment right now. I'm not angry with you; I'm angry with myself. I'm too old to be as gullible as I've been lately. A part of me knew it was all too easy, but I saw what I wanted to see. I wanted to believe in miracles, I guess."

Hope peed a little on the floor near her feet, and Hailey shook her head in resignation while cleaning it up. *Now there is a sign if there ever was one. Reality always crashes in.*

"Open the door, Hailey."

"Have you heard anything I've said?"

"Yes, but I'm not a boy anymore. I know what I want now. And that's you, Hailey. I lost you once because I wasn't ready. I'm ready now."

Hailey opened the door. They stood simply looking at each other for a long time. The attraction between them pulsed through them, complicating her feelings further. "That was an ugly scene."

"I know," he said.

"You were cruel to Delinda."

He rubbed a hand across the back of his neck. "I'm not proud of my behavior, but Delinda and I had to clear the air."

"And now that you have?"

"Oh, there are still glitches. My whole family is batshit crazy. There's no denying that."

Hope whined at Hailey's feet. "She needs to go out."

Spencer walked Hailey through the house and out to the backyard where Hope circled a few times before relieving herself. Hailey sat on a step as Hope bounced through the grass. Spencer took a seat beside her. The heat from his body warmed her side, igniting a desire she did her best to deny. He turned his head and looked like he might kiss her.

She raised a hand. "Don't."

He stayed where he was, but his eyes burned with a yearning she felt just as strongly. If only this, their hunger for each other, were enough.

She mustered irritation with him. "And don't look at me that way."

"Which way?" He leaned closer.

She couldn't look away, couldn't stop herself from flicking her tongue over her bottom lip. "Like there is any chance that you and I will—that there's something you could say that would—you know exactly how you're looking at me."

The corner of his mouth curled in a hint of a smile. "Yes, because you're looking at me the same way."

She shook her head, but couldn't tear her eyes from his. Being close to him—knowing that all she'd have to do was stretch ever so slightly to once again feel his lips on hers—made it difficult to remember why she was upset with him. "This isn't enough," she said for her own benefit as much as his. "I have responsibilities. I'm still trying to wrap my head around what Delinda did and what that means for me and Skye. If my talk with Delinda doesn't go well, I'm essentially homeless."

"That would never happen. You and Skye would come with me."

"To where?" she asked hoarsely. There was nowhere she could imagine bringing Skye that night.

"My place is big enough—"

"It's not that easy, Spencer. She doesn't know you. You haven't even met her. You may not like her."

An expression entered his eyes that she'd seen before, but this time it was more intense. "I don't have to meet her to know that I'll love her because she's part of you." He took out a box and opened it, revealing an enormous sparkling engagement ring. "I'm not asking you to move in with me. I'm asking you to marry me. There has never been anyone else for me. I love you, Hailey Tiverton."

Hailey blinked back tears, wanting to believe in second chances but afraid to. "This is too fast."

"Is it? I knew you were the one the first time around; I just wasn't ready to do anything about it."

I wasn't, either.

Don't—don't open yourself to hope again. It never ends well. "Did Delinda give you the ring?"

"Yes."

"When?"

He frowned, hesitating before answering. "Does it matter?"

"Maybe. Have you thought this through? Skye and I are a package deal, and parenting is a full-time gig. Skye takes riding lessons twice a week. Saturday shows. School starts in the fall. That will mean homework. She may take an instrument—maybe an ear-piercing one like violin."

"You're not scaring me."

"No?" Did he understand how big of a commitment it was? "She's getting to the age when she'll want friends to sleep over. That means girls giggling all night. I want her to have all of those experiences. She's not only my responsibility; she's also a priority. A wonderful, miraculous, sometimes terrifyingly overwhelming priority."

"Hailey?"

"Yes?"

"I had an amazing father who would have loved every moment of the life you're describing. I will as well. You think I can't handle giggling? I was raised with two sisters. In a pinch, I can braid hair and apply nail polish like a pro. It's not something I normally brag about, but I've got skills. I'm up for this. The question is—are you?"

Spencer held his breath. He didn't want to rush her, but he felt like he'd waited half of his life for this moment. In the movies, women broke into tears and threw their arms around a man who proposed, then the credits began to roll. Reality was much more gut-wrenching. Hailey went pale and hugged her stomach while leaning forward as if she were about to retch. *I'm a selfish bastard. She's been through hell and back, and all I can think about is making her mine before I lose her again. This isn't business, where closing the deal is all that matters.*

This is the woman I love, and she's scared.

He put an arm around her. "Talk to me. Say yes. Say no. It's okay. It won't change how I feel about you or how willing I am to help you. You are not alone. If you won't marry me, then I'll still be the best damn friend you've ever had—always."

She shook beneath his arm, and he hated that he hadn't done every step of this better. "Oh, Spencer. I want to marry you, but I can't move fast anymore. If we do this, we need to take it slow. I have to make sure Skye's okay—with all of this. She's been through so much."

Spencer closed the ring box, pocketed it, then gently turned her face toward him. "So have you. Let me carry some of the weight you think belongs solely on your shoulders. You don't have to do this alone."

He kissed her then. He intended to brush his lips across hers, but that light touch opened the floodgates for both of them. They kissed deeply, feverishly, like lovers who had gone too long without each other. He told himself to pull back, but the feel of her undoing the buttons of his shirt sent him over the edge.

He lifted her into his arms and carried her into the guesthouse, almost tripping over the puppy that darted between his legs when he opened the door. They continued to kiss as he carried her down a short hallway to where he guessed her bedroom would be. The puppy raced around them, yipping with excitement. Spencer raised his head and peered down at the creature. "What's his name?"

"Her name is Hope," Hailey said breathlessly, her face beautifully flushed with desire.

"As in 'I hope you have a crate for her'?" he asked.

She chuckled, then sobered. "More like I hope you forgive me when I say we can't do this. Skye could be back any moment."

Just outside the master bedroom door, Spencer slowly lowered Hailey to her feet and rested his forehead on hers. "I'm the one who should be apologizing. I don't know what happens to my brain around you."

She smiled. "I do because it happens to me, too."

"We're quite a pair."

"Yes, we are." She framed his face with her hands and tilted her head back so she could better meet his eyes. "There are women with so much less baggage than I have. Why choose me?"

It was a question he hadn't expected. "You might as well ask me why I choose to breathe. It has always been you, Hailey. Always. We can take it as slow or as fast as you want." He leaned down and picked up the puppy and held it up to his face. "Hope, huh? Good name. I tried life without you, and it sucked. Walking away was easier, avoiding my family was a hell of lot less messy, but I don't want that life. I didn't grow up that way, and I sure as hell don't want to die that way. So, Hope, how about you convince your mommy to marry me, and we'll give this whole messy family thing a shot?"

Hope gave Spencer a wet kiss on his cheek that he took as a yes.

"You're crazy—do you know that?"

He shot her a smile. "Crazy in a lovable, 'you can imagine spending the rest of your life with me' kind of way? Or 'put down my dog because I'm about to call the police'?"

Hailey burst out laughing. "Definitely the former."

"Good," Spencer said as he tucked Hope beneath his arm. Hailey hadn't accepted his proposal, but he now believed she would—in time. And that was okay because now there was hope. "Come on, my entire family is likely lingering in the driveway, waiting to see if you toss me out on my rear or forgive me."

He held out his hand to her. She hesitated.

"It's not about forgiving—not even with Delinda. Regardless of what her intentions were, Skye is happy again. Delinda did that." She searched his face. "I'm not angry with you. I'm—maybe I'm—"

"Scared," he supplied. *I know, Sunshine.* "We've been here before, haven't we? But we're not kids anymore. Sure there will be challenges, but they can only beat us if we let them."

She placed her hand in his. "Did you say your *entire* family?"

He smiled and led the way down the hall and out of the guest-house. "Jordan called them. When I heard that Delinda had blocked you from getting that job—he was probably right to sound the alarm. I was furious."

There was no one in the driveway, but all the cars were still there. Michael opened the door as Spencer and Hailey approached the house. "Everyone is on the back porch. Should I escort you?"

"You should," Hailey said. "Spencer, you must know Michael."

"Of course," Spencer said. "He's worked here for as long as I can remember."

Michael tipped his head in agreement.

Hailey touched Michael's forearm briefly. "Thank you, Michael, for everything."

Spencer and Michael shared a brief look. Whatever Delinda's butler had done for Hailey, Spencer was grateful. He shook Michael's hand firmly, letting that gesture express how he felt.

Michael turned and led the way to the porch that overlooked both the gardens and the ocean behind it. Stephanie, Dereck, and Delinda were seated. Brett, Alisha, Nicolette, and Rachelle were gathered in a loose circle. Everyone stopped and turned as Spencer and Hailey stepped onto the porch.

Delinda pushed out of her chair and walked toward them. "Hailey, a moment alone, please? This won't take long."

Spencer handed Hope to Michael, then while still holding Hailey's hand, said, "New family rule—no secrets. Our track record with them is horrible."

Delinda blinked several times quickly, then nodded. "Hailey, I shouldn't have brought you here without telling you the truth about why. I was desperate, and I saw you as a way to fix something I had broken. I never meant to hurt you. You and Skye have breathed life into this empty house and me as well. Can you forgive an old woman for loving her grandchildren so much she'd be willing to do anything to have them in her life?"

"She sure knows how to lay it on thick," Nicolette said in a stage whisper.

"Don't, Nicolette," Rachelle and Stephanie said in unison.

Nicolette raised both of her hands in mock surrender. "Am I the only one who thinks she's being too nice? It's actually making me nervous."

Spencer changed the subject by introducing Hailey to the group in general and then to each of them individually. For a group of people who were barely holding back their curiosity, they covered it pretty well. A few of them glanced at Hailey's left ring finger, then at Spencer, but they didn't say anything.

"Miss Skye has returned," Michael announced from the doorway of the main house.

Skye burst past him, then slowed as she appeared to realize that most of the people on the porch were strangers to her. She looked from one person to the next, but once she saw that Hailey and Spencer were holding hands, her eyes riveted to him. Slowly, she approached him. "I know you," Skye said, then turned to Delinda. "I know him."

Delinda nodded.

Skye's eyes flew to Hailey's. "I've seen pictures of him. Is your boyfriend Delinda's grandson?"

Hailey's hand held on to Spencer's tightly. She didn't seem to know how she should answer that.

Spencer looked from his mother's concerned expression to Dereck's somber one. Dereck could have announced to everyone that Spencer wasn't his. He hadn't. Delinda could have done the same. They had chosen to be his family—chosen, just as he was being given a chance to choose at that moment. He could easily deny Dereck and Delinda. Could anyone blame him if he did?

Family is what we make it. Spencer crouched down so he was eye level with Skye, then held out his hand. "That's me, Spencer Westerly. Arguably the best looking and most successful of all of her grandchildren."

His joke drew groans from his siblings, but flew right over Skye's head. She focused on the only part of what he'd said that mattered to her.

"Auntie Hailey, I love you." She hugged Hailey tightly. "You do want me to be happy. You really do."

Hailey kissed her niece on the top of her head. "Of course I do."

Skye bolted from Hailey to Delinda. She grabbed her hand with a confidence that surprised Spencer. Delinda had never been fond of physical displays of affection, but she welcomed Skye's touch. "Do you know what this means, Delinda? Do you? When they get married, I'll be your real granddaughter. Your real one. It'll be like I came out of your vagina."

The look on Delinda's face was priceless as a round of laughter erupted. Spencer knew right then that Skye would keep him laughing. He looked down at Hailey, who was holding back a laugh—barely. "Seems like you might want to go over that birds-and-bees talk again. She almost has it."

Skye's nose wrinkled in an expression Hailey sometimes made. "I'm right. Babies come out of vaginas. If you came out of her daughter's vagina and her daughter came out of her vagina, then you came out of her vagina because you were inside her daughter. Wait, Delinda, do you have a daughter?"

Above more shared laughter, Nicolette said, "Oh my God, I love her."

Skye looked around and frowned. "Auntie Hailey said vagina is not a bad word. It's part of a woman's body."

"I did say that," Hailey said, with tears of laughter in her eyes. "But you shouldn't say the word in public."

Skye waved her free hand at Hailey. "Why would you teach me words I can't use?"

Hailey shrugged helplessly and laughed. "I'm learning as I go."

Spencer walked up behind her and wrapped his arms around her. "If you need any help . . ."

She laced her fingers through his and gave him a smile over her shoulder that knocked the breath out of him. "I do, and I have my answer to the question you asked me earlier."

He tensed.

She relaxed back against him. "Yes. Yes. Yes a hundred times. Yes a thousand times. We can do this. I believe that now."

"Wait," Skye said. "If you get married, do we have to move?"

Hailey opened her mouth, then closed it without saying anything. "I—we—"

"We are going to take it slow, so this time we get it right," Spencer said.

Chapter Seventeen

Later that night, after Hailey tucked Skye into bed, she joined Spencer on the couch in the living room of the guesthouse. He opened his arms. She snuggled against his side and laid her head on his shoulder. "You know you're her hero now."

He kissed Hailey's temple. "Because I'm Delinda's grandson?"

Hailey rested her hand over his heart. "No, because you asked Delinda if she had the rest of the *Billy and the Lion* series and she did. Don't be surprised if Skye asks you to read a story to her soon. She's a wonderful reader, but Ryan had a way of making stories come to life for her."

"It's a good series. I can't believe I forgot it was Delinda who used to read it to me. I didn't think I had any good memories of her."

"She's a tough cookie, but she has her reasons."

"Yes, she does. My family is lucky Skye brings out the best in her. That's no easy feat. She's a remarkable child."

"She is."

"It's not shocking, though, because you're pretty damn amazing yourself."

"So are you." A lick of desire spread through Hailey, and Spencer tensed beside her.

He whistled softly. "I can see why some people call kids birth control. I'm enjoying a rather filthy fantasy of what I'd like to do with you, but it's not going to happen with your niece across the hall."

"Nope." Hailey smiled. "But she goes back to school soon. There's always long lunches."

He nodded slowly. "I like the way you think." He dug in the pocket of his trousers and produced the ring box again.

Hailey let out a shaky breath. Her life had been a series of highs and lows filled with both love and loss. She couldn't open herself to one without inviting the possibility of the other. *What's the alternative? To close myself off? To let my fears win? Like Spencer, I don't want to live or die that way. So here we go.*

Spencer moved to stand.

Hailey protested. "You don't have to—"

"I do. I want to do it right." He dropped to one knee and held out the ring.

With happy tears welling in her eyes, Hailey sat forward, eye to eye with the man she loved. "I love you."

With a huge smile, he wagged a finger at her. "Don't steal my lines. This isn't something a man has a chance to practice."

"Oh, sorry," Hailey said and tried to contain her amusement.

He cleared his throat, then winked. It was endearing and sexy and better than any version of that moment she'd ever allowed herself to imagine. The man kneeling before her was not just a lover, he was also a friend, and that added a whole new layer to what they had. *We're on the same team.*

"Hailey Tiverton, any worthwhile advancement in technology includes a period of trial and error. Things that should work—don't. Whole networks can crash from one faulty upgrade."

"Okay." Hailey tipped her head to one side. A joke was on the tip of her tongue, but she didn't voice it because he was being sincere.

"I don't measure the success of a project by how few mistakes I made along the way. I measure it by the end result. We didn't get here by the shortest route we could have taken, but we're here. We made it. Just as I can't imagine the world without the Internet, I can't imagine my life without you in it. Marry me, Hailey. I love you. You're my pie, my cake, the only damn pastry I need."

The man who was on one knee before her was a combination of the boy she'd once loved and the man he'd become. Although he had morphed from football player to successful businessman, his core was still all geek, and she loved him more because of it. She threw her arms around his neck and kissed him soundly. When she raised her head, she said, "How could I refuse a man who can integrate coding issues and sugary analogies into a proposal? I'm sold. Where do I sign?"

He placed the ring on her finger before rising to his feet and pulling her up and into his arms. "I can think of a better way to seal the deal."

The bulge of his excitement pulsed against her. "Really? I never would have guessed."

He laughed, kissed her gently, then sat back onto the couch and patted the place beside her. "You're heartless."

"And yet you want to marry me," she said. Their relationship was the best of what they'd once had and so much more.

He growled playfully and swung her up and across his lap. "That's because I'm a dick."

She burst out laughing.

He joined in.

It was a moment that should have ended in a kiss, and would have had they been alone in the house. Instead, she forced her attention away from him and to the rock on her hand. "How do I wear this without being a nervous wreck that I'll lose it?"

"You don't like it?"

It was stunning. Flawless. Probably worth more than the total income she'd made since she started working at sixteen. She twirled it on her finger. "It's too much—too big. I'm not sure I could ever feel like it was mine."

He ran his hand through her hair in an intimate, possessive caress. "Delinda knew you'd feel that way. Before you give it back, I think you should hear the story of the ring. It just might change your mind."

A month ago, hell, as recently as that morning, had someone told Spencer that he would be holding Hailey in his arms and quoting Delinda, he would have laughed it off as impossible. One day, one conversation, had changed his perspective of many things.

He took Hailey's hand in his and turned it so the large diamond shimmered in the light of the lamp beside them. "This ring has been in the Westerly family for at least four generations. Delinda said she told you about her husband and her family."

"Yes. It's a sad story."

"Not all of it. Delinda's husband, Oliver, didn't come to her with money, but he did have one possession that was said to be worth enough that he could have started his own business had he sold it."

"The ring?" Hailey's eyes rounded as she looked down at it.

"Yes. Oliver had promised his mother, though, that he would never sell it. Generations of Westerlys have treasured that ring. Delinda said that instead of it being given to the oldest son, it was given to the one who could be most trusted to uphold the tradition of passing it on. Tradition, she said, is a bridge to the past that has only lost favor in this generation. The ring doesn't represent wealth, but in fact, the opposite. Restraint, loyalty, family—above the luxuries that selling it could provide. In the end, everything else is temporary and insignificant, but family endures."

Hailey's eyes flew to his. "I completely agree."

Emotion tightened Spencer's throat. "Dereck gave it to my mother, but she returned it to Delinda after they divorced. According to

Delinda, Dereck felt that he had failed both the generation before and after him."

"That's heartbreaking."

"If you weigh the sum of something by the number of mistakes taken to create it, yes. When Delinda gave me the ring, she said I am 100 percent Westerly. In her heart I have always been and will always be her grandchild, regardless of the blood that runs through my veins. Hearing that meant more to me than any inheritance ever could. I guess that's the point of the ring."

"Your batshit-crazy family can be pretty wonderful sometimes."

"Who knew?" he joked as he nuzzled Hailey's neck. "And I'm glad you feel that way because they'll be your family soon."

Hailey sighed happily, then hugged him tightly. "Family. Up until now, when I looked back at this year I wanted to cringe because all I saw was what I did wrong, but I prefer the way you think. I may not have done everything right, but somehow I got us here. And here is pretty damn amazing."

Despite the fact that he was living in a state of perma-arousal, he totally agreed with her. "Yes, it is." They kissed deeply, testing each other's restraint like the inexperienced teenagers they'd once been. Rather than being flat-out torture, this time around anticipation was tempered by the knowledge that they had forever. "And it's only going to get better."

Epilogue

Two months later, Hailey found herself wildly hunting through Delinda's house for Skye. The ceremony was about to begin and, as the flower girl, Skye was the first one scheduled to walk down the aisle. Keeping Skye calm and at her side had quickly become impossible as soon as the Andrade clan had arrived with a large number of children in tow. Small garden wedding? There had to be three hundred people gathered on the lawn beneath a white tent, and families were still arriving. All those guests and the army of staff would have been enough to overwhelm most people, but Delinda took it surprisingly well.

I wonder what she'd think if she knew I have no idea where Skye is.

A sparkle from the large diamond on her left hand briefly caught her attention. It stood out here as much as it did against the office clothes Hailey wore for her new job at WorkChat. She'd been reluctant to take the position at first, but all of her worries had quickly fallen away. The purchasing negotiation skills she'd honed in retail were an asset that both Spencer and Jordan said they appreciated.

Jordan, Spencer, and Hailey—together again—and the mix was just as good this time around. Jordan credited Hailey with bringing laughter back to the office.

"Hailey!" Alisha, Brett's soon-to-be bride, stopped Hailey as she was about to rush by her.

If she asks about Skye, I'm going to lie and say I know where she is. No upsetting the bride; isn't that what people say? Especially not a pregnant bride. Hailey took a deep, calming breath. "Is it time to gather?"

"It is," Alisha said. "We're meeting in the room before the solarium. Have you seen Eric? Brett is so excited he's here. I was afraid he'd call last minute and say he needed to be on location for his next movie, but he came. He's probably with Brett now. At least, I hope so."

"I'm sure he is." Hailey scanned the room for Skye. "The solarium. Check. We'll be right there."

"Hey, thank you for helping Rachelle hold my dress in the bathroom. I'm sure that wasn't the duty you thought you'd signed up for when you agreed to be a bridesmaid. I would have waited for Nicolette, but when you're pregnant, it's better not to risk it."

"Anytime," Hailey said with a smile. Alisha was exactly the kind of sister-in-law Hailey had always dreamed of having. She was humble, funny, and shockproof, and best of all, she loved Skye.

"Okay, well, if you see anyone else from the bridal party tell them to come now."

"Absolutely."

Shit.

As soon as Alisha left the foyer, Hailey rushed from room to room searching. She literally bumped into Alessandro on her way from the library to the solarium. "Sorry. Have you seen Skye?"

"I have." The twinkle in his eye made Hailey's stomach lurch from nerves.

"Where?"

"She's in the bounce house."

"Where?" *No, he couldn't have. She's in a white dress.*

"Out front with Spencer."

"He let her go in a bounce house?"

"Don't worry; he's in there with her."

"What?" Hailey shook her head, sure she'd misunderstood.

Alessandro led the way out the front of the house to where there was now a bounce house and blow-up slide. Children of all ages were enjoying both. Hailey walked toward them. A large black pair of dress shoes were lined up beside a much smaller white pair of sandals. The two of them laughed right along with several children.

Alessandro said, "It's beautiful, no?"

"No," Hailey said with growing horror. Skye's hair had fallen free of its clip.

Alessandro gave Hailey's shoulder a sympathetic pat. "I was here when she said she wanted to go in, but was afraid because there were so many children she didn't know in there. Spencer took his shoes right off. He's going to be a good father to her."

Hailey nodded. "I know he is, but he couldn't have waited until after the ceremony? What if she ruins her dress?"

Alessandro shrugged. "When Skye remembers this day, do you think it will be because her dress was pristine or do you think it will be because of that?" He pointed to Spencer organizing the children in a circle so he could jump in the middle and send all of them flying. "And what will you choose to remember?" Squeals and laughter filled the air, and all of Hailey's worries fell away.

"You're right, but do you mind giving the same talk to Alisha and Delinda?" Hailey said with a laugh.

"Alisha is expecting a child. She won't be bothered by mussed hair or a stained dress. And Delinda adores you and Skye. You could do no wrong according to her. Go, get your family—the wedding will be just as beautiful a few minutes late."

"You're trouble; do you know that, Alessandro?" Hailey teased.

"My wife tells me that frequently," he answered with another shrug and a pleased smile.

Hailey walked over to the bounce house. "Spencer. Skye. It's time to go."

Skye kept bouncing. Spencer stood in the middle, looking shamelessly pleased with himself. "I forgot how much fun these things are. Designing something like this in a simulator wouldn't be easy, but I bet I could do it."

"We can talk about all of that later. Alisha's calling everyone to gather. Skye, we need to get out of there and cleaned up."

"Bounce with us, Auntie Hailey. Just one bounce. It's so much fun."

"Maybe later. There's no time. Come on out, you two."

Skye's bottom lip quivered. "Please? Just one bounce. I promise."

There was a light of challenge in Spencer's eyes. "That is, unless you're afraid I can bounce better than you."

"She's not afraid of anything. Right, Auntie Hailey? Show him you can out-bounce him."

Hailey was about to refuse and cite her still-immaculate hairstyle and dress when she glanced at Alessandro. With his small nod of encouragement, suddenly being perfect didn't matter as much to her as being part of that memory. She kicked off her shoes, hiked up her dress, and climbed in.

A moment later, she was holding hands with Spencer, taking turns jumping high to see which of them could toss the children farther— and laughing. Skye joined them, linking her hands with theirs, and they began to jump in unison. It was a time Hailey knew she would never forget, and regardless of when they said their own vows, it was when they truly became a family.

Alessandro was headed back into the house to tell the bride that the wedding would start a few minutes late, when he came across a concerned-looking Delinda.

"The wedding procession is waiting on one groomsman, one bridesmaid, and a flower girl. You wouldn't have any idea where they are, would you?"

Alessandro led her out onto the step and pointed toward the bounce house where Hailey, Spencer, and Skye were still laughing and jumping around. He expected Delinda to voice her displeasure, but she nodded in approval. "I knew she could make him happy."

Although Alessandro adored Delinda, that didn't hold him back from voicing his own concern. "You were lucky with this one, Delinda. It could have gone bad in so many ways."

Delinda linked her arm with his and shot him a bright smile. "But it didn't, and there's three left to go."

"Does that mean I'll be invited over for tea again soon?" a redhead asked from beside them.

Alessandro frowned. "You shouldn't encourage her."

Alethea's wide smile mirrored Delinda's. "Encourage her? I'm taking notes."

Delinda looked the younger woman up and down with a critical eye. "You should be. The man you brought here with you today, Marc Stone—you've been engaged to him for years? It's obvious he loves you, and since I can't imagine many men being able to handle someone like you, you should seal that deal."

Alethea and Alessandro exchanged a look, then both burst out laughing.

Still laughing, Alethea leaned in. "Delinda Westerly, will you adopt me? Please?"

Alessandro shook his head while smiling. "Someone needs to separate the two of you. You're each bad enough on your own."

Looking quite unimpressed, Delinda said, "By 'bad' he means so good it puts all else to shame."

Alethea winked at Delinda and joked, "Don't hate us 'cause you ain't us."

Delinda looked like she was about to correct Alethea, then stopped and nodded in approval instead. "Exactly."

Acknowledgments

I am so grateful to everyone who was part of the process of creating *Up for Heir*.

Thank you to:

Montlake Romance for supporting my addiction to alpha billionaires.

My very patient beta readers. You know who you are. Thank you for kicking my butt when I need it.

My editors: Karen Lawson, Janet Hitchcock, Marion Archer, Krista Stroever, and Marlene Engel.

My Roadies for making me smile each day when I log on to my computer. So many of you have become my friends. Was there life before the Roadies? I'm sure there was, but it wasn't as much fun.

Thank you to my husband, Tony, who is a saint—simple as that.

About the Author

Ruth Cardello is a *New York Times* bestselling author who loves writing about rich alpha men and the strong women who tame them. She was born the youngest of eleven children in a small city in northern Rhode Island. She's lived in Boston, Paris, Orlando, New York, and Rhode Island again before moving to Massachusetts, where she now lives with her husband and three children. Before turning her attention to writing, Ruth was an educator for two decades, including eleven years as a kindergarten teacher. *Up for Heir* is the second book in her Westerly Billionaire series. Learn about Ruth's new releases by signing up for her newsletter at www.RuthCardello.com.